P9-EEH-808

BOLLINGEN SERIES LXXX

# The Divine Comedy

◇

## Purgatorio

### 1: Italian Text and Translation

DANTE ALIGHIERI

# The Divine Comedy

TRANSLATED, WITH A COMMENTARY, BY

CHARLES S. SINGLETON

## Purgatorio

### 1: Italian Text and Translation

BOLLINGEN SERIES LXXX

PRINCETON UNIVERSITY PRESS

THIS IS VOLUME II, PART I, OF

THE DIVINE COMEDY OF DANTE ALIGHIERI

CONSTITUTING NUMBER LXXX IN BOLLINGEN SERIES

SPONSORED BY BOLLINGEN FOUNDATION.

THIS VOLUME, PURGATORIO,

IS IN TWO PARTS: ITALIAN TEXT AND TRANSLATION,

AND COMMENTARY.

*The pagination of the paperback edition is the same as that of the original cloth edition.*

Library of Congress Catalogue card number 68-57090

ISBN 0-691-01909-6

Printed in the United States of America

by Princeton University Press, Princeton, New Jersey

*Second printing, with corrections, 1977*

First Princeton/Bollingen Paperback printing, 1982

Sixth Paperback printing, and

First paperback edition in two volumes, 1991

12 11 10 9 8 7 6

# Purgatorio

## Italian Text and Translation

# PURGATORIO

PER CORRER miglior acque alza le vele
omai la navicella del mio ingegno,
che lascia dietro a sé mar sì crudele; 3
e canterò di quel secondo regno
dove l'umano spirito si purga
e di salire al ciel diventa degno. 6
Ma qui la morta poesì resurga,
o sante Muse, poi che vostro sono;
e qui Calïopè alquanto surga, 9
seguitando il mio canto con quel suono
di cui le Piche misere sentiro
lo colpo tal, che disperar perdono. 12
Dolce color d'orïental zaffiro,
che s'accoglieva nel sereno aspetto
del mezzo, puro infino al primo giro, 15
a li occhi miei ricominciò diletto,
tosto ch'io usci' fuor de l'aura morta
che m'avea contristati li occhi e 'l petto. 18

# CANTO I

To course over better waters the little bark of my genius now hoists her sails, leaving behind her a sea so cruel; and I will sing of that second realm where the human spirit is purged and becomes fit to ascend to Heaven. But here let dead poetry rise again, O holy Muses, since I am yours; and here let Calliope rise up somewhat, accompanying my song with that strain whose stroke the wretched Pies felt so that they despaired of pardon.

Sweet hue of oriental sapphire which was gathering in the serene face of the sky, pure even to the first circle, to my eyes restored delight, as soon as I issued forth from the dead air that had afflicted my eyes and breast.

Lo bel pianeto che d'amar conforta
faceva tutto rider l'orïente,
velando i Pesci ch'erano in sua scorta. *21*

I' mi volsi a man destra, e puosi mente
a l'altro polo, e vidi quattro stelle
non viste mai fuor ch'a la prima gente. *24*

Goder pareva 'l ciel di lor fiammelle:
oh settentrïonal vedovo sito,
poi che privato se' di mirar quelle! *27*

Com' io da loro sguardo fui partito,
un poco me volgendo a l'altro polo,
là onde 'l Carro già era sparito, *30*

vidi presso di me un veglio solo,
degno di tanta reverenza in vista,
che più non dee a padre alcun figliuolo. *33*

Lunga la barba e di pel bianco mista
portava, a' suoi capelli simigliante,
de' quai cadeva al petto doppia lista. *36*

Li raggi de le quattro luci sante
fregiavan sì la sua faccia di lume,
ch'i' 'l vedea come 'l sol fosse davante. *39*

"Chi siete voi che contro al cieco fiume
fuggita avete la pregione etterna?"
diss' el, movendo quelle oneste piume. *42*

"Chi v'ha guidati, o che vi fu lucerna,
uscendo fuor de la profonda notte
che sempre nera fa la valle inferna? *45*

Son le leggi d'abisso così rotte?
o è mutato in ciel novo consiglio,
che, dannati, venite a le mie grotte?" *48*

The fair planet that prompts to love was making the whole East smile, veiling the Fishes that were in her train. I turned to the right and gave heed to the other pole, and saw four stars never seen before save by the first people. The heavens seemed to rejoice in their flames. O northern widowed clime, that are deprived of beholding them!

When I had withdrawn my gaze from them, turning a little to the other pole, there whence the Wain had already disappeared, I saw close to me an old man alone, worthy in his looks of so great reverence that no son owes more to his father. His beard was long and streaked with white, like his locks of which a double tress fell on his breast. The rays of the four holy lights so adorned his face with brightness that I saw him as if the sun were before him.

"Who are you that, against the blind stream, have fled the eternal prison?" said he, moving those venerable plumes. "Who has guided you, or what was a lamp to you issuing forth from the deep night that ever makes the infernal valley black? Are the laws of the abyss thus broken? Or is some new counsel changed in Heaven that though damned you come to my rocks?"

Lo duca mio allor mi diè di piglio,
e con parole e con mani e con cenni
reverenti mi fé le gambe e 'l ciglio. *51*
Poscia rispuose lui: "Da me non venni:
donna scese del ciel, per li cui prieghi
de la mia compagnia costui sovvenni. *54*
Ma da ch'è tuo voler che più si spieghi
di nostra condizion com' ell' è vera,
esser non puote il mio che a te si nieghi. *57*
Questi non vide mai l'ultima sera;
ma per la sua follia le fu sì presso,
che molto poco tempo a volger era. *60*
Sì com' io dissi, fui mandato ad esso
per lui campare; e non li era altra via
che questa per la quale i' mi son messo. *63*
Mostrata ho lui tutta la gente ria;
e ora intendo mostrar quelli spirti
che purgan sé sotto la tua balìa. *66*
Com' io l'ho tratto, saria lungo a dirti;
de l'alto scende virtù che m'aiuta
conducerlo a vederti e a udirti. *69*
Or ti piaccia gradir la sua venuta:
libertà va cercando, ch'è sì cara,
come sa chi per lei vita rifiuta. *72*
Tu 'l sai, ché non ti fu per lei amara
in Utica la morte, ove lasciasti
la vesta ch'al gran dì sarà sì chiara. *75*
Non son li editti etterni per noi guasti,
ché questi vive e Minòs me non lega;
ma son del cerchio ove son li occhi casti *78*

My leader then laid hold on me, and with speech and hand and sign made reverent my legs and brow. Then he answered him, "Of myself I came not. A lady descended from Heaven through whose prayers I succored this man with my company. But since it is your will that more of our condition be unfolded to you as it truly is, mine it cannot be that to you this be denied. This man has not seen his last evening, but by his folly was so near to it that very little time was left to run. Even as I said, I was sent to him to rescue him, and there was no other way than this along which I have set myself. I have shown him all the guilty people, and now I intend to show him those spirits that purge themselves under your charge. How I have brought him would be long to tell you: from on high descends power that aids me to conduct him to see you and to hear you. Now may it please you to approve his coming. He goes seeking freedom, which is so precious, as he knows who renounces life for it; you know it, for death for its sake was not bitter to you in Utica, where you did leave the raiment which on the great day will be so bright. The eternal edicts are not violated by us, for this one is alive and Minos does not bind me; but I am of the circle where are the chaste eyes

di Marzia tua, che 'n vista ancor ti priega,
o santo petto, che per tua la tegni:
per lo suo amore adunque a noi ti piega. *81*
Lasciane andar per li tuoi sette regni;
grazie riporterò di te a lei,
se d'esser mentovato là giù degni." *84*
"Marzïa piacque tanto a li occhi miei
mentre ch'i' fu' di là," diss' elli allora,
"che quante grazie volse da me, fei. *87*
Or che di là dal mal fiume dimora,
più muover non mi può, per quella legge
che fatta fu quando me n'usci' fora. *90*
Ma se donna del ciel ti move e regge,
come tu di', non c'è mestier lusinghe:
bastisi ben che per lei mi richegge. *93*
Va dunque, e fa che tu costui ricinghe
d'un giunco schietto e che li lavi 'l viso,
sì ch'ogne sucidume quindi stinghe; *96*
ché non si converria, l'occhio sorpriso
d'alcuna nebbia, andar dinanzi al primo
ministro, ch'è di quei di paradiso. *99*
Questa isoletta intorno ad imo ad imo,
là giù colà dove la batte l'onda,
porta di giunchi sovra 'l molle limo: *102*
null' altra pianta che facesse fronda
o indurasse, vi puote aver vita,
però ch'a le percosse non seconda. *105*
Poscia non sia di qua vostra reddita;
lo sol vi mosterrà, che surge omai,
prendere il monte a più lieve salita." *108*

of your Marcia, who in her look still prays you, O holy breast, that you hold her for your own. For love of her, then, incline yourself to us: let us go on through your seven realms. I will report to her your kindness, if you deign to be mentioned there below."

"Marcia so pleased my eyes while I was yonder," he then said, "that every kindness she wished of me I did. Now that she dwells beyond the evil stream no more may she move me, by the law which was made when I came forth from there. But if a lady of Heaven moves and directs you, as you say, there is no need of flattery: let it fully suffice that for her sake you ask me. Go, then, and see that you gird him with a smooth rush, and that you bathe his face so that you remove all defilement from it, for with eye dimmed by any mist it would not be fitting to go before the first minister of those of Paradise. This little island, round about its very base, down there where the wave beats it, bears rushes on its soft mud. No other plant which would put forth leaf or harden can live there, because it yields not to the buffetings. Then let not your return be this way. The sun, which is now rising, will show you where to take the mountain at an easier ascent."

Così sparì; e io sù mi levai
  sanza parlare, e tutto mi ritrassi
  al duca mio, e li occhi a lui drizzai. *111*
El cominciò: "Figliuol, segui i miei passi:
  volgianci in dietro, ché di qua dichina
  questa pianura a' suoi termini bassi." *114*
L'alba vinceva l'ora mattutina
  che fuggia innanzi, sì che di lontano
  conobbi il tremolar de la marina. *117*
Noi andavam per lo solingo piano
  com' om che torna a la perduta strada,
  che 'nfino ad essa li pare ire in vano. *120*
Quando noi fummo là 've la rugiada
  pugna col sole, per essere in parte
  dove, ad orezza, poco si dirada, *123*
ambo le mani in su l'erbetta sparte
  soavemente 'l mio maestro pose:
  ond' io, che fui accorto di sua arte, *126*
porsi ver' lui le guance lagrimose;
  ivi mi fece tutto discoverto
  quel color che l'inferno mi nascose. *129*
Venimmo poi in sul lito diserto,
  che mai non vide navicar sue acque
  omo, che di tornar sia poscia esperto. *132*
Quivi mi cinse sì com' altrui piacque:
  oh maraviglia! ché qual elli scelse
  l'umile pianta, cotal si rinacque
subitamente là onde l'avelse. *136*

So he vanished; and I rose up, without speaking, and drew all close to my leader and turned my eyes to him. "Son," he began, "follow my steps: let us turn back, for this plain slopes that way to its low limits."

The dawn was vanquishing the matin hour which fled before it, so that I recognized from afar the trembling of the sea. We were making our way across the solitary plain, like a man who returns to the road he has lost and, till he comes to it, seems to go in vain. When we came there where the dew strives with the sun, for being in a place where, in the breeze, it is little dispersed, my master gently laid both hands outspread on the grass. I therefore, aware of his purpose, reached toward him my tear-stained cheeks, and on them he wholly disclosed that color of mine which Hell had hidden.

Then we came on to the desert shore, that never saw any man navigate its waters who afterwards had experience of return. There, even as pleased another, he girded me. O marvel! that such as he plucked the humble plant, even such did it instantly spring up again, there whence he had uprooted it.

# PURGATORIO

GIÀ ERA 'l sole a l'orizzonte giunto
lo cui meridïan cerchio coverchia
Ierusalèm col suo più alto punto; *3*
e la notte, che opposita a lui cerchia,
uscia di Gange fuor con le Bilance,
che le caggion di man quando soverchia; *6*
sì che le bianche e le vermiglie guance,
là dov' i' era, de la bella Aurora
per troppa etate divenivan rance. *9*
Noi eravam lunghesso mare ancora,
come gente che pensa a suo cammino,
che va col cuore e col corpo dimora. *12*
Ed ecco, qual, sorpreso dal mattino,
per li grossi vapor Marte rosseggia
giù nel ponente sovra 'l suol marino, *15*
cotal m'apparve, s'io ancor lo veggia,
un lume per lo mar venir sì ratto,
che 'l muover suo nessun volar pareggia. *18*

## CANTO II

The sun had now reached the horizon whose meridian circle covers Jerusalem with its highest point; and night, circling opposite to him, was issuing forth from Ganges with the Scales, which fall from her hand when she exceeds, so that there where I was the white and rosy cheeks of fair Aurora were turning orange through too great age.

We were alongside the ocean yet, like folk who ponder on their road, who go in heart and linger in body; and lo, as when, suffused by dawn, Mars glows ruddy through the thick vapors low in the west over the ocean floor, so to me appeared—may I see it again! —a light coming over the sea so swiftly that no flight is equal to its motion;

Dal qual com' io un poco ebbi ritratto
l'occhio per domandar lo duca mio,
rividil più lucente e maggior fatto. 21

Poi d'ogne lato ad esso m'appario
un non sapeva che bianco, e di sotto
a poco a poco un altro a lui uscìo. 24

Lo mio maestro ancor non facea motto,
mentre che i primi bianchi apparver ali;
allor che ben conobbe il galeotto, 27

gridò: "Fa, fa che le ginocchia cali.
Ecco l'angel di Dio: piega le mani;
omai vedrai di sì fatti officiali. 30

Vedi che sdegna li argomenti umani,
sì che remo non vuol, né altro velo
che l'ali sue, tra liti sì lontani. 33

Vedi come l'ha dritte verso 'l cielo,
trattando l'aere con l'etterne penne,
che non si mutan come mortal pelo." 36

Poi, come più e più verso noi venne
l'uccel divino, più chiaro appariva;
per che l'occhio da presso nol sostenne, 39

ma chinail giuso; e quei sen venne a riva
con un vasello snelletto e leggero,
tanto che l'acqua nulla ne 'nghiottiva. 42

Da poppa stava il celestial nocchiero,
tal che parea beato per iscripto;
e più di cento spirti entro sediero. 45

"*In exitu Isräel de Aegypto*"
cantavan tutti insieme ad una voce
con quanto di quel salmo è poscia scripto. 48

from which when I had taken my eyes for a little in order to question my leader, I again saw it grown brighter and bigger. Then on each side of it appeared to me a something white, and from beneath it, little by little, came forth another whiteness. My master still said not a word, until the first whitenesses appeared as wings; then, when he clearly discerned the pilot, he cried, "Bend, bend your knees! Behold the angel of God! Clasp your hands: henceforth you shall see such ministers. Look how he scorns all human instruments, and will have no oar, nor other sail than his own wings between such distant shores; see how he holds them straight toward heaven, fanning the air with his eternal feathers that are not changed like mortal plumage."

Then, as the divine bird came nearer and nearer to us, the brighter did he appear, so that close up my eyes could not endure him and I cast them down; and he came on to the shore with a vessel so swift and light that the water took in naught of it. At the stern stood the celestial steersman, such, that blessedness seemed to be inscribed upon him; and within sat more than a hundred spirits. "*In exitu Israel de Aegypto*" all of them were singing together with one voice, with the rest of that psalm as it is written.

Poi fece il segno lor di santa croce;
ond' ei si gittar tutti in su la piaggia:
ed el sen gì, come venne, veloce. *51*

La turba che rimase lì, selvaggia
parea del loco, rimirando intorno
come colui che nove cose assaggia. *54*

Da tutte parti saettava il giorno
lo sol, ch'avea con le saette conte
di mezzo 'l ciel cacciato Capricorno, *57*

quando la nova gente alzò la fronte
ver' noi, dicendo a noi: "Se voi sapete,
mostratene la via di gire al monte." *60*

E Virgilio rispuose: "Voi credete
forse che siamo esperti d'esto loco;
ma noi siam peregrin come voi siete. *63*

Dianzi venimmo, innanzi a voi un poco,
per altra via, che fu sì aspra e forte,
che lo salire omai ne parrà gioco." *66*

L'anime, che si fuor di me accorte,
per lo spirare, ch'i' era ancor vivo,
maravigliando diventaro smorte. *69*

E come a messagger che porta ulivo
tragge la gente per udir novelle,
e di calcar nessun si mostra schivo, *72*

così al viso mio s'affisar quelle
anime fortunate tutte quante,
quasi oblïando d'ire a farsi belle. *75*

Io vidi una di lor trarresi avante
per abbracciarmi, con sì grande affetto,
che mosse me a far lo somigliante. *78*

Then he made the sign of holy cross upon them, whereon they all flung themselves upon the strand, and he went away swift as he had come.

The crowd which remained there seemed strange to the place, gazing about like those who essay new things. The sun was shooting forth the day on all sides and with his deft arrows had chased Capricorn from mid-heaven, when the new people raised their faces towards us, saying to us, "If you know, show us the way up the mountain."

And Virgil answered, "Perhaps you think we are acquainted with this place; but we are pilgrims, like yourselves. We came but now, a little while before you, by another road which was so rough and hard that henceforth the climb will seem but play to us."

The souls, who had perceived from my breathing that I was yet alive, marveling grew pale; and as to a messenger who bears an olive-branch the people crowd to hear the news, and no one shows himself shy of trampling, so did all of these fortunate souls fix their eyes on my face, as though forgetting to go to make themselves fair.

I saw one of them with such great affection drawing forward to embrace me that he moved me to do the same.

Ohi ombre vane, fuor che ne l'aspetto!
tre volte dietro a lei le mani avvinsi,
e tante mi tornai con esse al petto. *81*
Di maraviglia, credo, mi dipinsi;
per che l'ombra sorrise e si ritrasse,
e io, seguendo lei, oltre mi pinsi. *84*
Soavemente disse ch'io posasse;
allor conobbi chi era, e pregai
che, per parlarmi, un poco s'arrestasse. *87*
Rispuosemi: "Così com' io t'amai
nel mortal corpo, così t'amo sciolta:
però m'arresto; ma tu perché vai?" *90*
"Casella mio, per tornar altra volta
là dov' io son, fo io questo vïaggio,"
diss' io; "ma a te com' è tanta ora tolta?" *93*
Ed elli a me: "Nessun m'è fatto oltraggio,
se quei che leva quando e cui li piace,
più volte m'ha negato esto passaggio; *96*
ché di giusto voler lo suo si face:
veramente da tre mesi elli ha tolto
chi ha voluto intrar, con tutta pace. *99*
Ond' io, ch'era ora a la marina vòlto
dove l'acqua di Tevero s'insala,
benignamente fu' da lui ricolto. *102*
A quella foce ha elli or dritta l'ala,
però che sempre quivi si ricoglie
qual verso Acheronte non si cala." *105*
E io: "Se nuova legge non ti toglie
memoria o uso a l'amoroso canto
che mi solea quetar tutte mie voglie, *108*

O empty shades except in aspect! Three times I clasped my hands behind him and as often brought them back to my breast. Wonder, I think, was painted in my looks, whereat the shade smiled and drew back, and I, following him, pressed forward. Gently he bade me stand; then I knew who it was, and begged him that he would stay a little and talk with me.

He answered me, "Even as I loved you in my mortal body, so do I love you freed from it; therefore I stay. But you, why do you go?"

"My Casella, to return here once again where I am I make this journey," I said, "but how has so much time been taken from you?"

And he to me, "No wrong is done me if he who takes up whom and when he will has denied me this passage many times, for of a just will his own is made. Truly, for three months now he has taken with all peace whoever would embark. I, therefore, who was now turned to the seashore where the water of Tiber grows salt, was kindly gathered in by him. To that river-mouth he has now set his wings, for there the souls are always gathering that sink not down to Acheron."

And I, "If a new law does not take from you memory or practice of the songs of love which used to quiet in me all my longings,

di ciò ti piaccia consolare alquanto
l'anima mia, che, con la sua persona
venendo qui, è affannata tanto!" 111
"*Amor che ne la mente mi ragiona*"
cominciò elli allor sì dolcemente,
che la dolcezza ancor dentro mi suona. 114
Lo mio maestro e io e quella gente
ch'eran con lui parevan sì contenti,
come a nessun toccasse altro la mente. 117
Noi eravam tutti fissi e attenti
a le sue note; ed ecco il veglio onesto
gridando: "Che è ciò, spiriti lenti? 120
qual negligenza, quale stare è questo?
Correte al monte a spogliarvi lo scoglio
ch'esser non lascia a voi Dio manifesto." 123
Come quando, cogliendo biado o loglio,
li colombi adunati a la pastura,
queti, sanza mostrar l'usato orgoglio, 126
se cosa appare ond' elli abbian paura,
subitamente lasciano star l'esca,
perch' assaliti son da maggior cura; 129
così vid' io quella masnada fresca
lasciar lo canto, e fuggir ver' la costa,
com' om che va, né sa dove rïesca;
né la nostra partita fu men tosta. 133

may it please you therewith to comfort my soul somewhat, which coming hither with its body is so wearied."

"*Love that discourses in my mind,*" he then began so sweetly that the sweetness still within me sounds. My master and I and that folk who were with him appeared content as if naught else touched the mind of any. We were all rapt and attentive to his notes, when lo, the venerable old man, crying, "What is this, you laggard spirits? What negligence, what stay is this? Haste to the mountain to strip off the slough that lets not God be manifest to you."

As doves, when gathering wheat or tares, assembled all at their repast and quiet, without their usual show of pride, if something appears that frightens them, suddenly leave their food because they are assailed by a greater care; so I saw that new troop leave the song and hasten toward the hillside, like one who goes, but knows not where he may come forth; nor was our departure less quick.

AVVEGNA che la subitana fuga
dispergesse color per la campagna,
rivolti al monte ove ragion ne fruga, 3
i' mi ristrinsi a la fida compagna:
e come sare' io sanza lui corso?
chi m'avria tratto su per la montagna? 6
El mi parea da sé stesso rimorso:
o dignitosa coscïenza e netta,
come t'è picciol fallo amaro morso! 9
Quando li piedi suoi lasciar la fretta,
che l'onestade ad ogn' atto dismaga,
la mente mia, che prima era ristretta, 12
lo 'ntento rallargò, sì come vaga,
e diedi 'l viso mio incontr' al poggio
che 'nverso 'l ciel più alto si dislaga. 15
Lo sol, che dietro fiammeggiava roggio,
rotto m'era dinanzi a la figura,
ch'avëa in me de' suoi raggi l'appoggio. 18

# CANTO III

ALTHOUGH their sudden flight was scattering them over the plain, turned to the mountain where justice probes us, I drew close to my faithful companion. And how should I have sped without him? who would have brought me up the mountain? He seemed to me smitten with self-reproach. O pure and noble conscience, how bitter a sting is a little fault to you!

When his feet left off haste, which takes seemliness from every act, my mind, which at first had been restrained, widened its scope as in eager search, and I turned my face to the hill that rises highest heavenward from the sea. The sun, which was flaming red behind, was broken in front of me by the figure which was formed by the staying of its rays upon me.

Io mi volsi dallato con paura
d'essere abbandonato, quand' io vidi
solo dinanzi a me la terra oscura; 21
e 'l mio conforto: "Perché pur diffidi?"
a dir mi cominciò tutto rivolto;
"non credi tu me teco e ch'io ti guidi? 24
Vespero è già colà dov' è sepolto
lo corpo dentro al quale io facea ombra;
Napoli l'ha, e da Brandizio è tolto. 27
Ora, se innanzi a me nulla s'aombra,
non ti maravigliar più che d'i cieli
che l'uno a l'altro raggio non ingombra. 30
A sofferir tormenti, caldi e geli
simili corpi la Virtù dispone
che, come fa, non vuol ch'a noi si sveli. 33
Matto è chi spera che nostra ragione
possa trascorrer la infinita via
che tiene una sustanza in tre persone. 36
State contenti, umana gente, al *quia*;
ché, se potuto aveste veder tutto,
mestier non era parturir Maria; 39
e disïar vedeste sanza frutto
tai che sarebbe lor disio quetato,
ch'etternalmente è dato lor per lutto: 42
io dico d'Aristotile e di Plato
e di molt' altri"; e qui chinò la fronte,
e più non disse, e rimase turbato. 45
Noi divenimmo intanto a piè del monte;
quivi trovammo la roccia sì erta,
che 'ndarno vi sarien le gambe pronte. 48

I turned to my side, fearing that I was abandoned, when I saw the ground darkened before me only. And my comfort, turning full round, began to say to me, "Why do you still distrust? Do you not believe that I am with you and that I guide you? It is now evening in the place where the body is buried within which I made shadow: Naples has it, and it was taken from Brindisi. If in front of me now there is no shadow, do not marvel more than at the heavens, that one obstructs not the light from the other. To suffer torments, heat, and frost, bodies such as these that Power ordains, which wills not that the way of Its working be revealed to us. Foolish is he who hopes that our reason may compass the infinite course taken by One Substance in Three Persons. Be content, human race, with the *quia*; for if you had been able to see everything, no need was there for Mary to give birth; and you have seen desiring fruitlessly men such that their desire would have been satisfied which is given them for eternal grief: I speak of Aristotle and of Plato and of many others." And here he bent his brow and said no more, and remained troubled.

We came meanwhile to the foot of the mountain. Here we found the cliff so steep that in vain would legs be nimble there.

Tra Lerice e Turbìa la più diserta,
la più rotta ruina è una scala,
verso di quella, agevole e aperta. 51
"Or chi sa da qual man la costa cala,"
disse 'l maestro mio fermando 'l passo,
"sì che possa salir chi va sanz' ala?" 54
E mentre ch'e' tenendo 'l viso basso
essaminava del cammin la mente,
e io mirava suso intorno al sasso, 57
da man sinistra m'apparì una gente
d'anime, che movieno i piè ver' noi,
e non pareva, sì venïan lente. 60
"Leva," diss' io, "maestro, li occhi tuoi:
ecco di qua chi ne darà consiglio,
se tu da te medesmo aver nol puoi." 63
Guardò allora, e con libero piglio
rispuose: "Andiamo in là, ch'ei vegnon piano;
e tu ferma la spene, dolce figlio." 66
Ancora era quel popol di lontano,
i' dico dopo i nostri mille passi,
quanto un buon gittator trarria con mano, 69
quando si strinser tutti ai duri massi
de l'alta ripa, e stetter fermi e stretti
com' a guardar, chi va dubbiando, stassi. 72
"O ben finiti, o già spiriti eletti,"
Virgilio incominciò, "per quella pace
ch'i' credo che per voi tutti s'aspetti, 75
ditene dove la montagna giace,
sì che possibil sia l'andare in suso;
ché perder tempo a chi più sa più spiace." 78

Between Lerici and Turbia the most deserted, the most broken landslip is a stairway easy and free compared with that.

"Now who knows on which hand the hillside slopes," said my master, staying his step, "so that he can ascend who goes without wings?" And while he held his face low, searching his mind about the road, and I was looking up around the rock, on the left appeared to me a company of souls who were moving their feet towards us and yet seemed not to approach, they came on so slowly.

"Master," said I, "lift up your eyes: behold yonder those who will give us counsel, if you cannot find it in yourself."

Then he looked, and with an air of relief replied, "Let us go thither, for they come slowly; and do you make firm your hope, dear son."

As yet that people were still as far (I mean, after a thousand paces of ours) as a good thrower would cast with his hand, when they all pressed close to the hard rocks of the steep cliff and stood still and close together, as men stop to look who are in doubt.

"O you who have made a good end, spirits already elect," Virgil began, "by that peace which, I believe, awaits you all, tell us where the mountain slopes so that it is possible to go up, for time lost irks him most who knows most."

Come le pecorelle escon del chiuso
a una, a due, a tre, e l'altre stanno
timidette atterrando l'occhio e 'l muso; 81
e ciò che fa la prima, e l'altre fanno,
addossandosi a lei, s'ella s'arresta,
semplici e quete, e lo 'mperché non sanno; 84
sì vid' io muovere a venir la testa
di quella mandra fortunata allotta,
pudica in faccia e ne l'andare onesta. 87
Come color dinanzi vider rotta
la luce in terra dal mio destro canto,
sì che l'ombra era da me a la grotta, 90
restaro, e trasser sé in dietro alquanto,
e tutti li altri che venieno appresso,
non sappiendo 'l perché, fenno altrettanto. 93
"Sanza vostra domanda io vi confesso
che questo è corpo uman che voi vedete;
per che 'l lume del sole in terra è fesso. 96
Non vi maravigliate, ma credete
che non sanza virtù che da ciel vegna
cerchi di soverchiar questa parete." 99
Così 'l maestro; e quella gente degna
"Tornate," disse, "intrate innanzi dunque,"
coi dossi de le man faccendo insegna. 102
E un di loro incominciò: "Chiunque
tu se', così andando, volgi 'l viso:
pon mente se di là mi vedesti unque." 105
Io mi volsi ver' lui e guardail fiso:
biondo era e bello e di gentile aspetto,
ma l'un de' cigli un colpo avea diviso. 108

As sheep come forth from the fold by one and two and three, and the rest stand timid, bending eyes and muzzle to the ground; and what the first does the others also do, huddling themselves to it if it stops, simple and quiet, and know not why; so saw I then the head of that happy flock move to come on, modest in countenance, in movement dignified.

When those in front saw the light broken on the ground at my right side, so that my shadow was from me to the cliff, they halted and drew back somewhat; and all the others that came after did the same, not knowing why. "Without your asking I confess to you that this is a human body which you see, whereby the light of the sun is cleft on the ground. Do not marvel, but believe that not without power which comes from Heaven does he seek to scale this wall." Thus my master. And that worthy company said, "Turn back then and go on before us," with the backs of their hands making sign. And one of them began, "Whoever you are, turn your face as you thus go: consider if ever you saw me yonder." I turned to him, and looked at him fixedly: blond he was, and handsome, and of noble mien, but a blow had cloven one of his eyebrows.

Quand' io mi fui umilmente disdetto
d'averlo visto mai, el disse: "Or vedi";
e mostrommi una piaga a sommo 'l petto. *111*
Poi sorridendo disse: "Io son Manfredi,
nepote di Costanza imperadrice;
ond' io ti priego che, quando tu riedi, *114*
vadi a mia bella figlia, genitrice
de l'onor di Cicilia e d'Aragona,
e dichi 'l vero a lei, s'altro si dice. *117*
Poscia ch'io ebbi rotta la persona
di due punte mortali, io mi rendei,
piangendo, a quei che volontier perdona. *120*
Orribil furon li peccati miei;
ma la bontà infinita ha sì gran braccia,
che prende ciò che si rivolge a lei. *123*
Se 'l pastor di Cosenza, che a la caccia
di me fu messo per Clemente allora,
avesse in Dio ben letta questa faccia, *126*
l'ossa del corpo mio sarieno ancora
in co del ponte presso a Benevento,
sotto la guardia de la grave mora. *129*
Or le bagna la pioggia e move il vento
di fuor dal regno, quasi lungo 'l Verde,
dov' e' le trasmutò a lume spento. *132*
Per lor maladizion sì non si perde,
che non possa tornar l'etterno amore,
mentre che la speranza ha fior del verde. *135*

When I had humbly disclaimed ever to have seen him, he said, "Look now," and showed me a wound high on his breast, then said smiling, "I am Manfred, grandson of the Empress Constance. Therefore I beg of you that when you return you go to my fair daughter, mother of the pride of Sicily and of Aragon, and tell her the truth, if aught else be told. After I had my body pierced by two mortal stabs I gave myself weeping to Him who pardons willingly; horrible were my sins, but the Infinite Goodness has such wide arms that It receives all who turn to It. If Cosenza's pastor, who was then sent by Clement to hunt me down, had well read that page in God, the bones of my body would yet be at the bridge-head near Benevento, under the guard of the heavy cairn. Now the rain washes them and the wind stirs them, beyond the Kingdom, hard by the Verde, whither he transported them with tapers quenched. By curse of theirs none is so lost that the Eternal Love cannot return, so long as hope keeps aught of green.

Vero è che quale in contumacia more
di Santa Chiesa, ancor ch'al fin si penta,
star li convien da questa ripa in fore, *138*
per ognun tempo ch'elli è stato, trenta,
in sua presunzïon, se tal decreto
più corto per buon prieghi non diventa. *141*
Vedi oggimai se tu mi puoi far lieto,
revelando a la mia buona Costanza
come m'hai visto, e anco esto divieto;
ché qui per quei di là molto s'avanza." *145*

True it is that whoso dies in contumacy of Holy Church, even though he repent at the last, must stay outside upon this bank thirtyfold for all the time that he has lived in his presumption, if such decree is not made shorter by holy prayers. See now if you can make me glad by revealing to my good Constance how you have seen me, as well as this ban: for much is gained here through those who are yonder."

QUANDO per dilettanze o ver per doglie,
che alcuna virtù nostra comprenda,
l'anima bene ad essa si raccoglie, 3
par ch'a nulla potenza più intenda;
e questo è contra quello error che crede
ch'un'anima sovr' altra in noi s'accenda. 6
E però, quando s'ode cosa o vede
che tegna forte a sé l'anima volta,
vassene 'l tempo e l'uom non se n'avvede; 9
ch'altra potenza è quella che l'ascolta,
e altra è quella c'ha l'anima intera:
questa è quasi legata e quella è sciolta. 12
Di ciò ebb' io esperïenza vera,
udendo quello spirto e ammirando;
ché ben cinquanta gradi salito era 15
lo sole, e io non m'era accorto, quando
venimmo ove quell' anime ad una
gridaro a noi: "Qui è vostro dimando." 18
Maggiore aperta molte volte impruna
con una forcatella di sue spine
l'uom de la villa quando l'uva imbruna, 21

# CANTO IV

When through impression of pleasure, or of pain, which some one of our faculties receives, the soul is wholly centered thereon, it seems that it gives heed to no other of its powers; and this is contrary to that error which holds that one soul above another is kindled within us; and therefore when aught is heard or seen which holds the soul strongly bent to it, the time passes away and we perceive it not, for one faculty is that which notes it, and another that which possesses the entire soul, the latter as it were bound, the former free. Of this I had true experience as I listened to that spirit and marveled; for full fifty degrees the sun had climbed and I had not perceived it, when we came to where those souls with one voice cried out to us, "Here is what you ask."

A bigger opening many a time the man of the farm hedges up with a little forkful of his thorns, when the grape is darkening,

che non era la calla onde salìne
  lo duca mio, e io appresso, soli,
  come da noi la schiera si partìne. 24

Vassi in Sanleo e discendesi in Noli,
  montasi su Bismantova in cacume
  con esso i piè; ma qui convien ch'om voli; 27

dico con l'ale snelle e con le piume
  del gran disio, di retro a quel condotto
  che speranza mi dava e facea lume. 30

Noi salavam per entro 'l sasso rotto,
  e d'ogne lato ne stringea lo stremo,
  e piedi e man volea il suol di sotto. 33

Poi che noi fummo in su l'orlo suppremo
  de l'alta ripa, a la scoperta piaggia,
  "Maestro mio," diss' io, "che via faremo?" 36

Ed elli a me: "Nessun tuo passo caggia;
  pur su al monte dietro a me acquista,
  fin che n'appaia alcuna scorta saggia." 39

Lo sommo er' alto che vincea la vista,
  e la costa superba più assai
  che da mezzo quadrante a centro lista. 42

Io era lasso, quando cominciai:
  "O dolce padre, volgiti, e rimira
  com' io rimango sol, se non restai." 45

"Figliuol mio," disse, "infin quivi ti tira,"
  additandomi un balzo poco in sùe
  che da quel lato il poggio tutto gira. 48

Sì mi spronaron le parole sue,
  ch'i' mi sforzai carpando appresso lui,
  tanto che 'l cinghio sotto i piè mi fue. 51

than was the gap by which my leader mounted, and I after him, we two alone, when that troop had parted from us. One can walk to San Leo and descend to Noli, one can mount Bismantova to the summit, with feet alone; but here a man must fly, I mean with the swift wings and the plumes of great desire, behind that leader, who gave me hope and was a light to me. We were climbing within the cleft rock, and the surface on either side pressed close on us, and the ground beneath required both feet and hands.

After we were upon the upper edge of the high bank, out on the open slope, "My master," I said, "what way shall we take?" And he to me, "Let no step of yours descend, but ever up the mountain win your way behind me until some wise escort appear to us."

So high was the top that it surpassed my sight, and the slope was steeper far than a line from mid-quadrant to center. I was weary when I began, "O sweet father, turn and look how I remain alone if you do not stop!"

"My son," he said, "drag yourself up as far as here," pointing out to me a ledge a little higher up, which on that side circles all the mountain. His words so spurred me on that I forced myself to creep after him until the ledge was beneath my feet.

A seder ci ponemmo ivi ambedui
  vòlti a levante ond' eravam saliti,
  che suole a riguardar giovare altrui. *54*
Li occhi prima drizzai ai bassi liti;
  poscia li alzai al sole, e ammirava
  che da sinistra n'eravam feriti. *57*
Ben s'avvide il poeta ch'ïo stava
  stupido tutto al carro de la luce,
  ove tra noi e Aquilone intrava. *60*
Ond' elli a me: "Se Castore e Poluce
  fossero in compagnia di quello specchio
  che sù e giù del suo lume conduce, *63*
tu vedresti il Zodïaco rubecchio
  ancora a l'Orse più stretto rotare,
  se non uscisse fuor del cammin vecchio. *66*
Come ciò sia, se 'l vuoi poter pensare,
  dentro raccolto, imagina Sïòn
  con questo monte in su la terra stare *69*
sì, ch'amendue hanno un solo orizzòn
  e diversi emisperi; onde la strada
  che mal non seppe carreggiar Fetòn, *72*
vedrai come a costui convien che vada
  da l'un, quando a colui da l'altro fianco,
  se lo 'ntelletto tuo ben chiaro bada." *75*
"Certo, maestro mio," diss' io, "unquanco
  non vid' io chiaro sì com' io discerno
  là dove mio ingegno parea manco, *78*
che 'l mezzo cerchio del moto superno,
  che si chiama Equatore in alcun' arte,
  e che sempre riman tra 'l sole e 'l verno, *81*

There we both sat down, turned towards the East whence we had climbed, for to look back that way is wont to encourage a man. I first directed my eyes to the shores below, then raised them to the sun, marveling that we were struck by it on the left side. Right well the poet perceived that I was all amazed at the chariot of the light where it was entering between us and Aquilo; wherefore he to me, "If Castor and Pollux were in company of that mirror which conducts its light up and down, you would see the ruddy Zodiac revolve yet closer to the Bears, unless it strayed from its old road. If you would conceive how this can be, concentrate within you and imagine Zion and this mountain to be so placed on the earth that they have one sole horizon and different hemispheres; then you will see that the way which Phaëthon, unhappily for him, knew not how to drive, must needs pass this mountain on the one side when it passes that mountain on the other, if your mind right clearly apprehends."

"Surely, my master," I said, "never did I see so clearly as I now discern, where my wit seemed lacking, that the mid-circle of the celestial motion, which is called the Equator in a certain science, and which lies always between the sun and the winter,

per la ragion che di', quinci si parte
verso settentrïon, quanto li Ebrei
vedevan lui verso la calda parte. *84*

Ma se a te piace, volontier saprei
quanto avemo ad andar; ché 'l poggio sale
più che salir non posson li occhi miei." *87*

Ed elli a me: "Questa montagna è tale,
che sempre al cominciar di sotto è grave;
e quant' om più va sù, e men fa male. *90*

Però, quand' ella ti parrà soave
tanto, che sù andar ti fia leggero
com' a seconda giù andar per nave, *93*

allor sarai al fin d'esto sentiero;
quivi di riposar l'affanno aspetta.
Più non rispondo, e questo so per vero." *96*

E com' elli ebbe sua parola detta,
una voce di presso sonò: "Forse
che di sedere in pria avrai distretta!" *99*

Al suon di lei ciascun di noi si torse,
e vedemmo a mancina un gran petrone,
del qual né io né ei prima s'accorse. *102*

Là ci traemmo; e ivi eran persone
che si stavano a l'ombra dietro al sasso
come l'uom per negghienza a star si pone. *105*

E un di lor, che mi sembiava lasso,
sedeva e abbracciava le ginocchia,
tenendo 'l viso giù tra esse basso. *108*

"O dolce segnor mio," diss' io, "adocchia
colui che mostra sé più negligente
che se pigrizia fosse sua serocchia." *111*

for the reason that you tell, departs here toward the north, as far as the Hebrews used to see it toward the hot climes. But, if it please you, I would fain know how far we have to go, for the hillside rises higher than my eyes can reach."

And he to me, "This mountain is such that ever at the beginning below it is toilsome, but the higher one goes the less it wearies. Therefore, when it shall seem to you so pleasant that the going up is as easy for you as going downstream in a boat, then will you be at the end of this path: hope there to rest your weariness; no more I answer, and this I know for true."

And when he had spoken these words, there sounded a voice close by, "Perhaps before then you'll need to sit!" At the sound of it each of us turned, and we saw on our left a great boulder which neither he nor I had noticed before. We went over to it, and there were persons lounging in the shade behind the rock, even as men who settle themselves to rest for laziness; and one of them, who seemed to me weary, was sitting and clasping his knees, holding his face low down between them.

"O my sweet lord," said I, "set your eye on that one who shows himself lazier than if sloth were his sister!"

Allor si volse a noi e puose mente,
movendo 'l viso pur su per la coscia,
e disse: "Or va tu sù, che se' valente!" *114*
Conobbi allor chi era, e quella angoscia
che m'avacciava un poco ancor la lena,
non m'impedì l'andare a lui; e poscia *117*
ch'a lui fu' giunto, alzò la testa a pena,
dicendo: "Hai ben veduto come 'l sole
da l'omero sinistro il carro mena?" *120*
Li atti suoi pigri e le corte parole
mosser le labbra mie un poco a riso;
poi cominciai: "Belacqua, a me non dole *123*
di te omai; ma dimmi: perché assiso
quiritto se'? attendi tu iscorta,
o pur lo modo usato t'ha' ripriso?" *126*
Ed elli: "O frate, andar in sù che porta?
ché non mi lascerebbe ire a' martìri
l'angel di Dio che siede in su la porta. *129*
Prima convien che tanto il ciel m'aggiri
di fuor da essa, quanto fece in vita,
per ch'io 'ndugiai al fine i buon sospiri, *132*
se orazïone in prima non m'aita
che surga sù di cuor che in grazia viva;
l'altra che val, che 'n ciel non è udita?" *135*
E già il poeta innanzi mi saliva,
e dicea: "Vienne omai; vedi ch'è tocco
meridïan dal sole, e a la riva
cuopre la notte già col piè Morrocco." *139*

Then he turned to us and gave heed, barely moving his look up along his thigh, and said, "Then you go on up who are so sturdy!"

Then I knew who he was, and that toil which still quickened my breath a little did not hinder my going to him; and when I had got to him, he scarcely lifted his head, saying, "Have you truly seen how the sun drives his chariot on your left side?"

His lazy actions and his brief words moved my lips to smile a little, then I began, "Belacqua, I am not grieved for you now; but tell me, why are you sitting here? Are you waiting for an escort? Or have you only resumed your old ways?"

And he, "O brother, what's the use of going up? For God's angel who sits at the gate would not let me pass to the torments. First must the heavens revolve around me outside it, so long as they did during my life, because I delayed good sighs until the end—unless prayer first aid me which rises from a heart that lives in grace. What avails the other, which is not heard in Heaven?"

And now the poet was climbing before me and saying, "Come on now: see, the meridian is touched by the sun, and on the shore night now sets its foot on Morocco."

# PURGATORIO

Io ERA già da quell' ombre partito,
  e seguitava l'orme del mio duca,
  quando di retro a me, drizzando 'l dito, *3*
una gridò: "Ve' che non par che luca
  lo raggio da sinistra a quel di sotto,
  e come vivo par che si conduca!" *6*
Li occhi rivolsi al suon di questo motto,
  e vidile guardar per maraviglia
  pur me, pur me, e 'l lume ch'era rotto. *9*
"Perché l'animo tuo tanto s'impiglia,"
  disse 'l maestro, "che l'andare allenti?
  che ti fa ciò che quivi si pispiglia? *12*
Vien dietro a me, e lascia dir le genti:
  sta come torre ferma, che non crolla
  già mai la cima per soffiar di venti; *15*
ché sempre l'omo in cui pensier rampolla
  sovra pensier, da sé dilunga il segno,
  perché la foga l'un de l'altro insolla." *18*

# CANTO V

I HAD NOW parted from those shades and was following in the steps of my leader, when one behind me, pointing his finger, cried, "See, the rays do not seem to shine on the left of him below, and he seems to bear himself like one who is alive!"

I turned my eyes at the sound of these words, and saw them gazing in astonishment at me alone, at me alone, and the light that was broken.

"Why is your mind so entangled," said the master, "that you slacken your pace? What matters to you what is whispered here? Follow me and let the people talk. Stand as a firm tower which never shakes its summit for blast of winds; for always the man in whom thought wells up on thought sets back his mark, for the one thought weakens the force of the other."

Che potea io ridir, se non "Io vegno"?
Dissilo, alquanto del color consperso
che fa l'uom di perdon talvolta degno. 21
E 'ntanto per la costa di traverso
venivan genti innanzi a noi un poco,
cantando "*Miserere*" a verso a verso. 24
Quando s'accorser ch'i' non dava loco
per lo mio corpo al trapassar d'i raggi,
mutar lor canto in un "oh!" lungo e roco; 27
e due di loro, in forma di messaggi,
corsero incontr' a noi e dimandarne:
"Di vostra condizion fatene saggi." 30
E 'l mio maestro: "Voi potete andarne
e ritrarre a color che vi mandaro
che 'l corpo di costui è vera carne. 33
Se per veder la sua ombra restaro,
com' io avviso, assai è lor risposto:
fàccianli onore, ed esser può lor caro." 36
Vapori accesi non vid' io sì tosto
di prima notte mai fender sereno,
né, sol calando, nuvole d'agosto, 39
che color non tornasser suso in meno;
e, giunti là, con li altri a noi dier volta,
come schiera che scorre sanza freno. 42
"Questa gente che preme a noi è molta,
e vegnonti a pregar," disse 'l poeta:
"però pur va, e in andando ascolta." 45
"O anima che vai per esser lieta
con quelle membra con le quai nascesti,"
venian gridando, "un poco il passo queta. 48

What could I answer if not, "I come"? I said it, overspread somewhat with that color which sometimes makes a man worthy of pardon.

And meanwhile across the mountain slope came people a little in front of us, singing the *Miserere* verse by verse. When they perceived that I gave no place to the passage of the rays through my body, they changed their song into an "Oh!" long and hoarse; and two of them, as messengers, ran to meet us, and asked of us, "Let us know of your condition."

And my master said, "You may go back and report to those who sent you that this man's body is true flesh. If they stopped for seeing his shadow, as I suppose, they have sufficient answer. Let them do him honor, and it may be dear to them."

Never did I see kindled vapors cleave the bright sky at early night, or August clouds at sunset, so swiftly as these returned above; and, arrived there, they with the others wheeled round towards us, like a troop that runs without curb.

"These people that press to us are many, and they come to entreat you," said the poet; "but do you continue on your way and, while going, listen."

"O soul that go to your bliss with those members with which you were born," they came crying, "stay your steps for a little;

Guarda s'alcun di noi unqua vedesti,
sì che di lui di là novella porti:
deh, perché vai? deh, perché non t'arresti? 51
Noi fummo tutti già per forza morti,
e peccatori infino a l'ultima ora;
quivi lume del ciel ne fece accorti, 54
sì che, pentendo e perdonando, fora
di vita uscimmo a Dio pacificati,
che del disio di sé veder n'accora." 57
E io: "Perché ne' vostri visi guati,
non riconosco alcun; ma s'a voi piace
cosa ch'io possa, spiriti ben nati, 60
voi dite, e io farò per quella pace
che, dietro a' piedi di sì fatta guida,
di mondo in mondo cercar mi si face." 63
E uno incominciò: "Ciascun si fida
del beneficio tuo sanza giurarlo,
pur che 'l voler nonpossa non ricida. 66
Ond' io, che solo innanzi a li altri parlo,
ti priego, se mai vedi quel paese
che siede tra Romagna e quel di Carlo, 69
che tu mi sie di tuoi prieghi cortese
in Fano, sì che ben per me s'adori
pur ch'i' possa purgar le gravi offese. 72
Quindi fu' io; ma li profondi fóri
ond' uscì 'l sangue in sul quale io sedea,
fatti mi fuoro in grembo a li Antenori, 75
là dov' io più sicuro esser credea:
quel da Esti il fé far, che m'avea in ira
assai più là che dritto non volea. 78

look if you have ever seen any of us, so that you may carry news of him yonder. Ah, why do you go? Ah, why do you not stay? We were all done to death by violence, and sinners up to the last hour. Then light from Heaven made us mindful, so that, repenting and pardoning, we came forth from life at peace with God, who fills our hearts with sad longing to see Him."

And I, "Although I gaze upon your faces, I do not recognize any; but if aught that I can do be pleasing to you, spirits well-born, speak, and I will do it, by that peace which, following in the steps of such a guide, makes me pursue it from world to world."

And one began, "Each of us trusts in your good offices without your oath, if only lack of power thwart not the will; wherefore I, who speak alone before the others, do beg of you, if ever you see that country which lies between Romagna and that of Charles, that you be courteous to me with your prayers in Fano, so that holy orison be made for me, that I may purge away my grievous sins. Thence I sprang; but the deep wounds whence flowed the blood in which I had my life were dealt me in the bosom of the Antenori, there where I thought to be most secure: he of Este had it done, who held me in wrath far beyond what justice warranted;

Ma s'io fosse fuggito inver' la Mira,
quando fu' sovragiunto ad Orïaco,
ancor sarei di là dove si spira. *81*

Corsi al palude, e le cannucce e 'l braco
m'impigliar sì ch'i' caddi; e lì vid' io
de le mie vene farsi in terra laco." *84*

Poi disse un altro: "Deh, se quel disio
si compia che ti tragge a l'alto monte,
con buona pïetate aiuta il mio! *87*

Io fui di Montefeltro, io son Bonconte;
Giovanna o altri non ha di me cura;
per ch'io vo tra costor con bassa fronte." *90*

E io a lui: "Qual forza o qual ventura
ti travïò sì fuor di Campaldino,
che non si seppe mai tua sepultura?" *93*

"Oh!" rispuos' elli, "a piè del Casentino
traversa un'acqua c'ha nome l'Archiano,
che sovra l'Ermo nasce in Apennino. *96*

Là 've 'l vocabol suo diventa vano,
arriva' io forato ne la gola,
fuggendo a piede e sanguinando il piano. *99*

Quivi perdei la vista e la parola;
nel nome di Maria fini', e quivi
caddi, e rimase la mia carne sola. *102*

Io dirò vero, e tu 'l ridì tra ' vivi:
l'angel di Dio mi prese, e quel d'inferno
gridava: 'O tu del ciel, perché mi privi? *105*

Tu te ne porti di costui l'etterno
per una lagrimetta che 'l mi toglie;
ma io farò de l'altro altro governo!' *108*

but if I had fled toward La Mira when I was surprised at Oriaco I should yet be yonder where men breathe. I ran to the marsh, and the reeds and the mire so entangled me that I fell, and there I saw form on the ground a pool from my veins."

Then said another, "Ah, so may that desire be fulfilled which draws you up the lofty mountain, do you with gracious pity help my own. I was of Montefeltro, I am Buonconte. Giovanna, or any other, has no care for me, so that I go among these with downcast brow."

And I to him, "What force or what chance so carried you astray from Campaldino that your burial-place was never known?"

"Oh!" he answered, "at the foot of the Casentino a stream crosses, named the Archiano, which rises in the Apennines above the Hermitage. To the place where its name is lost I came, wounded in the throat, flying on foot and bloodying the plain. There I lost my sight and speech. I ended on the name of Mary, and there I fell, and my flesh remained alone. I will tell the truth, and do you repeat it among the living. The Angel of God took me, and he from Hell cried, 'O you from Heaven, why do you rob me? You carry off with you the eternal part of him for one little tear which takes him from me; but of the rest I will make other disposal!'

Ben sai come ne l'aere si raccoglie
quell' umido vapor che in acqua riede,
tosto che sale dove 'l freddo il coglie. 111
Giunse quel mal voler che pur mal chiede
con lo 'ntelletto, e mosse il fummo e 'l vento
per la virtù che sua natura diede. 114
Indi la valle, come 'l dì fu spento,
da Pratomagno al gran giogo coperse
di nebbia; e 'l ciel di sopra fece intento, 117
sì che 'l pregno aere in acqua si converse;
la pioggia cadde, e a' fossati venne
di lei ciò che la terra non sofferse; 120
e come ai rivi grandi si convenne,
ver' lo fiume real tanto veloce
si ruinò, che nulla la ritenne. 123
Lo corpo mio gelato in su la foce
trovò l'Archian rubesto; e quel sospinse
ne l'Arno, e sciolse al mio petto la croce 126
ch'i' fe' di me quando 'l dolor mi vinse;
voltòmmi per le ripe e per lo fondo,
poi di sua preda mi coperse e cinse." 129
"Deh, quando tu sarai tornato al mondo
e riposato de la lunga via,"
seguitò 'l terzo spirito al secondo, 132
"ricorditi di me, che son la Pia;
Siena mi fé, disfecemi Maremma:
salsi colui che 'nnanellata pria
disposando m'avea con la sua gemma." 136

"You know well how in the air is condensed that moist vapor which turns to water soon as it rises where the cold seizes it. Evil will that seeks only evil he joined with intellect, and, by the power his nature gave, stirred the mists and the wind; then when day was spent, he covered with clouds the valley from Pratomagno to the great mountain chain and so charged the sky overhead that the pregnant air was turned to water. The rain fell, and that which the ground refused came to the gulleys and, gathering in great torrents, so swiftly rushed toward the royal river that nothing stayed its course. The raging Archiano found my frozen body at its mouth and swept it into the Arno and loosed the cross on my breast which I had made of me when pain overcame me. It rolled me along its banks and along its bottom, then covered and wrapped me with its spoils."

"Pray, when you have returned to the world and have rested from your long journey," the third spirit followed on the second, "remember me, who am la Pia. Siena made me, Maremma unmade me, as he knows who with his ring had plighted me to him in wedlock."

# PURGATORIO

QUANDO si parte il gioco de la zara,
colui che perde si riman dolente,
repetendo le volte, e tristo impara; *3*
con l'altro se ne va tutta la gente;
qual va dinanzi, e qual di dietro il prende,
e qual dallato li si reca a mente; *6*
el non s'arresta, e questo e quello intende;
a cui porge la man, più non fa pressa;
e così da la calca si difende. *9*
Tal era io in quella turba spessa,
volgendo a loro, e qua e là, la faccia,
e promettendo mi sciogliea da essa. *12*
Quiv' era l'Aretin che da le braccia
fiere di Ghin di Tacco ebbe la morte,
e l'altro ch'annegò correndo in caccia. *15*
Quivi pregava con le mani sporte
Federigo Novello, e quel da Pisa
che fé parer lo buon Marzucco forte. *18*

# CANTO VI

WHEN THE game of hazard breaks up, the loser is left disconsolate, repeating the throws and sadly learns. With the other all the people go along: one goes in front, one plucks him from behind, and at his side one brings himself to mind. He does not stop, but listens to this one and that one; each to whom he reaches forth his hand presses on him no longer, and thus from the throng he defends himself. Such was I in that dense crowd, turning my face to them this way and that and, by promising, I got free from them. Here was the Aretine who met his death at the fierce hands of Ghino di Tacco; and the other who was drowned as he fled in the rout; here Federigo Novello was imploring with outstretched hands, and he of Pisa who made the good Marzucco show fortitude.

Vidi conte Orso e l'anima divisa
dal corpo suo per astio e per inveggia,
com' e' dicea, non per colpa commisa; 21
Pier da la Broccia dico; e qui proveggia,
mentr' è di qua, la donna di Brabante,
sì che però non sia di peggior greggia. 24
Come libero fui da tutte quante
quell' ombre che pregar pur ch'altri prieghi,
sì che s'avacci lor divenir sante, 27
io cominciai: "El par che tu mi nieghi,
o luce mia, espresso in alcun testo
che decreto del cielo orazion pieghi; 30
e questa gente prega pur di questo:
sarebbe dunque loro speme vana,
o non m'è 'l detto tuo ben manifesto?" 33
Ed elli a me: "La mia scrittura è piana;
e la speranza di costor non falla,
se ben si guarda con la mente sana; 36
ché cima di giudicio non s'avvalla
perché foco d'amor compia in un punto
ciò che de' sodisfar chi qui s'astalla; 39
e là dov' io fermai cotesto punto,
non s'ammendava, per pregar, difetto,
perché 'l priego da Dio era disgiunto. 42
Veramente a così alto sospetto
non ti fermar, se quella nol ti dice
che lume fia tra 'l vero e lo 'ntelletto. 45
Non so se 'ntendi: io dico di Beatrice;
tu la vedrai di sopra, in su la vetta
di questo monte, ridere e felice." 48

I saw Count Orso; and the soul severed from its body by spite and by envy, as it said, and not for fault committed, Pierre de la Brosse, I mean: and let the Lady of Brabant look to it, while she is here, so that for this she be not of the worse flock.

As soon as I was free of all those shades, whose one prayer was that others should pray, so that their way to blessedness may be sped, I began, "It seems to me, O my light, that you deny expressly in a certain passage that prayer bends the decree of heaven; and these people pray but for this—shall then their hope be vain, or are your words not rightly clear to me?"

And he to me, "My writing is plain and the hope of these souls is not fallacious, if with sound judgment you consider well; for the summit of justice is not lowered because the fire of love fulfil in a moment that which he must satisfy who sojourns here; and there where I affirmed that point, default could not be amended by prayer, because the prayer was disjoined from God. But do not rest in so profound a doubt, except she tell you who shall be a light between the truth and the intellect. I know not if you understand: I speak of Beatrice. You will see her above, smiling and happy, on the summit of this mountain."

E io: "Segnore, andiamo a maggior fretta,
chè già non m'affatico come dianzi,
e vedi omai che 'l poggio l'ombra getta." 51
"Noi anderem con questo giorno innanzi,"
rispuose, "quanto più potremo omai;
ma 'l fatto è d'altra forma che non stanzi. 54
Prima che sie là sù, tornar vedrai
colui che già si cuopre de la costa,
sì che ' suoi raggi tu romper non fai. 57
Ma vedi là un'anima che, posta
sola soletta, inverso noi riguarda:
quella ne 'nsegnerà la via più tosta." 60
Venimmo a lei: o anima lombarda,
come ti stavi altera e disdegnosa
e nel mover de li occhi onesta e tarda! 63
Ella non ci dicëa alcuna cosa,
ma lasciavane gir, solo sguardando
a guisa di leon quando si posa. 66
Pur Virgilio si trasse a lei, pregando
che ne mostrasse la miglior salita;
e quella non rispuose al suo dimando, 69
ma di nostro paese e de la vita
ci 'nchiese; e 'l dolce duca incominciava
"Mantüa . . . ," e l'ombra, tutta in sé romita, 72
surse ver' lui del loco ove pria stava,
dicendo: "O Mantoano, io son Sordello
de la tua terra!"; e l'un l'altro abbracciava. 75
Ahi serva Italia, di dolore ostello,
nave sanza nocchiere in gran tempesta,
non donna di provincie, ma bordello! 78

And I, "My lord, let us go on with greater haste, for now I do not weary as before, and see how the hill now casts its shadow."

"We will go forward with this day," he answered, "as far as yet we may, but the fact is quite other than you suppose. Before you are there above you will see him return that is now hidden by the slope, so that you do not break his beams. But see yonder a soul seated all alone, who is looking towards us; he will point out to us the quickest way."

We came to him: O Lombard soul, how lofty and disdainful was your bearing, and the movement of your eyes how grave and slow! He said nothing to us, but let us go on, watching only after the fashion of a couching lion; but Virgil drew on towards him, asking him to show us the best ascent; and he did not reply to his question, but inquired of our country and condition. And the gentle leader began, "Mantua—"; and the shade, all in himself recluse, rose toward him from his place there, saying, "O Mantuan, I am Sordello of your city!"—and they embraced each other.

Ah, servile Italy, hostel of grief, ship without pilot in great tempest, no mistress of provinces, but brothel!

Quell' anima gentil fu così presta,
sol per lo dolce suon de la sua terra,
di fare al cittadin suo quivi festa; *81*
e ora in te non stanno sanza guerra
li vivi tuoi, e l'un l'altro si rode
di quei ch'un muro e una fossa serra. *84*
Cerca, misera, intorno da le prode
le tue marine, e poi ti guarda in seno,
s'alcuna parte in te di pace gode. *87*
Che val perché ti racconciasse il freno
Iustinïano, se la sella è vòta?
Sanz' esso fora la vergogna meno. *90*
Ahi gente che dovresti esser devota,
e lasciar seder Cesare in la sella,
se bene intendi ciò che Dio ti nota, *93*
guarda come esta fiera è fatta fella
per non esser corretta da li sproni,
poi che ponesti mano a la predella. *96*
O Alberto tedesco ch'abbandoni
costei ch'è fatta indomita e selvaggia,
e dovresti inforcar li suoi arcioni, *99*
giusto giudicio da le stelle caggia
sovra 'l tuo sangue, e sia novo e aperto,
tal che 'l tuo successor temenza n'aggia! *102*
ch'avete tu e 'l tuo padre sofferto,
per cupidigia di costà distretti,
che 'l giardin de lo 'mperio sia diserto. *105*
Vieni a veder Montecchi e Cappelletti,
Monaldi e Filippeschi, uom sanza cura:
color già tristi, e questi con sospetti! *108*

So eager was that noble soul, only at the sweet name of his city, to give glad welcome there to his fellow-citizen—and now in you your living abide not without war, and of those whom one wall and one moat shut in, one gnaws at the other! Search, wretched one, round the shores of your seas, and then look within your bosom, if any part of you enjoy peace! What avails it that Justinian should refit the bridle, if the saddle is empty? But for that the shame were less!

Ah, people that ought to be obedient and let Caesar sit in the saddle, if you rightly understand what God notes to you! See how this beast has grown vicious, through not being corrected by the spurs, since you did put your hand to the bridle!

O German Albert, who do abandon her that is become wanton and wild and who should bestride her saddle-bows, may just judgment fall from the stars upon your blood, and be it so strange and manifest that your successor may have fear thereof! For you and your father, held back yonder by greed, have suffered the garden of the Empire to be laid waste. Come to see Montecchi and Cappelletti, Monaldi and Filippeschi, you man without care, those already wretched and these in dread.

Vien, crudel, vieni, e vedi la pressura
d'i tuoi gentili, e cura lor magagne;
e vedrai Santafior com' è oscura! 111
Vieni a veder la tua Roma che piagne
vedova e sola, e dì e notte chiama:
"Cesare mio, perché non m'accompagne?" 114
Vieni a veder la gente quanto s'ama!
e se nulla di noi pietà ti move,
a vergognar ti vien de la tua fama. 117
E se licito m'è, o sommo Giove
che fosti in terra per noi crucifisso,
son li giusti occhi tuoi rivolti altrove? 120
O è preparazion che ne l'abisso
del tuo consiglio fai per alcun bene
in tutto de l'accorger nostro scisso? 123
Ché le città d'Italia tutte piene
son di tiranni, e un Marcel diventa
ogne villan che parteggiando viene. 126
Fiorenza mia, ben puoi esser contenta
di questa digression che non ti tocca,
mercé del popol tuo che si argomenta. 129
Molti han giustizia in cuore, e tardi scocca
per non venir sanza consiglio a l'arco;
ma il popol tuo l'ha in sommo de la bocca. 132
Molti rifiutan lo comune incarco;
ma il popol tuo solicito risponde
sanza chiamare, e grida: "I' mi sobbarco!" 135
Or ti fa lieta, ché tu hai ben onde:
tu ricca, tu con pace e tu con senno!
S'io dico 'l ver, l'effetto nol nasconde. 138

Come, cruel one, come and see the distress of your nobles, and heal their hurts; and you will see Santafiora, how forlorn it is. Come see your Rome that weeps, widowed and alone, crying day and night, "My Caesar, why do you abandon me?" Come see your people, how they love one another; and if no pity for us moves you, come to be shamed by your own renown!

And if it be lawful for me, O Jove supreme that on earth wast crucified for us, are Thy just eyes turned elsewhere, or is it preparation Thou makest in the depths of Thy counsel for some good quite cut off from our perception? For all the cities of Italy are full of tyrants, and every yokel who comes to play the partisan becomes a Marcellus.

O my Florence, you may indeed rejoice at this digression which does not touch you, thanks to your people who are so resourceful. Many others have justice at heart, but slowly it is let fly, because the shaft does not come without counsel to the bow; but your people has it ever on its lips! Many others refuse the public burden; but your people answers eagerly without being called, crying, "I'll shoulder it!" Now make you glad, for you have good cause: you rich, you at peace, you so wise! If I speak the truth, the result does not conceal it.

Atene e Lacedemona, che fenno
  l'antiche leggi e furon sì civili,
  fecero al viver bene un picciol cenno *141*
verso di te, che fai tanto sottili
  provedimenti, ch'a mezzo novembre
  non giugne quel che tu d'ottobre fili. *144*
Quante volte, del tempo che rimembre,
  legge, moneta, officio e costume
  hai tu mutato, e rinovate membre! *147*
E se ben ti ricordi e vedi lume,
  vedrai te somigliante a quella inferma
  che non può trovar posa in su le piume,
ma con dar volta suo dolore scherma. *151*

Athens and Lacedaemon, that framed the laws of old and were so grown in civil arts, offered but the merest suggestion of right living, compared with you that make such subtle provisions that what you spin in October lasts not to mid-November. How many times within your memory have you changed laws, coinage, offices, and customs, and renewed your members! And if you well bethink you, and see clear, you will see yourself like the sick woman who cannot find repose upon the down, but with her tossing seeks to ease her pain.

Poscia che l'accoglienze oneste e liete
furo iterate tre e quattro volte,
Sordel si trasse, e disse: "Voi, chi siete?" *3*
"Anzi che a questo monte fosser volte
l'anime degne di salire a Dio,
fur l'ossa mie per Ottavian sepolte. *6*
Io son Virgilio; e per null' altro rio
lo ciel perdei che per non aver fé."
Così rispuose allora il duca mio. *9*
Qual è colui che cosa innanzi sé
sùbita vede ond' e' si maraviglia,
che crede e non, dicendo "Ella è . . . non è . . . ," *12*
tal parve quelli; e poi chinò le ciglia,
e umilmente ritornò ver' lui,
e abbracciòl là 've 'l minor s'appiglia. *15*
"O gloria di Latin," disse, "per cui
mostrò ciò che potea la lingua nostra,
o pregio etterno del loco ond' io fui, *18*

# CANTO VII

After the courteous and joyful greetings had been repeated three and four times, Sordello drew back and said, "But who are you?"

"Before the souls worthy to ascend to God were turned to this mountain, my bones were buried by Octavian; I am Virgil, and for no other fault did I lose Heaven than for not having faith." Thus answered my leader then.

As one who of a sudden sees a thing before him that he marvels at, who believes and believes not, saying, "It is, it is not,"—such seemed the other, and then he bent down his brow and humbly approached him again and embraced him where the inferior embraces. "O glory of the Latins," said he, "through whom our tongue showed forth its power, O eternal praise of the place whence I sprang,

qual merito o qual grazia mi ti mostra?
S'io son d'udir le tue parole degno,
dimmi se vien d'inferno, e di qual chiostra." 21
"Per tutt' i cerchi del dolente regno,"
rispuose lui, "son io di qua venuto;
virtù del ciel mi mosse, e con lei vegno. 24
Non per far, ma per non fare ho perduto
a veder l'alto Sol che tu disiri
e che fu tardi per me conosciuto. 27
Luogo è là giù non tristo di martìri,
ma di tenebre solo, ove i lamenti
non suonan come guai, ma son sospiri. 30
Quivi sto io coi pargoli innocenti
dai denti morsi de la morte avante
che fosser da l'umana colpa essenti; 33
quivi sto io con quei che le tre sante
virtù non si vestiro, e sanza vizio
conobber l'altre e seguir tutte quante. 36
Ma se tu sai e puoi, alcuno indizio
dà noi per che venir possiam più tosto
là dove purgatorio ha dritto inizio." 39
Rispuose: "Loco certo non c'è posto;
licito m'è andar suso e intorno;
per quanto ir posso, a guida mi t'accosto. 42
Ma vedi già come dichina il giorno,
e andar sù di notte non si puote;
però è buon pensar di bel soggiorno. 45
Anime sono a destra qua remote;
se mi consenti, io ti merrò ad esse,
e non sanza diletto ti fier note." 48

what merit or what favor shows you to me? If I am worthy to hear your words, tell me if you come from Hell, and from which cloister?"

"Through all the circles of the woeful kingdom," he answered him, "I have come hither. A power from Heaven moved me, and by its help I come. Not for doing, but for not doing, have I lost the sight of the high Sun that you desire and that was known by me too late. A place there is below, not sad with torments but with darkness only, where the lamentations sound not as wailings, but are sighs. There I abide with the little innocents, seized by the fangs of death before they were exempted from human guilt; there I abide with those who were not clothed with the three holy virtues, and without sin knew the others and followed all of them. But if you know and can, give us some direction whereby we may come more speedily to where Purgatory has its true beginning."

He answered, "No fixed place is set for us; it is permitted me to go up and round, and as far as I may go I will accompany you as guide. But see now how the day declines, and to go up by night is not possible, therefore it is well to take thought of a good resting-place. There are souls on the right here, apart: with your consent I will lead you to them, and not without delight will they be known to you."

"Com' è ciò?" fu risposto. "Chi volesse
salir di notte, fora elli impedito
d'altrui, o non sarria ché non potesse?" 51
E 'l buon Sordello in terra fregò 'l dito,
dicendo: "Vedi? sola questa riga
non varcheresti dopo 'l sol partito: 54
non però ch'altra cosa desse briga,
che la notturna tenebra, ad ir suso;
quella col nonpoder la voglia intriga. 57
Ben si poria con lei tornare in giuso
e passeggiar la costa intorno errando,
mentre che l'orizzonte il dì tien chiuso." 60
Allora il mio segnor, quasi ammirando,
"Menane," disse, "dunque là 've dici
ch'aver si può diletto dimorando." 63
Poco allungati c'eravam di lici,
quand' io m'accorsi che 'l monte era scemo,
a guisa che i vallon li sceman quici. 66
"Colà," disse quell' ombra, "n'anderemo
dove la costa face di sé grembo;
e là il novo giorno attenderemo." 69
Tra erto e piano era un sentiero schembo,
che ne condusse in fianco de la lacca,
là dove più ch'a mezzo muore il lembo. 72
Oro e argento fine, cocco e biacca,
indaco legno lucido e sereno,
fresco smeraldo in l'ora che si fiacca, 75
da l'erba e da li fior, dentr' a quel seno
posti, ciascun saria di color vinto,
come dal suo maggiore è vinto il meno. 78

"How is that?" was answered; "he who wished to climb by night, would he be hindered by others, or would he not climb because he had not the power?" And the good Sordello drew his finger on the ground, saying, "Look, even this line you would not cross after the sun is set. Not that aught else save the nocturnal darkness hinders the going up: that hampers the will with impotence. Truly by night one might return downwards, and walk wandering around the mountainside while the horizon holds the day closed."

Then my lord, as though marveling, said, "Lead us therefore whither you say we may have delight in tarrying."

We had gone from there but a little way when I perceived that the mountain was hollowed out, even as valleys hollow out mountains here. "Thither will we go," said the shade, "to where the slope makes a lap of itself, and wait there for the new day." There was a slanting path, between steep and level, which brought us to the side of that hollow, there where its edge more than half dies away. Gold and fine silver, cochineal and white lead, Indian wood bright and clear, fresh emerald at the moment it is split, would all be surpassed in color, if placed within that valley, by the grass and by the flowers growing there, as the less is surpassed by the greater.

Non avea pur natura ivi dipinto,
  ma di soavità di mille odori
  vi facea uno incognito e indistinto. *81*
"*Salve, Regina*" in sul verde e 'n su' fiori
  quindi seder cantando anime vidi,
  che per la valle non parean di fuori. *84*
"Prima che 'l poco sole omai s'annidi,"
  cominciò 'l Mantoan che ci avea vòlti,
  "tra color non vogliate ch'io vi guidi. *87*
Di questo balzo meglio li atti e ' volti
  conoscerete voi di tutti quanti,
  che ne la lama giù tra essi accolti. *90*
Colui che più siede alto e fa sembianti
  d'aver negletto ciò che far dovea,
  e che non move bocca a li altrui canti, *93*
Rodolfo imperador fu, che potea
  sanar le piaghe c'hanno Italia morta,
  sì che tardi per altri si ricrea. *96*
L'altro che ne la vista lui conforta,
  resse la terra dove l'acqua nasce
  che Molta in Albia, e Albia in mar ne porta: *99*
Ottacchero ebbe nome, e ne le fasce
  fu meglio assai che Vincislao suo figlio
  barbuto, cui lussuria e ozio pasce. *102*
E quel nasetto che stretto a consiglio
  par con colui c'ha sì benigno aspetto,
  morì fuggendo e disfiorando il giglio: *105*
guardate là come si batte il petto!
  L'altro vedete c'ha fatto a la guancia
  de la sua palma, sospirando, letto. *108*

Nature had not only painted there, but of the sweetness of a thousand scents she made there one unknown to us and blended. From there I saw, seated upon the green grass and the flowers, singing "*Salve, Regina*," souls who because of the valley were not visible from without.

"Before the lessening sun sinks to its nest," began the Mantuan who had brought us thither, "do not ask me to lead you among them there. From this bank you will distinguish better the acts and countenances of all of them, than if you were received among them on the level below. He who sits highest and has the look of having neglected what he ought to have done, and does not move his lips with the others' song, was Rudolf the Emperor, who might have healed the wounds that were the death of Italy, so that through another she is succored too late. The other, who appears to be comforting him, ruled the land where the waters spring that the Moldau carries to the Elbe, and the Elbe to the sea: his name was Ottokar, and in swaddling-bands he was better far than bearded Wenceslaus, his son, who is fed by lust and idleness. And he with the small nose, who seems close in counsel with him that has so kindly a mien, died in flight and disflowering the lily: look there how he beats his breast. See the other that, sighing, has made a bed for his cheek with the palm of his hand.

Padre e suocero son del mal di Francia:
  sanno la vita sua viziata e lorda,
  e quindi viene il duol che sì li lancia. *111*
Quel che par sì membruto e che s'accorda,
  cantando, con colui dal maschio naso,
  d'ogne valor portò cinta la corda; *114*
e se re dopo lui fosse rimaso
  lo giovanetto che retro a lui siede,
  ben andava il valor di vaso in vaso, *117*
che non si puote dir de l'altre rede;
  Iacomo e Federigo hanno i reami;
  del retaggio miglior nessun possiede. *120*
Rade volte risurge per li rami
  l'umana probitate; e questo vole
  quei che la dà, perché da lui si chiami. *123*
Anche al nasuto vanno mie parole
  non men ch'a l'altro, Pier, che con lui canta,
  onde Puglia e Proenza già si dole. *126*
Tant' è del seme suo minor la pianta,
  quanto, più che Beatrice e Margherita,
  Costanza di marito ancor si vanta. *129*
Vedete il re de la semplice vita
  seder là solo, Arrigo d'Inghilterra:
  questi ha ne' rami suoi migliore uscita. *132*
Quel che più basso tra costor s'atterra,
  guardando in suso, è Guiglielmo marchese,
  per cui e Alessandria e la sua guerra
fa pianger Monferrato e Canavese." *136*

They are the father and the father-in-law of the plague of France; they know his wicked and foul life, and hence comes the grief that pierces them so. He that seems so stout of limb and who accords his singing with him of the virile nose was begirt with the cord of every worth; and if the youth who is sitting behind him had followed him as king, then indeed his worth had passed from vessel to vessel, which cannot be said of the other heirs; James and Frederick have the realms; the better heritage no one possesses. Rarely does human worth rise through the branches, and this He wills who gives it, in order that it may be asked from Him. My words apply also to the large-nosed one no less than to the other, Peter, who is singing with him, wherefore Apulia and Provence are now in grief; as much is the plant inferior to its seed as Constance yet boasts of her husband more than Beatrice and Margaret of theirs. See the king of the simple life sitting there alone, Henry of England: he in his branches has a better issue. He that sits on the ground lowest among them, looking up, is William the marquis, because of whom Alessandria and its war make Montferrat and the Canavese mourn."

# PURGATORIO

ERA GIÀ l'ora che volge il disio
ai navicanti e 'ntenerisce il core
lo dì c'han detto ai dolci amici addio; *3*
e che lo novo peregrin d'amore
punge, se ode squilla di lontano
che paia il giorno pianger che si more; *6*
quand' io incominciai a render vano
l'udire e a mirare una de l'alme
surta, che l'ascoltar chiedea con mano. *9*
Ella giunse e levò ambo le palme,
ficcando li occhi verso l'orïente,
come dicesse a Dio: "D'altro non calme." *12*
"*Te lucis ante*" sì devotamente
le uscìo di bocca e con sì dolci note,
che fece me a me uscir di mente; *15*
e l'altre poi dolcemente e devote
seguitar lei per tutto l'inno intero,
avendo li occhi a le superne rote. *18*
Aguzza qui, lettor, ben li occhi al vero,
ché 'l velo è ora ben tanto sottile,
certo che 'l trapassar dentro è leggero. *21*

# CANTO VIII

It was now the hour that turns back the longing of seafaring folk and melts their heart the day they have bidden sweet friends farewell, and that pierces the new pilgrim with love if he hears from afar a bell that seems to mourn the dying day, when I began to annul my hearing and to gaze on one of the souls, uprisen, who was signing with his hand to be heard. He joined and lifted both his palms, fixing his eyes on the East, as if he said to God, "For naught else do I care." "*Te lucis ante*" came from his lips so devoutly and with such sweet notes that it rapt me from myself. Then the rest joined him sweetly and devoutly through the whole hymn, keeping their eyes fixed on the supernal wheels.

Reader, here sharpen well your eyes to the truth, for the veil is now indeed so thin that certainly to pass within is easy.

Io vidi quello essercito gentile
tacito poscia riguardare in sùe,
quasi aspettando, palido e umìle; *24*
e vidi uscir de l'alto e scender giùe
due angeli con due spade affocate,
tronche e private de le punte sue. *27*
Verdi come fogliette pur mo nate
erano in veste, che da verdi penne
percosse traean dietro e ventilate. *30*
L'un poco sovra noi a star si venne,
e l'altro scese in l'opposita sponda,
sì che la gente in mezzo si contenne. *33*
Ben discernëa in lor la testa bionda;
ma ne la faccia l'occhio si smarria,
come virtù ch'a troppo si confonda. *36*
"Ambo vegnon del grembo di Maria,"
disse Sordello, "a guardia de la valle,
per lo serpente che verrà vie via." *39*
Ond' io, che non sapeva per qual calle,
mi volsi intorno, e stretto m'accostai,
tutto gelato, a le fidate spalle. *42*
E Sordello anco: "Or avvalliamo omai
tra le grandi ombre, e parleremo ad esse;
grazïoso fia lor vedervi assai." *45*
Solo tre passi credo ch'i' scendesse,
e fui di sotto, e vidi un che mirava
pur me, come conoscer mi volesse. *48*
Temp' era già che l'aere s'annerava,
ma non sì che tra li occhi suoi e ' miei
non dichiarisse ciò che pria serrava. *51*

Then I saw that noble army silently gaze upward as if expectant, pallid and humble; and I saw come forth from above and descend two angels with flaming swords, broken short and deprived of their points. Their robes were green as newborn leaves, which they trailed behind them, smitten and fanned by their green wings. One came and took his stand a little above us, and the other alighted on the opposite bank, so that the company was contained in the middle. I clearly discerned their blond heads, but in their faces my sight was dazzled, like a faculty confounded by excess.

"Both come from Mary's bosom," said Sordello, "to guard the valley, because of the serpent that will presently come." Whereat I, who knew not by what path, turned round all chilled and pressed close to the trusty shoulders. And Sordello continued, "Let us go down into the valley among the great shades, and we will speak with them: it will be well pleasing to them to see you."

I believe I descended but three steps and was below, and saw one who was gazing only at me, as if he would recognize me. It was now the time when the air was darkening, yet not so dark that it did not make plain between his eyes and mine what it had shut off before.

Ver' me si fece, e io ver' lui mi fei:
  giudice Nin gentil, quanto mi piacque
  quando ti vidi non esser tra ' rei! *54*
Nullo bel salutar tra noi si tacque;
  poi dimandò: "Quant' è che tu venisti
  a piè del monte per le lontane acque?" *57*
"Oh!" diss' io lui, "per entro i luoghi tristi
  venni stamane, e sono in prima vita,
  ancor che l'altra, sì andando, acquisti." *60*
E come fu la mia risposta udita,
  Sordello ed elli in dietro si raccolse
  come gente di sùbito smarrita. *63*
L'uno a Virgilio e l'altro a un si volse
  che sedea lì, gridando: "Sù, Currado!
  vieni a veder che Dio per grazia volse." *66*
Poi, vòlto a me: "Per quel singular grado
  che tu dei a colui che sì nasconde
  lo suo primo perché, che non li è guado, *69*
quando sarai di là da le larghe onde,
  dì a Giovanna mia che per me chiami
  là dove a li 'nnocenti si risponde. *72*
Non credo che la sua madre più m'ami,
  poscia che trasmutò le bianche bende,
  le quai convien che, misera!, ancor brami. *75*
Per lei assai di lieve si comprende
  quanto in femmina foco d'amor dura,
  se l'occhio o 'l tatto spesso non l'accende. *78*
Non le farà sì bella sepultura
  la vipera che Melanesi accampa,
  com' avria fatto il gallo di Gallura." *81*

He moved toward me and I toward him: noble Judge Nino, how I rejoiced to see you there, and not among the damned! No fair salutation was silent between us; then he asked, "How long is it since you came to the foot of the mountain over the far waters?"

"Oh," I said to him, "from within the woeful places I came this morning, and I am in my first life, albeit by this my journeying I gain the other." And when they heard my answer, Sordello and he drew back like folk suddenly bewildered, the one to Virgil and the other turned to one who was seated there, crying, "Up, Currado, come see what God, of His grace, has willed!" Then, turning to me, "By that singular gratitude you owe to Him who so hides His primal purpose that there is no fording thereunto, when you are beyond the wide waters, tell my Giovanna that she pray for me there where the innocent are heard. I do not think her mother loves me longer since changing her white wimples which she, in her wretchedness, needs must yet long for. By her right easily may be known how long the fire of love lasts in woman, if eye or touch do not often kindle it. The viper that leads afield the Milanese will not make her so fair a tomb as Gallura's cock would have done."

Così dicea, segnato de la stampa,
nel suo aspetto, di quel dritto zelo
che misuratamente in core avvampa. *84*
Li occhi miei ghiotti andavan pur al cielo,
pur là dove le stelle son più tarde,
sì come rota più presso a lo stelo. *87*
E 'l duca mio: "Figliuol, che là sù guarde?"
E io a lui: "A quelle tre facelle
di che 'l polo di qua tutto quanto arde." *90*
Ond' elli a me: "Le quattro chiare stelle
che vedevi staman, son di là basse,
e queste son salite ov' eran quelle." *93*
Com' ei parlava, e Sordello a sé il trasse
dicendo: "Vedi là 'l nostro avversaro";
e drizzò il dito perché 'n là guardasse. *96*
Da quella parte onde non ha riparo
la picciola vallea, era una biscia,
forse qual diede ad Eva il cibo amaro. *99*
Tra l'erba e ' fior venìa la mala striscia,
volgendo ad ora ad or la testa, e 'l dosso
leccando come bestia che si liscia. *102*
Io non vidi, e però dicer non posso,
come mosser li astor celestïali;
ma vidi bene e l'uno e l'altro mosso. *105*
Sentendo fender l'aere a le verdi ali,
fuggì 'l serpente, e li angeli dier volta,
suso a le poste rivolando iguali. *108*
L'ombra che s'era al giudice raccolta
quando chiamò, per tutto quello assalto
punto non fu da me guardare sciolta. *111*

Thus he spoke, his aspect stamped with the mark of that righteous zeal which in due measure glows in the heart.

My greedy eyes kept going to the sky just where the stars are slowest, as in a wheel nearest the axle. And my leader, "Son, what are you gazing at up there?" And I to him, "At those three torches with which the pole here is all aflame." And he to me, "The four bright stars you saw this morning are low on the other side, and these are risen where those were."

As he was speaking, lo! Sordello drew him to himself, saying, "See there our adversary!" and pointed with his finger that he should look that way. At that part where the little valley has no rampart was a snake, perhaps such as gave to Eve the bitter food. Through the grass and the flowers came the evil streak, turning from time to time its head and licking its back like a beast that sleeks itself. I did not see and therefore cannot tell how the celestial falcons moved, but well did I see both one and the other in motion. Hearing the green wings cleave the air, the serpent fled; and the angels wheeled round, flying alike back up to their posts.

The shade that had drawn close to the judge when he exclaimed, through all that assault had not for an instant loosed his gaze from me.

"Se la lucerna che ti mena in alto
truovi nel tuo arbitrio tanta cera
quant' è mestiere infino al sommo smalto," *114*
cominciò ella, "se novella vera
di Val di Magra o di parte vicina
sai, dillo a me, che già grande là era. *117*
Fui chiamato Currado Malaspina;
non son l'antico, ma di lui discesi;
a' miei portai l'amor che qui raffina." *120*
"Oh!" diss' io lui, "per li vostri paesi
già mai non fui; ma dove si dimora
per tutta Europa ch'ei non sien palesi? *123*
La fama che la vostra casa onora,
grida i segnori e grida la contrada,
sì che ne sa chi non vi fu ancora; *126*
e io vi giuro, s'io di sopra vada,
che vostra gente onrata non si sfregia
del pregio de la borsa e de la spada. *129*
Uso e natura sì la privilegia,
che, perché il capo reo il mondo torca,
sola va dritta e 'l mal cammin dispregia." *132*
Ed elli: "Or va; che 'l sol non si ricorca
sette volte nel letto che 'l Montone
con tutti e quattro i piè cuopre e inforca, *135*
che cotesta cortese oppinïone
ti fia chiavata in mezzo de la testa
con maggior chiovi che d'altrui sermone,
se corso di giudicio non s'arresta." *139*

"So may the light that leads you on high find in your will as much wax as is needed up to the enamelled summit," he began, "if you know true news of Val di Magra or of the neighboring region, tell it to me, who once was great there. I was called Currado Malaspina: I am not the old Currado, but from him I am descended. To my own I bore the love that is refined here."

"Oh," said I to him, "through your lands I have never been, but where do men dwell in all Europe that they are not renowned? The fame that honors your house proclaims alike its lords and its district, so that he knows of them who has never been there; and I swear to you, so may I go above, that your honored race does not strip itself of the glory of the purse and of the sword. Custom and nature so privilege it, that though the wicked head turn the world awry, it alone goes right and scorns the evil path."

And he, "Now go, for the sun shall not lie seven times in the bed that the Ram covers and bestrides with all four feet before this courteous opinion will be nailed in the midst of your head, with stronger nails than men's talk, if course of judgment be not stayed."

PURGATORIO

LA CONCUBINA di Titone antico
già s'imbiancava al balco d'orïente,
fuor de le braccia del suo dolce amico; *3*
di gemme la sua fronte era lucente,
poste in figura del freddo animale
che con la coda percuote la gente; *6*
e la notte, de' passi con che sale,
fatti avea due nel loco ov' eravamo,
e 'l terzo già chinava in giuso l'ale; *9*
quand' io, che meco avea di quel d'Adamo,
vinto dal sonno, in su l'erba inchinai
là 've già tutti e cinque sedavamo. *12*
Ne l'ora che comincia i tristi lai
la rondinella presso a la mattina,
forse a memoria de' suo' primi guai, *15*
e che la mente nostra, peregrina
più da la carne e men da' pensier presa,
a le sue visïon quasi è divina, *18*

# CANTO IX

THE CONCUBINE of old Tithonus was now showing white on the balcony of the East, forth from her sweet lover's arms; her forehead was glittering with gems, set in the form of the cold animal that strikes men with its tail. And in the place where we were night had taken two of the steps with which she climbs, and already the third was bending down its wings when I, who had somewhat of Adam with me, being overcome with sleep, lay me down on the grass there where all five of us were already seated.

At the hour near morning when the swallow begins her sad lays, perhaps in memory of her former woes, and when our mind, more a pilgrim from the flesh and less captive to thoughts, is in its visions almost divine,

in sogno mi parea veder sospesa
un'aguglia nel ciel con penne d'oro,
con l'ali aperte e a calare intesa; 21
ed esser mi parea là dove fuoro
abbandonati i suoi da Ganimede,
quando fu ratto al sommo consistoro. 24
Fra me pensava: "Forse questa fiede
pur qui per uso, e forse d'altro loco
disdegna di portarne suso in piede." 27
Poi mi parea che, poi rotata un poco,
terribil come folgor discendesse,
e me rapisse suso infino al foco. 30
Ivi parea che ella e io ardesse;
e sì lo 'ncendio imaginato cosse,
che convenne che 'l sonno si rompesse. 33
Non altrimenti Achille si riscosse,
li occhi svegliati rivolgendo in giro
e non sappiendo là dove si fosse, 36
quando la madre da Chirón a Schiro
trafuggò lui dormendo in le sue braccia,
là onde poi li Greci il dipartiro; 39
che mi scoss' io, sì come da la faccia
mi fuggì 'l sonno, e diventa' ismorto,
come fa l'uom che, spaventato, agghiaccia. 42
Dallato m'era solo il mio conforto,
e 'l sole er' alto già più che due ore,
e 'l viso m'era a la marina torto. 45
"Non aver tema," disse il mio segnore;
"fatti sicur, ché noi semo a buon punto;
non stringer, ma rallarga ogne vigore. 48

I seemed to see, in a dream, an eagle poised in the sky, with feathers of gold, its wings outspread, and prepared to swoop. And I seemed to be in the place where Ganymede abandoned his own company, when he was caught up to the supreme consistory; and I thought within myself, "Perhaps it is wont to strike only here, and perhaps disdains to carry anyone upward in its claws from any other place." Then it seemed to me that, having wheeled a while, it descended terrible as a thunderbolt and snatched me upwards as far as the fire: there it seemed that it and I burned; and the imagined fire so scorched me that perforce my sleep was broken.

Even as Achilles started up, turning his awakened eyes about him and not knowing where he was, when his mother carried him off, sleeping in her arms, from Chiron to Skyros, whence later the Greeks took him away; so did I start, as soon as sleep fled from my face, and I grew pale, like one who is chilled with terror. My comfort was alone beside me, and the sun was already more than two hours high, and my face was turned to the sea.

"Have no fear," said my lord, "take confidence, for all is well with us; do not hold back, but put forth all your strength.

Tu se' omai al purgatorio giunto:
vedi là il balzo che 'l chiude dintorno;
vedi l'entrata là 've par digiunto. 51
Dianzi, ne l'alba che procede al giorno,
quando l'anima tua dentro dormia,
sovra li fiori ond' è là giù addorno 54
venne una donna, e disse: 'I' son Lucia;
lasciatemi pigliar costui che dorme;
sì l'agevolerò per la sua via.' 57
Sordel rimase e l'altre genti forme;
ella ti tolse, e come 'l dì fu chiaro,
sen venne suso; e io per le sue orme. 60
Qui ti posò, ma pria mi dimostraro
li occhi suoi belli quella intrata aperta;
poi ella e 'l sonno ad una se n'andaro." 63
A guisa d'uom che 'n dubbio si raccerta
e che muta in conforto sua paura,
poi che la verità li è discoperta, 66
mi cambia' io; e come sanza cura
vide me 'l duca mio, su per lo balzo
si mosse, e io di rietro inver' l'altura. 69
Lettor, tu vedi ben com' io innalzo
la mia matera, e però con più arte
non ti maravigliar s'io la rincalzo. 72
Noi ci appressammo, ed eravamo in parte
che là dove pareami prima rotto,
pur come un fesso che muro diparte, 75
vidi una porta, e tre gradi di sotto
per gire ad essa, di color diversi,
e un portier ch'ancor non facea motto. 78

You are now arrived at Purgatory: see the cliff there that encloses it about; see the entrance there where it appears cleft. A while ago, in the dawn that precedes the day, when your soul was sleeping within you, upon the flowers that adorn the place down there, came a lady who said, 'I am Lucy; let me take this man who is sleeping, so will I speed him on his way.' Sordello remained, and the other noble souls. She took you, and when the day was bright she went on upwards and I in her steps. Here she laid you down; but first her beautiful eyes showed me that open entrance; then she and slumber together went away."

Like a perplexed man who is reassured, whose fear changes to confidence when the truth is revealed to him, so I was changed; and when my leader saw me free from care he moved on up the slope, and I behind him, toward the height.

You see well, reader, that I uplift my theme: do not wonder, therefore, if I sustain it with greater art.

We drew near and came to a point from which, where at first there appeared to be merely a break, like a fissure that divides a wall, I saw a gate, with three steps beneath for going up to it, of different colors, and a warder who as yet spoke not a word.

E come l'occhio più e più v'apersi,
vidil seder sovra 'l grado sovrano,
tal ne la faccia ch'io non lo soffersi; 81

e una spada nuda avëa in mano,
che reflettëa i raggi sì ver' noi,
ch'io dirizzava spesso il viso in vano. 84

"Dite costinci: che volete voi?"
cominciò elli a dire, "ov' è la scorta?
Guardate che 'l venir sù non vi nòi." 87

"Donna del ciel, di queste cose accorta,"
rispuose 'l mio maestro a lui, "pur dianzi
ne disse: 'Andate là: quivi è la porta.'" 90

"Ed ella i passi vostri in bene avanzi,"
ricominciò il cortese portinaio:
"Venite dunque a' nostri gradi innanzi." 93

Là ne venimmo; e lo scaglion primaio
bianco marmo era sì pulito e terso,
ch'io mi specchiai in esso qual io paio. 96

Era il secondo tinto più che perso,
d'una petrina ruvida e arsiccia,
crepata per lo lungo e per traverso. 99

Lo terzo, che di sopra s'ammassiccia,
porfido mi parea, sì fiammeggiante
come sangue che fuor di vena spiccia. 102

Sovra questo tenëa ambo le piante
l'angel di Dio sedendo in su la soglia
che mi sembiava pietra di diamante. 105

Per li tre gradi sù di buona voglia
mi trasse il duca mio, dicendo: "Chiedi
umilemente che 'l serrame scioglia." 108

And as I looked more and more intently I saw that he was seated upon the topmost step, and in his face he was such that I endured it not. In his hand he had a naked sword, which so reflected the rays on us that often in vain I directed my eyes upon it.

"Say from there, what is it you seek?" he began to say; "Where is the escort? Take care lest the coming upward be to your hurt."

"A heavenly lady who knows these things well," my master answered him, "said to us just now: 'Go that way, there is the gate.'"

"And may she speed your steps to good!" began again the courteous doorkeeper; "Come forward, then, to our stairs."

We then came on, and the first step was white marble so polished and clear that I mirrored myself in it in my true likeness; the second was darker than perse and was of a stone rugged and burnt, cracked in its length and in its breadth. The third, which lies massy above, seemed to me of porphyry as flaming red as blood that spurts from a vein. Upon this step the angel of God held both his feet, seated upon the threshold that seemed to me to be of adamant. Up by the three steps, with my good will, my leader drew me, saying, "Beg him humbly that he withdraw the bolt."

Divoto mi gittai a' santi piedi;
misericordia chiesi e ch'el m'aprisse,
ma tre volte nel petto pria mi diedi. *111*
Sette P ne la fronte mi descrisse
col punton de la spada, e "Fa che lavi,
quando se' dentro, queste piaghe" disse. *114*
Cenere, o terra che secca si cavi,
d'un color fora col suo vestimento;
e di sotto da quel trasse due chiavi. *117*
L'una era d'oro e l'altra era d'argento;
pria con la bianca e poscia con la gialla
fece a la porta sì, ch'i' fu' contento. *120*
"Quandunque l'una d'este chiavi falla,
che non si volga dritta per la toppa,"
diss' elli a noi, "non s'apre questa calla. *123*
Più cara è l'una; ma l'altra vuol troppa
d'arte e d'ingegno avanti che diserri,
perch' ella è quella che 'l nodo digroppa. *126*
Da Pier le tegno; e dissemi ch'i' erri
anzi ad aprir ch'a tenerla serrata,
pur che la gente a' piedi mi s'atterri." *129*
Poi pinse l'uscio a la porta sacrata,
dicendo: "Intrate; ma facciovi accorti
che di fuor torna chi 'n dietro si guata." *132*
E quando fuor ne' cardini distorti
li spigoli di quella regge sacra,
che di metallo son sonanti e forti, *135*
non rugghiò sì né si mostrò sì acra
Tarpëa, come tolto le fu il buono
Metello, per che poi rimase macra. *138*

I threw myself devoutly at the holy feet; I besought for mercy's sake that he would open to me, but first I smote three times upon my breast. Seven P's he traced on my forehead with the point of his sword and said, "See that you wash away these wounds when you are within."

Ashes, or earth that is dug out dry, would be of one color with his vesture, and from beneath it he drew two keys, the one of gold and the other of silver. First with the white and then with the yellow he did so to the gate that I was content.

"Whenever one of these keys fails so that it does not turn rightly in the lock," he said to us, "this passage does not open. The one is more precious; but the other requires great skill and wisdom before it will unlock, for this is the one that disentangles the knot. From Peter I hold them, and he told me to err rather in opening than in keeping shut, if but the people prostrate themselves at my feet." Then he pushed open the door of the sacred portal, saying, "Enter; but I bid you know that he who looks back returns outside again."

When the pivots of that sacred portal, which are of metal resounding and strong, were turned within their hinges, Tarpea roared not so loud nor showed itself so stubborn, when the good Metellus was taken from it, leaving it lean thereafter.

Io mi rivolsi attento al primo tuono,
e "*Te Deum laudamus*" mi parea
udire in voce mista al dolce suono. *141*
Tale imagine a punto mi rendea
ciò ch'io udiva, qual prender si suole
quando a cantar con organi si stea;
ch'or sì or no s'intendon le parole. *145*

I turned attentive to the first note, and "*Te Deum laudamus*" I seemed to hear in a voice mingled with the sweet music. What I heard gave me the same impression we sometimes get when people are singing with an organ, and now the words are clear and now are not.

# PURGATORIO

POI FUMMO dentro al soglio de la porta
che 'l mal amor de l'anime disusa,
perché fa parer dritta la via torta, *3*
sonando la senti' esser richiusa;
e s'io avesse li occhi vòlti ad essa,
qual fora stata al fallo degna scusa? *6*
Noi salavam per una pietra fessa,
che si moveva e d'una e d'altra parte,
sì come l'onda che fugge e s'appressa. *9*
"Qui si conviene usare un poco d'arte,"
cominciò 'l duca mio, "in accostarsi
or quinci, or quindi al lato che si parte." *12*
E questo fece i nostri passi scarsi,
tanto che pria lo scemo de la luna
rigiunse al letto suo per ricorcarsi, *15*
che noi fossimo fuor di quella cruna;
ma quando fummo liberi e aperti
sù dove il monte in dietro si rauna, *18*
ïo stancato e amendue incerti
di nostra via, restammo in su un piano
solingo più che strade per diserti. *21*

# CANTO X

When we were within the threshold of the gate which the souls' wrong love disuses, making the crooked way seem straight, I heard by its resounding that it was closed again; and if I had turned my eyes to it, what would have been a fitting excuse for my fault?

We were climbing through a cleft in the rock, which kept bending one way and the other, like a wave that goes and comes. "Here must we use a little skill," my leader began, "in keeping close, now here, now there, to the side that recedes." And this made our steps so scant that the waning orb of the moon had regained its bed to sink to rest before we came forth from that needle's eye. But when we were free and out in the open above, where the mountain draws back, I weary and each of us uncertain of our way, we stopped on a level place more solitary than roads through deserts.

Da la sua sponda, ove confina il vano,
al piè de l'alta ripa che pur sale,
misurrebbe in tre volte un corpo umano; 24
e quanto l'occhio mio potea trar d'ale,
or dal sinistro e or dal destro fianco,
questa cornice mi parea cotale. 27
Là sù non eran mossi i piè nostri anco,
quand' io conobbi quella ripa intorno
che, dritta, di salita aveva manco, 30
esser di marmo candido e addorno
d'intagli sì, che non pur Policleto,
ma la natura lì avrebbe scorno. 33
L'angel che venne in terra col decreto
de la molt' anni lagrimata pace,
ch'aperse il ciel del suo lungo divieto, 36
dinanzi a noi pareva sì verace
quivi intagliato in un atto soave,
che non sembiava imagine che tace. 39
Giurato si saria ch'el dicesse "*Ave!*";
perché iv' era imaginata quella
ch'ad aprir l'alto amor volse la chiave; 42
e avea in atto impressa esta favella
"*Ecce ancilla Deï,*" propriamente
come figura in cera si suggella. 45
"Non tener pur ad un loco la mente,"
disse 'l dolce maestro, che m'avea
da quella parte onde 'l cuore ha la gente. 48
Per ch'i' mi mossi col viso, e vedea
di retro da Maria, da quella costa
onde m'era colui che mi movea, 51

From its edge, bordering the void, to the foot of the high bank which rises sheer, a human body would measure in three lengths; and as far as my eye could make its flight, now on the left and now on the right, such this terrace seemed to me. Not yet had we moved our feet on it when I perceived that the encircling bank (which, being vertical, lacked means of ascent) was of pure white marble, and was adorned with such carvings that not only Polycletus but Nature herself would there be put to shame.

The angel who came to earth with the decree of peace, wept for since many a year, which opened Heaven from its long ban, before us there appeared so vividly graven in gentle mien that it seemed not a silent image: one would have sworn that he was saying, "*Ave*," for there she was imaged who turned the key to open the supreme love, and these words were imprinted in her attitude: "*Ecce ancilla Dei*," as expressly as a figure is stamped on wax.

"Do not keep your mind on one part only," said the sweet master, who had me on the side where people have their heart; wherefore I moved my eyes and saw beyond Mary, on the same side as was he who prompted me,

un'altra storia ne la roccia imposta;
 per ch'io varcai Virgilio, e fe'mi presso,
 acciò che fosse a li occhi miei disposta. *54*
Era intagliato lì nel marmo stesso
 lo carro e ' buoi, traendo l'arca santa,
 per che si teme officio non commesso. *57*
Dinanzi parea gente; e tutta quanta,
 partita in sette cori, a' due mie' sensi
 faceva dir l'un "No," l'altro "Sì, canta." *60*
Similemente al fummo de li 'ncensi
 che v'era imaginato, li occhi e 'l naso
 e al sì e al no discordi fensi. *63*
Lì precedeva al benedetto vaso,
 trescando alzato, l'umile salmista,
 e più e men che re era in quel caso. *66*
Di contra, effigïata ad una vista
 d'un gran palazzo, Micòl ammirava
 sì come donna dispettosa e trista. *69*
I' mossi i piè del loco dov' io stava,
 per avvisar da presso un'altra istoria,
 che di dietro a Micòl mi biancheggiava. *72*
Quiv' era storïata l'alta gloria
 del roman principato, il cui valore
 mosse Gregorio a la sua gran vittoria; *75*
i' dico di Traiano imperadore;
 e una vedovella li era al freno,
 di lagrime atteggiata e di dolore. *78*
Intorno a lui parea calcato e pieno
 di cavalieri, e l'aguglie ne l'oro
 sovr' essi in vista al vento si movieno. *81*

another story set in the rock; wherefore I went past Virgil and drew near to it, that it might be displayed before my eyes. There, carved in the same marble, were the cart and the oxen drawing the holy ark, because of which men fear an office not given in charge. In front appeared people, and all the company, divided into seven choirs, made two of my senses say, the one "No," the other, "Yes, they are singing." In like manner, by the smoke of the incense that was imaged there my eyes and nose were made discordant with *yes* and *no*. There, preceding the blessed vessel, dancing girt up, was the humble Psalmist, and on that occasion he was both more and less than king. Opposite, figured at a window of a great palace, was Michal looking on, like a woman vexed and scornful.

I moved my feet from where I was to examine close at hand another story which I saw gleaming white beyond Michal. There storied was the high glory of the Roman prince whose worth moved Gregory to his great victory: I mean the Emperor Trajan. And a poor widow was at his bridle in attitude of weeping and of grief. Round about him appeared a trampling and throng of horsemen, and above them the eagles in gold moved visibly in the wind.

La miserella intra tutti costoro
pareva dir: "Segnor, fammi vendetta
di mio figliuol ch'è morto, ond' io m'accoro"; 84
ed elli a lei rispondere: "Or aspetta
tanto ch'i' torni"; e quella: "Segnor mio,"
come persona in cui dolor s'affretta, 87
"se tu non torni?"; ed ei: "Chi fia dov' io,
la ti farà"; ed ella: "L'altrui bene
a te che fia, se 'l tuo metti in oblio?"; 90
ond' elli: "Or ti conforta; ch'ei convene
ch'i' solva il mio dovere anzi ch'i' mova:
giustizia vuole e pietà mi ritene." 93
Colui che mai non vide cosa nova
produsse esto visibile parlare,
novello a noi perché qui non si trova. 96
Mentr' io mi dilettava di guardare
l'imagini di tante umilitadi,
e per lo fabbro loro a veder care, 99
"Ecco di qua, ma fanno i passi radi,"
mormorava il poeta, "molte genti:
questi ne 'nvïeranno a li alti gradi." 102
Li occhi miei, ch'a mirare eran contenti
per veder novitadi ond' e' son vaghi,
volgendosi ver' lui non furon lenti. 105
Non vo' però, lettor, che tu ti smaghi
di buon proponimento per udire
come Dio vuol che 'l debito si paghi. 108
Non attender la forma del martìre:
pensa la succession; pensa ch'al peggio
oltre la gran sentenza non può ire. 111

Among all these the poor woman seemed to say, "My lord, do me vengeance for my son who is slain, wherefore my heart is pierced." And he seemed to answer her, "Wait now till I return." And she, "My lord," like one whose grief is urgent, "and if you do not return?" And he, "He who shall be in my place will do it for you." And she, "What shall another's welldoing avail you, if you forget your own?" He then, "Now take comfort, for I must discharge my duty before I go: justice requires it, and pity bids me stay."

He who never beheld any new thing wrought this visible speech, new to us because here it is not found.

While I was taking delight in gazing on the images of humilities so great, and for their Craftsman's sake precious to behold, "Lo, here are many people," murmured the poet, "but they come with slow step: they will direct us on to the high stairs." My eyes, which were content to behold novelties whereof they are fain, were not slow in turning towards him.

But, reader, I would not have you turned from good resolution for hearing how God wills the debt shall be paid. Heed not the form of the pain: think what follows, think that at the worst beyond the great Judgment it cannot go.

Io cominciai: "Maestro, quel ch'io veggio
muovere a noi, non mi sembian persone,
e non so che, sì nel veder vaneggio." *114*
Ed elli a me: "La grave condizione
di lor tormento a terra li rannicchia,
sì che ' miei occhi pria n'ebber tencione. *117*
Ma guarda fiso là, e disviticchia
col viso quel che vien sotto a quei sassi:
già scorger puoi come ciascun si picchia." *120*
O superbi cristian, miseri lassi,
che, de la vista de la mente infermi,
fidanza avete ne' retrosi passi, *123*
non v'accorgete voi che noi siam vermi
nati a formar l'angelica farfalla,
che vola a la giustizia sanza schermi? *126*
Di che l'animo vostro in alto galla,
poi siete quasi antomata in difetto,
sì come vermo in cui formazion falla? *129*
Come per sostentar solaio o tetto,
per mensola talvolta una figura
si vede giugner le ginocchia al petto, *132*
la qual fa del non ver vera rancura
nascere 'n chi la vede; così fatti
vid' io color, quando puosi ben cura. *135*
Vero è che più e meno eran contratti
secondo ch'avien più e meno a dosso;
e qual più pazïenza avea ne li atti,
piangendo parea dicer: "Più non posso." *139*

"Master," I began, "what I see moving towards us does not seem to me persons, but what it is I do not know, my sight wanders so." And he to me, "The grievous condition of their torment doubles them to the ground, so that my own eyes at first had contention therewith. But look closely there and with your sight disentangle that which comes beneath those stones: already you may discern how each beats his breast."

O proud Christians, wretched and weary, who, sick in mental vision, put trust in backward steps: are you not aware that we are worms, born to form the angelic butterfly that flies unto judgment without defenses? Why does your mind soar up aloft, since you are as it were imperfect insects, even as the worm in which full form is wanting?

As for corbel to support a ceiling or a roof, sometimes a figure is seen to join the knees to the breast—which, unreal, begets real distress in one who sees it—so fashioned did I see these when I gave good heed. They were truly more or less contracted according as they had more and less upon their backs; and he who showed the most suffering in his looks, seemed to say, weeping, "I can no more."

# PURGATORIO

"O Padre nostro, che ne' cieli stai,
non circunscritto, ma per più amore
ch'ai primi effetti di là sù tu hai, *3*
laudato sia 'l tuo nome e 'l tuo valore
da ogne creatura, com' è degno
di render grazie al tuo dolce vapore. *6*
Vegna ver' noi la pace del tuo regno,
ché noi ad essa non potem da noi,
s'ella non vien, con tutto nostro ingegno. *9*
Come del suo voler li angeli tuoi
fan sacrificio a te, cantando *osanna*,
così facciano li uomini de' suoi. *12*
Dà oggi a noi la cotidiana manna,
sanza la qual per questo aspro diserto
a retro va chi più di gir s'affanna. *15*
E come noi lo mal ch'avem sofferto
perdoniamo a ciascuno, e tu perdona
benigno, e non guardar lo nostro merto. *18*

# CANTO XI

"OUR FATHER, who art in Heaven, not circumscribed, but through the greater love Thou hast for Thy first works on high,

"Praisèd be Thy name and Thy worth by every creature, as it is meet to render thanks to Thy sweet effluence.

"May the peace of Thy kingdom come to us, for we cannot reach it of ourselves, if it come not, for all our striving.

"As Thine angels make sacrifice to Thee of their will, singing Hosanna, so let men make of theirs.

"Give us this day our daily manna, without which he backward goes through this harsh desert who most labors to advance.

"And as we forgive everyone the wrong we have suffered, even do Thou in loving-kindness pardon, and regard not our desert.

Nostra virtù che di legger s'adona,
non spermentar con l'antico avversaro,
ma libera da lui che sì la sprona. *21*
Quest' ultima preghiera, segnor caro,
già non si fa per noi, ché non bisogna,
ma per color che dietro a noi restaro." *24*
Così a sé e noi buona ramogna
quell' ombre orando, andavan sotto 'l pondo,
simile a quel che talvolta si sogna, *27*
disparmente angosciate tutte a tondo
e lasse su per la prima cornice,
purgando la caligine del mondo. *30*
Se di là sempre ben per noi si dice,
di qua che dire e far per lor si puote
da quei c'hanno al voler buona radice? *33*
Ben si de' loro atar lavar le note
che portar quinci, sì che, mondi e lievi,
possano uscire a le stellate ruote. *36*
"Deh, se giustizia e pietà vi disgrievi
tosto, sì che possiate muover l'ala,
che secondo il disio vostro vi lievi, *39*
mostrate da qual mano inver' la scala
si va più corto; e se c'è più d'un varco,
quel ne 'nsegnate che men erto cala; *42*
ché questi che vien meco, per lo 'ncarco
de la carne d'Adamo onde si veste,
al montar sù, contra sua voglia, è parco." *45*
Le lor parole, che rendero a queste
che dette avea colui cu' io seguiva,
non fur da cui venisser manifeste; *48*

"Our strength, which is easily overcome, put not to trial with the old adversary, but deliver us from him, who so spurs it.

"This last petition, dear Lord, we make not now for ourselves, for there is no need, but for those who remain behind us."

Thus, praying good speed for themselves and for us, those shades were going under the burden, like that of which one sometimes dreams, unequally anguished all of them, wearily making their rounds on the first terrace, purging away the mists of the world. If there they always ask good for us, what for them can here be said or done, by those who have their will rooted in good? Truly we ought to help them wash away the stains they have borne hence, so that pure and light they may go forth to the starry wheels.

"Ah, so may justice and pity soon disburden you, that you may spread your wing which may uplift you according to your desire, show us on which hand we may go most quickly to the stair; and if there is more than one passage, show us that which is least steep, for he who comes with me here, for the burden of Adam's flesh wherewith he is clothed, against his will is slow at climbing up."

It was not plain from whom came the words that were returned to these my leader had spoken,

ma fu detto: "A man destra per la riva
con noi venite, e troverete il passo
possibile a salir persona viva. 51
E s'io non fossi impedito dal sasso
che la cervice mia superba doma,
onde portar convienmi il viso basso, 54
cotesti, ch'ancor vive e non si noma,
guardere' io, per veder s'i' 'l conosco,
e per farlo pietoso a questa soma. 57
Io fui latino e nato d'un gran Tosco:
Guiglielmo Aldobrandesco fu mio padre;
non so se 'l nome suo già mai fu vosco. 60
L'antico sangue e l'opere leggiadre
d'i miei maggior mi fer sì arrogante,
che, non pensando a la comune madre, 63
ogn' uomo ebbi in despetto tanto avante,
ch'io ne mori', come i Sanesi sanno,
e sallo in Campagnatico ogne fante. 66
Io sono Omberto; e non pur a me danno
superbia fa, ché tutti miei consorti
ha ella tratti seco nel malanno. 69
E qui convien ch'io questo peso porti
per lei, tanto che a Dio si sodisfaccia,
poi ch'io nol fe' tra ' vivi, qui tra ' morti." 72
Ascoltando chinai in giù la faccia;
e un di lor, non questi che parlava,
si torse sotto il peso che li 'mpaccia, 75
e videmi e conobbemi e chiamava,
tenendo li occhi con fatica fisi
a me che tutto chin con loro andava. 78

but they were, "Come with us to the right along this bank, and you will find the opening where it is possible for a living man to climb. And were I not hindered by the stone that subdues my proud neck, so that I must hold my face down, I would look at this man who is yet alive and is not named, to see if I know him, and make him piteous of this burden. I was Italian, the son of a great Tuscan: Guiglielmo Aldobrandesco was my father; I know not if his name was ever with you. The ancient blood and the gallant deeds of my ancestors made me so arrogant that, not thinking of our common mother, I held all men in such exceeding scorn that it was the death of me, as the Sienese know and every child in Campagnatico knows. I am Omberto; and not only to me does pride work ill, but it has dragged all my kinsfolk with it into calamity; and for this I must bear this weight, until God is satisfied, here among the dead, since I did it not among the living."

Listening, I bent down my face; and one of them, not he who spoke, twisted himself beneath the weight that encumbers them, and saw me and knew me, and was calling out, trying hard to keep his eyes fixed on me who all stooping went along with them.

"Oh!" diss' io lui, "non se' tu Oderisi,
  l'onor d'Agobbio e l'onor di quell' arte
  ch'alluminar chiamata è in Parisi?" *81*
"Frate," diss' elli, "più ridon le carte
  che pennelleggia Franco Bolognese;
  l'onore è tutto or suo, e mio in parte. *84*
Ben non sare' io stato sì cortese
  mentre ch'io vissi, per lo gran disio
  de l'eccellenza ove mio core intese. *87*
Di tal superbia qui si paga il fio;
  e ancor non sarei qui, se non fosse
  che, possendo peccar, mi volsi a Dio. *90*
Oh vana gloria de l'umane posse!
  com' poco verde in su la cima dura,
  se non è giunta da l'etati grosse! *93*
Credette Cimabue ne la pittura
  tener lo campo, e ora ha Giotto il grido,
  sì che la fama di colui è scura. *96*
Così ha tolto l'uno a l'altro Guido
  la gloria de la lingua; e forse è nato
  chi l'uno e l'altro caccerà del nido. *99*
Non è il mondan romore altro ch'un fiato
  di vento, ch'or vien quinci e or vien quindi,
  e muta nome perché muta lato. *102*
Che voce avrai tu più, se vecchia scindi
  da te la carne, che se fossi morto
  anzi che tu lasciassi il 'pappo' e 'l 'dindi,' *105*
pria che passin mill' anni? ch'è più corto
  spazio a l'etterno, ch'un muover di ciglia
  al cerchio che più tardi in cielo è torto. *108*

"Oh," I said to him, "are you not Oderisi, the honor of Gubbio and the honor of that art which in Paris is called 'illumination'?"

"Brother," he said," more smiling are the pages that Franco Bolognese paints: the honor is now all his—and mine in part. Truly I should not have been so courteous while I lived, because of the great desire for excellence whereon my heart was set. For such pride the fee is paid here; nor should I yet be here, were it not that, having power to sin, I turned to God. O empty glory of human powers! how briefly lasts the green upon the top, if it is not followed by barbarous times! Cimabue thought to hold the field in painting, and now Giotto has the cry, so that the other's fame is dim; so has the one Guido taken from the other the glory of our tongue—and he perchance is born that shall chase the one and the other from the nest. Earthly fame is naught but a breath of wind, which now comes hence and now comes thence, changing its name because it changes quarter. What greater fame will you have if you strip off your flesh when it is old than if you had died before giving up *pappo* and *dindi,* when a thousand years shall have passed, which is a shorter space compared to the eternal than the movement of the eyelids to that circle which is slowest turned in heaven?

Colui che del cammin sì poco piglia
  dinanzi a me, Toscana sonò tutta;
  e ora a pena in Siena sen pispiglia, *111*
ond' era sire quando fu distrutta
  la rabbia fiorentina, che superba
  fu a quel tempo sì com' ora è putta. *114*
La vostra nominanza è color d'erba,
  che viene e va, e quei la discolora
  per cui ella esce de la terra acerba." *117*
E io a lui: "Tuo vero dir m'incora
  bona umiltà, e gran tumor m'appiani;
  ma chi è quei di cui tu parlavi ora?" *120*
"Quelli è," rispuose, "Provenzan Salvani;
  ed è qui perché fu presuntüoso
  a recar Siena tutta a le sue mani. *123*
Ito è così e va, sanza riposo,
  poi che morì; cotal moneta rende
  a sodisfar chi è di là troppo oso." *126*
E io: "Se quello spirito ch'attende,
  pria che si penta, l'orlo de la vita,
  qua giù dimora e qua sù non ascende, *129*
se buona orazïon lui non aita,
  prima che passi tempo quanto visse,
  come fu la venuta lui largita?" *132*
"Quando vivea più glorïoso," disse,
  "liberamente nel Campo di Siena,
  ogne vergogna diposta, s'affisse; *135*
e lì, per trar l'amico suo di pena,
  ch'e' sostenea ne la prigion di Carlo,
  si condusse a tremar per ogne vena. *138*

With him who moves so slowly along the way in front of me all Tuscany resounded, and now there is scarcely a whisper of him in Siena, whereof he was lord when the rage of Florence was destroyed, which was as proud then as it is prostitute now. Your repute is as the hue of grass, which comes and goes, and he discolors it through whom it springs green from the ground."

And I to him, "Your true words fill my heart with good humility and abate in me a great swelling; but who is he of whom you just now spoke?"

"He is Provenzan Salvani," he answered, "and he is here because, in his presumption, he thought to bring all Siena into his grasp. Thus has he gone and thus he goes without rest, since he died: such coin does he pay in satisfaction who yonder is too daring."

And I, "If the spirit that awaits the verge of life before he repents abides there below and mounts not up here, unless holy prayers assist him, until as much time passes as he has lived, how was it granted him to come up here?"

"When he was living with greatest glory," said he, "he stationed himself of his own free will in the marketplace of Siena, putting away all shame; and there, to deliver his friend from the pains he was suffering in Charles' prison, he brought himself to tremble in every vein.

Più non dirò, e scuro so che parlo;
ma poco tempo andrà, che ' tuoi vicini
faranno sì che tu potrai chiosarlo.
Quest' opera li tolse quei confini." *142*

No more will I say, and I know that I speak darkly; but, short time will pass before your neighbors shall so act that you will be able to interpret this: such a deed released him from those confines."

DI PARI, come buoi che vanno a giogo,
m'andava io con quell' anima carca,
fin che 'l sofferse il dolce pedagogo. 3
Ma quando disse: "Lascia lui e varca;
ché qui è buono con l'ali e coi remi,
quantunque può, ciascun pinger sua barca"; 6
dritto sì come andar vuolsi rife'mi
con la persona, avvegna che i pensieri
mi rimanessero e chinati e scemi. 9
Io m'era mosso, e seguia volontieri
del mio maestro i passi, e amendue
già mostravam com' eravam leggeri; 12
ed el mi disse: "Volgi li occhi in giùe:
buon ti sarà, per tranquillar la via,
veder lo letto de le piante tue." 15
Come, perché di lor memoria sia,
sovra i sepolti le tombe terragne
portan segnato quel ch'elli eran pria, 18

# CANTO XII

Side by side, like oxen that go yoked, I went on beside that burdened soul, as long as the gentle teacher allowed it; but when he said, "Leave him and press on, for here it is well that with sail and oars each urge his bark along with all his might," I raised my body erect again as one should walk, though my thoughts remained bowed down and shrunken.

I had set out and was gladly following in my master's steps and both of us were now showing how light of foot we were, and he said to me, "Turn down your eyes: it will be well for you to solace your way by seeing the bed beneath your feet."

As, in order that there be memory of them, the stones in the church floor over the buried dead bear figured what they were before;

onde lì molte volte si ripiagne
per la puntura de la rimembranza,
che solo a' pïi dà de le calcagne; 21
sì vid' io lì, ma di miglior sembianza
secondo l'artificio, figurato
quanto per via di fuor del monte avanza. 24
Vedea colui che fu nobil creato
più ch'altra creatura, giù dal cielo
folgoreggiando scender, da l'un lato. 27
Vedëa Brïareo fitto dal telo
celestïal giacer, da l'altra parte,
grave a la terra per lo mortal gelo. 30
Vedea Timbreo, vedea Pallade e Marte,
armati ancora, intorno al padre loro,
mirar le membra d'i Giganti sparte. 33
Vedea Nembròt a piè del gran lavoro
quasi smarrito, e riguardar le genti
che 'n Sennaàr con lui superbi fuoro. 36
O Nïobè, con che occhi dolenti
vedea io te segnata in su la strada,
tra sette e sette tuoi figliuoli spenti! 39
O Saùl, come in su la propria spada
quivi parevi morto in Gelboè,
che poi non sentì pioggia né rugiada! 42
O folle Aragne, sì vedea io te
già mezza ragna, trista in su li stracci
de l'opera che mal per te si fé. 45
O Roboàm, già non par che minacci
quivi 'l tuo segno; ma pien di spavento
nel porta un carro, sanza ch'altri il cacci. 48

wherefore many a time men weep for them there, at the prick of memory that spurs only the faithful: so I saw sculptured there, but of better semblance in respect of skill, all that for pathway juts out from the mountain.

I saw, on the one side, him who was created nobler than any other creature fall as lightning from heaven.

I saw Briareus, on the other side, pierced by the celestial bolt, lying heavy on the ground in mortal chill.

I saw Thymbraeus, I saw Pallas and Mars, still armed, around their father, gazing on the scattered limbs of the giants.

I saw Nimrod at the foot of his great labor, as if bewildered; and there looking on were the people who were proud with him in Shinar.

O Niobe, with what grieving eyes did I see you traced on the roadway between seven and seven children slain!

O Saul, how upon your own sword did you appear there dead on Gilboa, which never thereafter felt rain or dew!

O mad Arachne, so did I see you already half spider, wretched on the shreds of the work which to your own hurt was wrought by you!

O Rehoboam, there your image does not seem to threaten now, but a chariot bears it off full of terror, and no one is in pursuit!

Mostrava ancor lo duro pavimento
come Almeon a sua madre fé caro
parer lo sventurato addornamento. 51
Mostrava come i figli si gittaro
sovra Sennacherìb dentro dal tempio,
e come, morto lui, quivi il lasciaro. 54
Mostrava la ruina e 'l crudo scempio
che fé Tamiri, quando disse a Ciro:
"Sangue sitisti, e io di sangue t'empio." 57
Mostrava come in rotta si fuggiro
li Assiri, poi che fu morto Oloferne,
e anche le reliquie del martiro. 60
Vedeva Troia in cenere e in caverne;
o Iliön, come te basso e vile
mostrava il segno che lì si discerne! 63
Qual di pennel fu maestro o di stile
che ritraesse l'ombre e ' tratti ch'ivi
mirar farieno uno ingegno sottile? 66
Morti li morti e i vivi parean vivi:
non vide mei di me chi vide il vero,
quant' io calcai, fin che chinato givi. 69
Or superbite, e via col viso altero,
figliuoli d'Eva, e non chinate il volto
sì che veggiate il vostro mal sentero! 72
Più era già per noi del monte vòlto
e del cammin del sole assai più speso
che non stimava l'animo non sciolto, 75
quando colui che sempre innanzi atteso
andava, cominciò: "Drizza la testa;
non è più tempo di gir sì sospeso. 78

It showed also, that hard pavement, how Alcmaeon made the luckless ornament seem costly to his mother.

It showed how his sons fell upon Sennacherib within the temple, and how they left him there slain.

It showed the destruction and the cruel slaughter which Tomyris wrought when she said to Cyrus, "You did thirst for blood, and with blood I fill you."

It showed how the Assyrians fled in the rout, when Holofernes was slain, and also the remains of that slaughter.

I saw Troy in ashes and in caverns: O Ilion, how cast down and vile it showed you—the sculpture which is there discerned!

What master was he of brush or of pencil who drew the forms and lineaments which there would make every subtle genius wonder? Dead the dead, and the living seemed alive. He who saw the reality of all I trod upon, while I went bent down, saw not better than I!

Now wax proud, and on with haughty visage, you children of Eve, and bend not down your face to see your evil path!

Already more of the mountain was circled by us and much more of the sun's course was sped than my mind, not free, had reckoned, when he who was always looking ahead as he went began, "Lift up your head, there is now no more time for going thus absorbed.

Vedi colà un angel che s'appresta
  per venir verso noi; vedi che torna
  dal servigio del dì l'ancella sesta. *81*
Di reverenza il viso e li atti addorna,
  sì che i diletti lo 'nvïarci in suso;
  pensa che questo dì mai non raggiorna!" *84*
Io era ben del suo ammonir uso
  pur di non perder tempo, sì che 'n quella
  materia non potea parlarmi chiuso. *87*
A noi venìa la creatura bella,
  biancovestito e ne la faccia quale
  par tremolando mattutina stella. *90*
Le braccia aperse, e indi aperse l'ale;
  disse: "Venite: qui son presso i gradi,
  e agevolemente omai si sale. *93*
A questo invito vegnon molto radi:
  o gente umana, per volar sù nata,
  perché a poco vento così cadi?" *96*
Menocci ove la roccia era tagliata;
  quivi mi batté l'ali per la fronte;
  poi mi promise sicura l'andata. *99*
Come a man destra, per salire al monte
  dove siede la chiesa che soggioga
  la ben guidata sopra Rubaconte, *102*
si rompe del montar l'ardita foga
  per le scalee che si fero ad etade
  ch'era sicuro il quaderno e la doga; *105*
così s'allenta la ripa che cade
  quivi ben ratta da l'altro girone;
  ma quinci e quindi l'alta pietra rade. *108*

See there an angel who is making ready to come towards us. See how the sixth handmaiden is returning from the service of the day. Adorn with reverence your bearing and your face, that it may please him to send us upward. Remember that this day will never dawn again."

Right well was I used to his admonitions never to lose time, so that in that matter his speech could not be dark to me.

The fair creature came towards us, clothed in white and such in his face as seems the tremulous morning star. He opened his arms and then spread his wings and said, "Come: the steps are at hand here, and henceforth the climb is easy. To this bidding there are very few that come: O race of men, born to fly upward, why do you fall so at a breath of wind?"

He brought us where the rock is cleft: there he struck his wings across my forehead and then promised me safe journeying. As on the right hand, for climbing the hill where stands the church above Rubaconte that dominates the well-guided city the bold scarp of the ascent is broken by the stairs which were made in a time when the record and the stave were safe, so the bank that falls there very steeply from the other circle is made easier, but the high rock presses close on this side and on that.

Noi volgendo ivi le nostre persone,
"*Beati pauperes spiritu!*" voci
cantaron sì, che nol diria sermone. 111
Ahi quanto son diverse quelle foci
da l'infernali! ché quivi per canti
s'entra, e là giù per lamenti feroci. 114
Già montavam su per li scaglion santi,
ed esser mi parea troppo più lieve
che per lo pian non mi parea davanti. 117
Ond' io: "Maestro, dì, qual cosa greve
levata s'è da me, che nulla quasi
per me fatica, andando, si riceve?" 120
Rispuose: "Quando i P che son rimasi
ancor nel volto tuo presso che stinti,
saranno, com' è l'un, del tutto rasi, 123
fier li tuoi piè dal buon voler sì vinti,
che non pur non fatica sentiranno,
ma fia diletto loro esser sù pinti." 126
Allor fec' io come color che vanno
con cosa in capo non da lor saputa,
se non che ' cenni altrui sospecciar fanno; 129
per che la mano ad accertar s'aiuta,
e cerca e truova e quello officio adempie
che non si può fornir per la veduta; 132
e con le dita de la destra scempie
trovai pur sei le lettere che 'ncise
quel da le chiavi a me sovra le tempie:
a che guardando, il mio duca sorrise. 136

As we were turning our steps there, "*Beati pauperes spiritu*" was sung so sweetly as no words would tell. Ah, how different these passages from those of Hell, for here the entrance is with songs, and down there with fierce laments.

Now we were mounting by the holy stairs, and it seemed to me I was far lighter than before, on the level; wherefore I said, "Master, tell me, what weight has been lifted from me that I feel almost no weariness as I go on?" He answered, "When the P's that are still left on your brow all but effaced shall be, as one is, quite erased, your feet shall be so conquered by good will that not only will they not feel fatigue, but it will be a delight to them to be urged upwards."

Then did I like those who go with something on their head unknown to them, save that the signs of others make them suspect, so that the hand lends its aid to make sure, and searches and finds, fulfilling the office which sight cannot accomplish; and with the spread fingers of my right hand I found only six of the letters that he of the keys had traced on my temples: and observing this my leader smiled.

# PURGATORIO

NOI ERAVAMO al sommo de la scala,
dove secondamente si risega
lo monte che salendo altrui dismala. *3*
Ivi così una cornice lega
dintorno il poggio, come la primaia;
se non che l'arco suo più tosto piega. *6*
Ombra non li è né segno che si paia:
parsi la ripa e parsi la via schietta
col livido color de la petraia. *9*
"Se qui per dimandar gente s'aspetta,"
ragionava il poeta, "io temo forse
che troppo avrà d'indugio nostra eletta." *12*
Poi fisamente al sole li occhi porse;
fece del destro lato a muover centro,
e la sinistra parte di sé torse. *15*
"O dolce lume a cui fidanza i' entro
per lo novo cammin, tu ne conduci,"
dicea, "come condur si vuol quinc' entro. *18*

# CANTO XIII

We were now at the top of the stairway where a second time the mountain is cut away which, by our ascent of it, frees us from evil. There a terrace girds the hill around, like the first, except that its arc makes a sharper curve. No figure is there, nor any image that may be seen, but only the bank and the bare road and the livid color of the stone.

"If to inquire one waits for people here," the poet was saying, "I fear that perhaps our choice may be delayed too long." Then he set his eyes fixedly on the sun, made of his right side a center for his movement, and brought round his left. "O sweet light, by trust in which I enter on this new road, do you guide us," he said, "with the guidance that is needful in this place.

Tu scaldi il mondo, tu sovr' esso luci;
  s'altra ragione in contrario non ponta,
  esser dien sempre li tuoi raggi duci." 21
Quanto di qua per un migliaio si conta,
  tanto di là eravam noi già iti,
  con poco tempo, per la voglia pronta; 24
e verso noi volar furon sentiti,
  non però visti, spiriti parlando
  a la mensa d'amor cortesi inviti. 27
La prima voce che passò volando
  "*Vinum non habent*" altamente disse,
  e dietro a noi l'andò reïterando. 30
E prima che del tutto non si udisse
  per allungarsi, un'altra "I' sono Oreste"
  passò gridando, e anco non s'affisse. 33
"Oh!" diss' io, "padre, che voci son queste?"
  E com' io domandai, ecco la terza
  dicendo: "Amate da cui male aveste." 36
E 'l buon maestro: "Questo cinghio sferza
  la colpa de la invidia, e però sono
  tratte d'amor le corde de la ferza. 39
Lo fren vuol esser del contrario suono;
  credo che l'udirai, per mio avviso,
  prima che giunghi al passo del perdono. 42
Ma ficca li occhi per l'aere ben fiso,
  e vedrai gente innanzi a noi sedersi,
  e ciascun è lungo la grotta assiso." 45
Allora più che prima li occhi apersi;
  guarda'mi innanzi, e vidi ombre con manti
  al color de la pietra non diversi. 48

You warm the world, you shed light upon it: if other reason urge not to the contrary, your beams must ever be our guide."

As far as here is counted for a mile, even so far there had we now gone, in but short time, because of ready will; and flying towards us were heard, but not seen, spirits uttering courteous invitations to the table of love. The first voice that passed flying, called out loudly, "*Vinum non habent,*" and passed on behind us repeating it; and before it had become wholly inaudible through distance, another passed, crying, "I am Orestes," and also did not stay.

"O father," said I, "what voices are these?" and even as I was asking, lo! the third voice saying, "Love them from whom you have suffered wrong." And my good master, "This circle scourges the sin of envy, and therefore from love the cords of the whip are drawn. The curb must be of the opposite sound: I think you will hear it, as I judge, before you come to the pass of pardon. But fix your eyes full steadily through the air and you will see people sitting there in front of us, and each is seated against the rock." Then more than before I opened my eyes: I looked in front of me and saw shades with cloaks not different in color from the stone.

E poi che fummo un poco più avanti,
udia gridar: "Maria, òra per noi":
gridar "Michele" e "Pietro" e "Tutti santi." 51
Non credo che per terra vada ancoi
omo sì duro, che non fosse punto
per compassion di quel ch'i' vidi poi; 54
ché, quando fui sì presso di lor giunto,
che li atti loro a me venivan certi,
per li occhi fui di grave dolor munto. 57
Di vil ciliccio mi parean coperti,
e l'un sofferia l'altro con la spalla,
e tutti da la ripa eran sofferti. 60
Così li ciechi a cui la roba falla,
stanno a' perdoni a chieder lor bisogna,
e l'uno il capo sopra l'altro avvalla, 63
perché 'n altrui pietà tosto si pogna,
non pur per lo sonar de le parole,
ma per la vista che non meno agogna. 66
E come a li orbi non approda il sole,
così a l'ombre quivi, ond' io parlo ora,
luce del ciel di sé largir non vole; 69
ché a tutti un fil di ferro i cigli fóra
e cusce sì, come a sparvier selvaggio
si fa però che queto non dimora. 72
A me pareva, andando, fare oltraggio,
veggendo altrui, non essendo veduto:
per ch'io mi volsi al mio consiglio saggio. 75
Ben sapev' ei che volea dir lo muto;
e però non attese mia dimanda,
ma disse: "Parla, e sie breve e arguto." 78

And when we were a little farther on, I heard cries of, "Mary, pray for us!" then "Michael" and "Peter" and "All Saints."

I do not believe there goes on earth today a man so hard that he would not have been pierced with pity at what I saw then, for when I had come so near that their condition came to me distinct, great grief was wrung from my eyes. They appeared to be covered with coarse haircloth, and one supported the other with his shoulder, and all were supported by the bank. Even so the blind who are destitute take their place at pardons to beg for their needs; and one sinks his head on the other, so that pity may quickly be awakened in others, not only by the sound of their words, but by their appearance, which pleads not less. And even as the sun profits not the blind, so to the shades in the place I speak of, heaven's light denies its bounty, for all their eyelids an iron wire pierces and stitches up, even as is done to an untamed hawk because it stays not quiet.

It seemed to me that I did them wrong as I went my way, seeing others, not being seen myself; wherefore I turned to my wise counsel. Well knew he what the dumb would say, and therefore did not wait for my question, but said, "Speak, and be brief and to the point."

Virgilio mi venìa da quella banda
de la cornice onde cader si puote,
perché da nulla sponda s'inghirlanda; *81*
da l'altra parte m'eran le divote
ombre, che per l'orribile costura
premevan sì, che bagnavan le gote. *84*
Volsimi a loro e: "O gente sicura,"
incominciai, "di veder l'alto lume
che 'l disio vostro solo ha in sua cura, *87*
se tosto grazia resolva le schiume
di vostra coscïenza sì che chiaro
per essa scenda de la mente il fiume, *90*
ditemi, ché mi fia grazioso e caro,
s'anima è qui tra voi che sia latina;
e forse lei sarà buon s'i' l'apparo." *93*
"O frate mio, ciascuna è cittadina
d'una vera città; ma tu vuo' dire
che vivesse in Italia peregrina." *96*
Questo mi parve per risposta udire
più innanzi alquanto che là dov' io stava,
ond' io mi feci ancor più là sentire. *99*
Tra l'altre vidi un'ombra ch'aspettava
in vista; e se volesse alcun dir "Come?"
lo mento a guisa d'orbo in sù levava. *102*
"Spirto," diss' io, "che per salir ti dome,
se tu se' quelli che mi rispondesti,
fammiti conto o per luogo o per nome." *105*
"Io fui sanese," rispuose, "e con questi
altri rimendo qui la vita ria,
lagrimando a colui che sé ne presti. *108*

Virgil was coming with me on that side of the terrace from which one could fall, since no parapet surrounds it; and on the other side of me were the devout shades that through the horrible seam were pressing out the tears that bathed their cheeks. I turned to them, and began, "O people assured of seeing the light on high which alone is the object of your desire, so may grace soon clear the scum of your conscience that the stream of memory may flow down through it pure, tell me, for it will be gracious and dear to me, if there is any soul here among you that is Italian—and perhaps it will be well for him if I know of it."

"O my brother, each one here is a citizen of a true city: but you mean one that lived in Italy while a pilgrim." This I seemed to hear for answer somewhat farther on from where I was, wherefore I made myself heard yet more that way; and among the rest I saw a shade that looked expectant, and if any would ask how, it was lifting up its chin in the manner of the blind.

"Spirit," I said, "who subdue yourself in order to ascend, if it be you who answered me, make yourself known to me either by place or name."

"I was of Siena," it replied, "and with these others here I mend my sinful life, weeping to Him, that He may grant himself to us.

Savia non fui, avvegna che Sapìa
fossi chiamata, e fui de li altrui danni
più lieta assai che di ventura mia. *111*
E perché tu non creda ch'io t'inganni,
odi s'i' fui, com' io ti dico, folle,
già discendendo l'arco d'i miei anni. *114*
Eran li cittadin miei presso a Colle
in campo giunti co' loro avversari,
e io pregava Iddio di quel ch'e' volle. *117*
Rotti fuor quivi e vòlti ne li amari
passi di fuga; e veggendo la caccia,
letizia presi a tutte altre dispari, *120*
tanto ch'io volsi in sù l'ardita faccia,
gridando a Dio: 'Omai più non ti temo!'
come fé 'l merlo per poca bonaccia. *123*
Pace volli con Dio in su lo stremo
de la mia vita; e ancor non sarebbe
lo mio dover per penitenza scemo, *126*
se ciò non fosse, ch'a memoria m'ebbe
Pier Pettinaio in sue sante orazioni,
a cui di me per caritate increbbe. *129*
Ma tu chi se', che nostre condizioni
vai dimandando, e porti li occhi sciolti,
sì com' io credo, e spirando ragioni?" *132*
"Li occhi," diss' io, "mi fieno ancor qui tolti,
ma picciol tempo, ché poca è l'offesa
fatta per esser con invidia vòlti. *135*
Troppa è più la paura ond' è sospesa
l'anima mia del tormento di sotto,
che già lo 'ncarco di là giù mi pesa." *138*

Sapient I was not, although Sapia was my name; and at others' hurt I rejoiced far more than at my own good fortune. But lest you think that I deceive you, hear if I was not mad, as I tell you, when I was already descending the arc of my years. My townsmen had joined battle near Colle with their adversaries, and I prayed God for that which He had willed: there were they routed and turned back in the bitter steps of flight; and, seeing the chase, I was filled with joy beyond all bounds, so much that I turned upwards my impudent face, crying out to God, 'Now I fear Thee no more,' as the blackbird did for a little fair weather. I sought peace with God on the brink of my life, and my debt would not yet be reduced by penitence, had not Pier Pettinaio remembered me in his holy prayers, who in his charity did grieve for me. But who are you that go asking of our condition and bear your eyes unsewn, as I believe, and breathing do speak?"

"My eyes," I said, "will yet be taken from me here, but for short time only, because they have little offended with looks of envy. Far greater is the fear that holds my soul in suspense, of the torment below, so that already the load down there is heavy upon me."

Ed ella a me: "Chi t'ha dunque condotto
qua sù tra noi, se giù ritornar credi?"
E io: "Costui ch'è meco e non fa motto. *141*

E vivo sono; e però mi richiedi,
spirito eletto, se tu vuo' ch'i' mova
di là per te ancor li mortai piedi." *144*

"Oh, questa è a udir sì cosa nuova,"
rispuose, "che gran segno è che Dio t'ami;
però col priego tuo talor mi giova. *147*

E cheggioti, per quel che tu più brami,
se mai calchi la terra di Toscana,
che a' miei propinqui tu ben mi rinfami. *150*

Tu li vedrai tra quella gente vana
che spera in Talamone, e perderagli
più di speranza ch'a trovar la Diana;
ma più vi perderanno li ammiragli." *154*

And she to me, "Who then has led you up here among us, if you think to return below?"

And I, "He that is with me here and is silent; and I am alive, and do you therefore ask of me, spirit elect, if you would that yonder I should yet move my mortal feet for you."

"Oh, this is so strange a thing to hear," she answered, "that it is a great token of God's love for you. Therefore help me sometimes with your prayers. And I pray you by all you most desire that, if ever you tread the soil of Tuscany, you restore my name among my kindred. You will see them among that vain people who put their trust in Talamone, and will lose more hope there than in finding the Diana—but there the admirals will lose the most."

# PURGATORIO

"Chi è costui che 'l nostro monte cerchia
prima che morte li abbia dato il volo,
e apre li occhi a sua voglia e coverchia?" *3*
"Non so chi sia, ma so ch'e' non è solo;
domandal tu che più li t'avvicini,
e dolcemente, sì che parli, acco'lo." *6*
Così due spirti, l'uno a l'altro chini,
ragionavan di me ivi a man dritta;
poi fer li visi, per dirmi, supini; *9*
e disse l'uno: "O anima che fitta
nel corpo ancora inver' lo ciel ten vai,
per carità ne consola e ne ditta *12*
onde vieni e chi se'; ché tu ne fai
tanto maravigliar de la tua grazia,
quanto vuol cosa che non fu più mai." *15*
E io: "Per mezza Toscana si spazia
un fiumicel che nasce in Falterona,
e cento miglia di corso nol sazia. *18*

# CANTO XIV

"WHO IS this that circles our mountain before death has given him flight, and opens and shuts his eyes at will?"

"I know not who he is, but I know he is not alone. Question him, since you are nearer, and greet him kindly, that he may speak."

Thus two spirits, leaning towards each other, were discoursing of me there on my right; then they turned up their faces to speak to me, and one of them said, "O soul that, still fixed in your body, go on toward Heaven, for charity console us and tell us whence you come and who you are: for you make us marvel so greatly at the grace that is given you as needs must something that never was before."

And I, "Through mid-Tuscany there winds a little stream that rises in Falterona, and a course of a hundred miles does not suffice for it.

Di sovr' esso rech' io questa persona:
  dirvi ch'i' sia, saria parlare indarno,
  ché 'l nome mio ancor molto non suona." *21*
"Se ben lo 'ntendimento tuo accarno
  con lo 'ntelletto," allora mi rispuose
  quei che diceva pria, "tu parli d'Arno." *24*
E l'altro disse lui: "Perché nascose
  questi il vocabol di quella riviera,
  pur com' om fa de l'orribili cose?" *27*
E l'ombra che di ciò domandata era,
  si sdebitò così: "Non so; ma degno
  ben è che 'l nome di tal valle pèra; *30*
ché dal principio suo, ov' è sì pregno
  l'alpestro monte ond' è tronco Peloro,
  che 'n pochi luoghi passa oltra quel segno, *33*
infin là 've si rende per ristoro
  di quel che 'l ciel de la marina asciuga,
  ond' hanno i fiumi ciò che va con loro, *36*
vertù così per nimica si fuga
  da tutti come biscia, o per sventura
  del luogo, o per mal uso che li fruga: *39*
ond' hanno sì mutata lor natura
  li abitator de la misera valle,
  che par che Circe li avesse in pastura. *42*
Tra brutti porci, più degni di galle
  che d'altro cibo fatto in uman uso,
  dirizza prima il suo povero calle. *45*
Botoli trova poi, venendo giuso,
  ringhiosi più che non chiede lor possa,
  e da lor disdegnosa torce il muso. *48*

From its banks I bring this body. To tell you who I am would be to speak in vain, for my name as yet makes no great sound."

"If I rightly penetrate your meaning," he that had spoken first then answered me, "you speak of the Arno."

And the other said to him, "Why did he conceal that river's name, even as one does some horrible thing?"

And the shade that was questioned acquitted himself thus, "I do not know, but it is fitting indeed that the name of such a valley should perish, for from its source (where the rugged mountain-chain from which Pelorus is cut off so teems with water that in few places is it surpassed) down to where it yields itself to replace that which the sky draws up from the sea, whence rivers have that which flows in them, virtue is fled from as an enemy by all, as if it were a snake, either through some misfortune of the place or from evil habit that goads them; wherefore the dwellers in the wretched valley have so changed their nature that it seems as though Circe had them at pasture. Among filthy hogs, fitter for acorns than for any food made for human use, it first directs its feeble course. Then, coming lower, it finds curs more snarling than their power warrants, and from them it scornfully turns away its snout.

Vassi caggendo; e quant' ella più 'ngrossa,
  tanto più trova di can farsi lupi
  la maladetta e sventurata fossa. 51
Discesa poi per più pelaghi cupi,
  trova le volpi sì piene di froda,
  che non temono ingegno che le occùpi. 54
Né lascerò di dir perch' altri m'oda;
  e buon sarà costui, s'ancor s'ammenta
  di ciò che vero spirto mi disnoda. 57
Io veggio tuo nepote che diventa
  cacciator di quei lupi in su la riva
  del fiero fiume, e tutti li sgomenta. 60
Vende la carne loro essendo viva;
  poscia li ancide come antica belva;
  molti di vita e sé di pregio priva. 63
Sanguinoso esce de la trista selva;
  lasciala tal, che di qui a mille anni
  ne lo stato primaio non si rinselva." 66
Com' a l'annunzio di dogliosi danni
  si turba il viso di colui ch'ascolta,
  da qual che parte il periglio l'assanni, 69
così vid' io l'altr' anima, che volta
  stava a udir, turbarsi e farsi trista,
  poi ch'ebbe la parola a sé raccolta. 72
Lo dir de l'una e de l'altra la vista
  mi fer voglioso di saper lor nomi,
  e dimanda ne fei con prieghi mista; 75
per che lo spirto che di pria parlòmi
  ricominciò: "Tu vuo' ch'io mi deduca
  nel fare a te ciò che tu far non vuo'mi. 78

It goes on falling, and the more it swells the more does the accursed and ill-fated ditch find the dogs turned to wolves. Then, after descending through many a deep gorge, it finds foxes so full of fraud that they have no fear that any trap may take them. Nor will I refrain from speech because another hears me (and it will be well for him if he keep in mind that which true prophecy discloses to me). I see your grandson who becomes a hunter of those wolves on the bank of the savage stream, and he strikes them all with terror; he sells their flesh still living, then slaughters them like worn-out cattle: many he deprives of life, himself of honor. Bloody he comes forth from the dismal wood: he leaves it such that in a thousand years from now it will not rewood itself as it was before."

As at the announcement of grievous ills the face of him who listens is troubled, from whatsoever side the danger may assail him, so I saw the other soul, who had turned to hear, become disturbed and sad, when it had taken in these words.

The speech of the one and the look of the other made me desire to know their names, and urgently I questioned them; wherefore the spirit who had spoken to me before began again, "You would have me consent to do for you what you will not for me;

Ma da che Dio in te vuol che traluca
  tanto sua grazia, non ti sarò scarso;
  però sappi ch'io fui Guido del Duca. *81*
Fu il sangue mio d'invidia sì rïarso,
  che se veduto avesse uom farsi lieto,
  visto m'avresti di livore sparso. *84*
Di mia semente cotal paglia mieto;
  o gente umana, perché poni 'l core
  là 'v' è mestier di consorte divieto? *87*
Questi è Rinier; questi è 'l pregio e l'onore
  de la casa da Calboli, ove nullo
  fatto s'è reda poi del suo valore. *90*
E non pur lo suo sangue è fatto brullo,
  tra 'l Po e 'l monte e la marina e 'l Reno,
  del ben richesto al vero e al trastullo; *93*
ché dentro a questi termini è ripieno
  di venenosi sterpi, sì che tardi
  per coltivare omai verrebber meno. *96*
Ov' è 'l buon Lizio e Arrigo Mainardi?
  Pier Traversaro e Guido di Carpigna?
  Oh Romagnuoli tornati in bastardi! *99*
Quando in Bologna un Fabbro si ralligna?
  quando in Faenza un Bernardin di Fosco,
  verga gentil di picciola gramigna? *102*
Non ti maravigliar s'io piango, Tosco,
  quando rimembro, con Guido da Prata,
  Ugolin d'Azzo che vivette nosco, *105*
Federigo Tignoso e sua brigata,
  la casa Traversara e li Anastagi
  (e l'una gente e l'altra è diretata), *108*

but since God wills that so much grace of His shine forth in you, I will not be chary with you; know therefore that I was Guido del Duca. My blood was so inflamed with envy that if I had seen a man become glad you would have seen me suffused with lividness. Of my sowing I reap such straw: O human race, why do you set your hearts where there must be exclusion of partnership?

"This is Rinieri, this is the glory and the honor of the house of Calboli, where none since has made himself heir to his worth. And not his blood alone, between the Po and the mountains and the sea and the Reno, has been stripped of the virtues required for earnest and for pastime, for within these bounds the land is so choked with poisonous growths that tardily would they now be rooted out by tillage. Where is the good Lizio and Arrigo Mainardi, Pier Traversaro and Guido di Carpigna? O men of Romagna turned to bastards! When will a Fabbro take root again in Bologna? when in Faenza a Bernardin di Fosco, noble scion of a lowly plant? Marvel not, Tuscan, if I weep when I remember Guido da Prata, and Ugolin d'Azzo who lived among us, Federigo Tignoso and his company, the Traversaro house and the Anastagi—the one family and the other now without an heir—

le donne e ' cavalier, li affanni e li agi
che ne 'nvogliava amore e cortesia
là dove i cuor son fatti sì malvagi. *111*

O Bretinoro, ché non fuggi via,
poi che gita se n'è la tua famiglia
e molta gente per non esser ria? *114*

Ben fa Bagnacaval, che non rifiglia;
e mal fa Castrocaro, e peggio Conio,
che di figliar tai conti più s'impiglia. *117*

Ben faranno i Pagan, da che 'l demonio
lor sen girà; ma non però che puro
già mai rimagna d'essi testimonio. *120*

O Ugolin de' Fantolin, sicuro
è 'l nome tuo, da che più non s'aspetta
chi far lo possa, tralignando, scuro. *123*

Ma va via, Tosco, omai; ch'or mi diletta
troppo di pianger più che di parlare,
sì m'ha nostra ragion la mente stretta." *126*

Noi sapavam che quell' anime care
ci sentivano andar; però, tacendo,
facëan noi del cammin confidare. *129*

Poi fummo fatti soli procedendo,
folgore parve quando l'aere fende,
voce che giunse di contra dicendo: *132*

"Anciderammi qualunque m'apprende";
e fuggì come tuon che si dilegua,
se sùbito la nuvola scoscende. *135*

Come da lei l'udir nostro ebbe triegua,
ed ecco l'altra con sì gran fracasso,
che somigliò tonar che tosto segua: *138*

the ladies and the knights, the toils and the sports to which love and courtesy moved us, there where hearts have become so wicked! O Bretinoro, why do you not flee away, now that your family has departed, with many another, in order to escape corruption? Bagnacaval does well that gets no sons; and Castrocaro ill, and Conio worse, that yet troubles to beget such counts. The Pagani will do well, when their Devil takes himself off, but not so that unsullied witness shall ever be left of them. O Ugolin de' Fantolini, your name is safe, since no more are looked for who might blacken it by degeneracy. But, Tuscan, go on your way now, for it now pleases me far more to weep than to talk, so has our discourse wrung my heart."

We knew that those dear souls heard us go, therefore by their silence they made us confident of the way. After we were left alone and were journeying on, a voice like lightning when it cleaves the air came counter to us, saying, "Everyone that finds me shall slay me," and fled like thunder that rolls away, if suddenly the cloud is rent. As soon as our hearing had respite from it, lo, the other with so loud a crash that it was like a thunderclap that follows quickly,

"Io sono Aglauro che divenni sasso";
e allor, per ristrignermi al poeta,
in destro feci, e non innanzi, il passo. *141*

Già era l'aura d'ogne parte queta;
ed el mi disse: "Quel fu 'l duro camo
che dovria l'uom tener dentro a sua meta. *144*

Ma voi prendete l'esca, sì che l'amo
de l'antico avversaro a sé vi tira;
e però poco val freno o richiamo. *147*

Chiamavi 'l cielo e 'ntorno vi si gira,
mostrandovi le sue bellezze etterne,
e l'occhio vostro pur a terra mira;
onde vi batte chi tutto discerne." *151*

"I am Aglauros that was turned to stone"; and then, to draw close to the poet I made a step to the right, not forward.

The air was now quiet on every side; and he said to me, "That was the hard bit which should hold man within his bounds: but you take the bait, so that the old adversary's hook draws you to him, and therefore little avails curb, or lure. The heavens call to you and circle about you, displaying to you their eternal splendors, and your eyes gaze only on the earth: wherefore He smites you who sees all."

# PURGATORIO

QUANTO tra l'ultimar de l'ora terza
  e 'l principio del dì par de la spera
  che sempre a guisa di fanciullo scherza, *3*
tanto pareva già inver' la sera
  essere al sol del suo corso rimaso;
  vespero là, e qui mezza notte era. *6*
E i raggi ne ferien per mezzo 'l naso,
  perché per noi girato era sì 'l monte,
  che già dritti andavamo inver' l'occaso, *9*
quand' io senti' a me gravar la fronte
  a lo splendore assai più che di prima,
  e stupor m'eran le cose non conte; *12*
ond' io levai le mani inver' la cima
  de le mie ciglia, e fecimi 'l solecchio,
  che del soverchio visibile lima. *15*
Come quando da l'acqua o da lo specchio
  salta lo raggio a l'opposita parte,
  salendo su per lo modo parecchio *18*

# CANTO XV

As much as between the end of the third hour and the beginning of the day appears of the sphere that is always playing like a child, so much now appeared to be left of the sun's course toward nightfall: it was evening there and here it was midnight. And the beams were striking us full in the face, for the mountain was now so far circled by us that we were going straight toward the sunset, when I felt my brow weighed down by the splendor far more than before, and the things not known were a wonder to me. Wherefore I lifted my hands above my eyebrows and made for me the shade that lessens excess of light.

As when the beam leaps from the water or the mirror to the opposite quarter, rising at the same angle

a quel che scende, e tanto si diparte
dal cader de la pietra in igual tratta,
sì come mostra esperïenza e arte; *21*
così mi parve da luce rifratta
quivi dinanzi a me esser percosso;
per che a fuggir la mia vista fu ratta. *24*
"Che è quel, dolce padre, a che non posso
schermar lo viso tanto che mi vaglia,"
diss' io, "e pare inver' noi esser mosso?" *27*
"Non ti maravigliar s'ancor t'abbaglia
la famiglia del cielo," a me rispuose:
"messo è che viene ad invitar ch'om saglia. *30*
Tosto sarà ch'a veder queste cose
non ti fia grave, ma fieti diletto
quanto natura a sentir ti dispuose." *33*
Poi giunti fummo a l'angel benedetto,
con lieta voce disse: "Intrate quinci
ad un scaleo vie men che li altri eretto." *36*
Noi montavam, già partiti di linci,
e "*Beati misericordes!*" fue
cantato retro, e "Godi tu che vinci!" *39*
Lo mio maestro e io soli amendue
suso andavamo; e io pensai, andando,
prode acquistar ne le parole sue; *42*
e dirizza'mi a lui sì dimandando:
"Che volse dir lo spirto di Romagna,
e 'divieto' e 'consorte' menzionando?" *45*
Per ch'elli a me: "Di sua maggior magagna
conosce il danno; e però non s'ammiri
se ne riprende perché men si piagna. *48*

as it descends, and at equal distance departs as much from the line of the falling stone, even as experiment and science show; so it seemed to me that I was struck by light reflected there in front of me, from which my sight was quick to flee.

"What is that, gentle father," I said, "from which I cannot screen my eyes so that it may avail me, and which seems to be moving towards us?"

"Do not marvel if the family of Heaven still dazzles you," he answered me; "this is a messenger that comes to invite to the ascent. Soon will it be that the seeing of these will not be hard for you, but as great a delight as nature has fitted you to feel."

When we had reached the blessed angel, with a glad voice he said, "Enter here to a stairway far less steep than the others."

We were mounting, having already departed thence, and "*Beati misericordes*" was sung behind, and "Rejoice, you that overcome."

My master and I, we two alone, were journeying upward, and I thought as we went to gain profit from his words, and I turned to him and asked, "What did the spirit of Romagna mean when he spoke of 'exclusion' and 'partnership'?" Whereupon he to me, "Of his own worst fault he knows the harm, and therefore it is little wonder if he reprove it, that it may be less mourned for.

Perché s'appuntano i vostri disiri
dove per compagnia parte si scema,
invidia move il mantaco a' sospiri. *51*
Ma se l'amor de la spera supprema
torcesse in suso il disiderio vostro,
non vi sarebbe al petto quella tema; *54*
ché, per quanti si dice più lì 'nostro,'
tanto possiede più di ben ciascuno,
e più di caritate arde in quel chiostro." *57*
"Io son d'esser contento più digiuno,"
diss' io, "che se mi fosse pria taciuto,
e più di dubbio ne la mente aduno. *60*
Com' esser puote ch'un ben, distributo
in più posseditor, faccia più ricchi
di sé che se da pochi è posseduto?" *63*
Ed elli a me: "Però che tu rificchi
la mente pur a le cose terrene,
di vera luce tenebre dispicchi. *66*
Quello infinito e ineffabil bene
che là sù è, così corre ad amore
com' a lucido corpo raggio vene. *69*
Tanto si dà quanto trova d'ardore;
sì che, quantunque carità si stende,
cresce sovr' essa l'etterno valore. *72*
E quanta gente più là sù s'intende,
più v'è da bene amare, e più vi s'ama,
e come specchio l'uno a l'altro rende. *75*
E se la mia ragion non ti disfama,
vedrai Beatrice, ed ella pienamente
ti torrà questa e ciascun' altra brama. *78*

Because your desires are centered there where the portion is lessened by partnership, envy moves the bellows to your sighs. But if the love of the highest sphere turned upwards your desire, that fear would not be at your heart. For there, the more they are who say 'ours,' the more of good does each possess, and the more of charity burns in that cloister."

"I am more hungering to be satisfied," I said, "than if I had at first been silent, and more of doubt do I assemble in my mind. How can it be that a good distributed can make more possessors richer with itself than if it is possessed by a few?"

And he to me, "Because you still set your mind on earthly things, you gather darkness from true light. That infinite and ineffable Good that is there above speeds to love as a ray of light comes to a bright body. So much it gives of itself as it finds of ardor, so that how far soever love extends, the more does the Eternal Goodness increase upon it; and the more souls there are that are enamored there above, the more there are for loving well, and the more love is there, and like a mirror one reflects to the other. And if my discourse does not appease your hunger, you shall see Beatrice and she will deliver you wholly from this and every other longing.

Procaccia pur che tosto sieno spente,
  come son già le due, le cinque piaghe,
  che si richiudon per esser dolente." 81
Com' io voleva dicer "Tu m'appaghe,"
  vidimi giunto in su l'altro girone,
  sì che tacer mi fer le luci vaghe. 84
Ivi mi parve in una visïone
  estatica di sùbito esser tratto,
  e vedere in un tempio più persone; 87
e una donna, in su l'entrar, con atto
  dolce di madre dicer: "Figliuol mio,
  perché hai tu così verso noi fatto? 90
Ecco, dolenti, lo tuo padre e io
  ti cercavamo." E come qui si tacque,
  ciò che pareva prima, dispario. 93
Indi m'apparve un'altra con quell' acque
  giù per le gote che 'l dolor distilla
  quando di gran dispetto in altrui nacque, 96
e dir: "Se tu se' sire de la villa
  del cui nome ne' dèi fu tanta lite,
  e onde ogne scïenza disfavilla, 99
vendica te di quelle braccia ardite
  ch'abbracciar nostra figlia, o Pisistràto."
  E 'l segnor mi parea, benigno e mite, 102
risponder lei con viso temperato:
  "Che farem noi a chi mal ne disira,
  se quei che ci ama è per noi condannato?" 105
Poi vidi genti accese in foco d'ira
  con pietre un giovinetto ancider, forte
  gridando a sé pur: "Martira, martira!" 108

Strive only that soon may be erased, as are the other two already, the five wounds, which are healed by being painful."

As I was about to say, "You satisfy me," I saw that I had reached the next circle, so that my eager eyes held me silent. There I seemed suddenly to be caught up in an ecstatic vision and to see persons in a temple, and a woman about to enter, with the tender attitude of a mother, saying "My son, why have you done so to us? Behold your father and I sought you, sorrowing"; and as she was silent, that which first appeared was there no more.

Then there appeared to me another woman, with those waters streaming down her cheeks that grief distills when it arises from great resentment against another, and she was saying, "If you are lord of the city for whose name was so great strife among the gods, and whence all knowledge sparkles, avenge you of those daring arms which embraced our daughter, O Pisistratus!" And her lord seemed to me kindly and gently to answer her, with placid mien, "What shall we do to one who desires ill to us, if he who loves us is condemned by us?"

Then I saw people, kindled with the fire of anger, stoning a youth to death, and ever crying out loudly to each other, "Kill, kill!"

E lui vedea chinarsi, per la morte
che l'aggravava già, inver' la terra,
ma de li occhi facea sempre al ciel porte, *111*
orando a l'alto Sire, in tanta guerra,
che perdonasse a' suoi persecutori,
con quello aspetto che pietà diserra. *114*
Quando l'anima mia tornò di fori
a le cose che son fuor di lei vere,
io riconobbi i miei non falsi errori. *117*
Lo duca mio, che mi potea vedere
far sì com' om che dal sonno si slega,
disse: "Che hai che non ti puoi tenere, *120*
ma se' venuto più che mezza lega
velando li occhi e con le gambe avvolte,
a guisa di cui vino o sonno piega?" *123*
"O dolce padre mio, se tu m'ascolte,
io ti dirò," diss' io, "ciò che m'apparve
quando le gambe mi furon sì tolte." *126*
Ed ei: "Se tu avessi cento larve
sovra la faccia, non mi sarian chiuse
le tue cogitazion, quantunque parve. *129*
Ciò che vedesti fu perché non scuse
d'aprir lo core a l'acque de la pace
che da l'etterno fonte son diffuse. *132*
Non dimandai 'Che hai?' per quel che face
chi guarda pur con l'occhio che non vede,
quando disanimato il corpo giace; *135*
ma dimandai per darti forza al piede:
così frugar conviensi i pigri, lenti
ad usar lor vigilia quando riede." *138*

and him I saw sink to the ground, for already death was heavy upon him, but of his eyes he ever made gates unto heaven, praying to the high Lord in such torture, with that look which unlocks pity, that He would forgive his persecutors.

When my mind returned outwardly to the things that are real outside of it, I recognized my not false errors. My leader, who could see me acting like one who frees himself from sleep, said, "What ails you, that you cannot control yourself, but have come more than half a league veiling your eyes and with staggering legs, like a man overcome by wine or sleep?"

"O my sweet father," I said, "if you will listen to me I will tell you what it was that appeared to me when my legs were so taken from me."

And he, "If you had a hundred masks upon your face, your thoughts however slight would not be hidden from me. That which you saw was shown you in order that you might not refuse to open your heart to the waters of peace, which are poured from the eternal fountain. I did not ask 'What ails you?' for the reason of one who looks only with unseeing eyes when another's body lies insensible, but I asked in order to give strength to your feet. So must the sluggish be spurred who are slow to use their waking hour when it returns."

Noi andavam per lo vespero, attenti
  oltre quanto potean li occhi allungarsi
  contra i raggi serotini e lucenti. *141*
Ed ecco a poco a poco un fummo farsi
  verso di noi come la notte oscuro;
  né da quello era loco da cansarsi.
Questo ne tolse li occhi e l'aere puro. *145*

We were journeying on through the evening, straining our eyes forward as far as we could against the bright late beams, when lo, little by little, a smoke dark as night, rolling towards us; nor was there room there to escape from it: this took from us our sight and the pure air.

Buio d'inferno e di notte privata
   d'ogne pianeto, sotto pover cielo,
   quant' esser può di nuvol tenebrata, *3*
non fece al viso mio sì grosso velo
   come quel fummo ch'ivi ci coperse,
   né a sentir di così aspro pelo, *6*
che l'occhio stare aperto non sofferse;
   onde la scorta mia saputa e fida
   mi s'accostò e l'omero m'offerse. *9*
Sì come cieco va dietro a sua guida
   per non smarrirsi e per non dar di cozzo
   in cosa che 'l molesti, o forse ancida, *12*
m'andava io per l'aere amaro e sozzo,
   ascoltando il mio duca che diceva
   pur: "Guarda che da me tu non sia mozzo." *15*
Io sentia voci, e ciascuna pareva
   pregar per pace e per misericordia
   l'Agnel di Dio che le peccata leva. *18*

# CANTO XVI

Gloom of hell, or night bereft of every planet under a barren sky obscured by clouds as much as it can be, never made a veil to my sight so thick nor of stuff so harsh to the sense, as that smoke which covered us there, so that it did not let the eye stay open; wherefore my wise and trusty escort drew to my side and offered me his shoulder. Even as a blind man goes behind his guide that he may not stray or knock against what might injure or perhaps kill him, so I went through that bitter and foul air, listening to my leader, who kept saying, "Take care that you are not cut off from me."

I heard voices, and each one seemed to pray for peace and for mercy to the Lamb of God that takes sins away.

Pur "*Agnus Dei*" eran le loro essordia;
 una parola in tutte era e un modo,
 sì che parea tra esse ogne concordia. *21*
"Quei sono spirti, maestro, ch'i' odo?"
 diss' io. Ed elli a me: "Tu vero apprendi,
 e d'iracundia van solvendo il nodo." *24*
"Or tu chi se' che 'l nostro fummo fendi,
 e di noi parli pur come se tue
 partissi ancor lo tempo per calendi?" *27*
Così per una voce detto fue;
 onde 'l maestro mio disse: "Rispondi,
 e domanda se quinci si va sùe." *30*
E io: "O creatura che ti mondi
 per tornar bella a colui che ti fece,
 maraviglia udirai, se mi secondi." *33*
"Io ti seguiterò quanto mi lece,"
 rispuose; "e se veder fummo non lascia,
 l'udir ci terrà giunti in quella vece." *36*
Allora incominciai: "Con quella fascia
 che la morte dissolve men vo suso,
 e venni qui per l'infernale ambascia. *39*
E se Dio m'ha in sua grazia rinchiuso,
 tanto che vuol ch'i' veggia la sua corte
 per modo tutto fuor del moderno uso, *42*
non mi celar chi fosti anzi la morte,
 ma dilmi, e dimmi s'i' vo bene al varco;
 e tue parole fier le nostre scorte." *45*
"Lombardo fui, e fu' chiamato Marco;
 del mondo seppi, e quel valore amai
 al quale ha or ciascun disteso l'arco. *48*

Their beginnings were always "*Agnus Dei*"; one word was with them all, and one measure, so that full concord seemed to be among them.

"Are these spirits, master, that I hear?" I said; and he answered me, "You judge aright, and they go loosening the knot of anger."

"Who then are you that cleave our smoke and speak of us even as if you still measured time by calends?" Thus spoke a voice; wherefore my master said, "Answer, and ask if by this way one goes up." And I, "O creature that are cleansing yourself to return fair to Him who made you, you shall hear a marvel if you follow me."

"I will follow you as far as is allowed me," it replied, "and if the smoke does not let us see, hearing will keep us together instead."

Then I began, "With those swaddling-bands which death unbinds I am journeying upwards, and I came here through the anguish of Hell; and since God has received me so far into His grace that He wills that I see His court in a manner wholly outside modern usage, do not hide from me who you were before death, but tell me, and tell me if I am on the right way to the passage; and your words shall be our escort."

"I was Lombard and was called Marco; I knew the world and loved that worth at which all now have unbent the bow.

Per montar sù dirittamente vai."
Così rispuose, e soggiunse: "I' ti prego
che per me prieghi quando sù sarai." 51
E io a lui: "Per fede mi ti lego
di far ciò che mi chiedi; ma io scoppio
dentro ad un dubbio, s'io non me ne spiego. 54
Prima era scempio, e ora è fatto doppio
ne la sentenza tua, che mi fa certo
qui, e altrove, quello ov' io l'accoppio. 57
Lo mondo è ben così tutto diserto
d'ogne virtute, come tu mi sone,
e di malizia gravido e coverto; 60
ma priego che m'addite la cagione,
sì ch'i' la veggia e ch'i' la mostri altrui;
ché nel cielo uno, e un qua giù la pone." 63
Alto sospir, che duolo strinse in "uhi!"
mise fuor prima; e poi cominciò: "Frate,
lo mondo è cieco, e tu vien ben da lui. 66
Voi che vivete ogne cagion recate
pur suso al cielo, pur come se tutto
movesse seco di necessitate. 69
Se così fosse, in voi fora distrutto
libero arbitrio, e non fora giustizia
per ben letizia, e per male aver lutto. 72
Lo cielo i vostri movimenti inizia;
non dico tutti, ma, posto ch'i' 'l dica,
lume v'è dato a bene e a malizia, 75
e libero voler; che, se fatica
ne le prime battaglie col ciel dura,
poi vince tutto, se ben si notrica. 78

For mounting up you are going aright." Thus he replied, then added, "I pray you that you pray for me when you are above."

And I to him, "I pledge my faith to you to do what you ask of me. But I am bursting from a doubt within if I do not free myself from it. At first it was simple, and now it is made double by your statement, which makes certain to me, both here and elsewhere, that with which I couple it. The world is indeed as utterly deserted by every virtue as you declare to me, and pregnant and overspread with iniquity, but I beg you to point out to me the cause, so that I may see it and show it to men, for one places it in the heavens and another here below."

He first heaved a deep sigh which grief wrung into "Ah me!" then began, "Brother, the world is blind, and truly you come from it! You who are living refer every cause upward to the heavens alone, as if they of necessity moved all things with them. If this were so, free will would be destroyed in you, and there would be no justice in happiness for good or grief for evil. The heavens initiate your movements: I do not say all of them, but supposing I did say so, a light is given you to know good and evil, and free will, which if it endure fatigue in its first battles with the heavens, afterwards, if it is well nurtured, it conquers completely.

A maggior forza e a miglior natura
 liberi soggiacete; e quella cria
 la mente in voi, che 'l ciel non ha in sua cura. *81*
Però, se 'l mondo presente disvia,
 in voi è la cagione, in voi si cheggia;
 e io te ne sarò or vera spia. *84*
Esce di mano a lui che la vagheggia
 prima che sia, a guisa di fanciulla
 che piangendo e ridendo pargoleggia, *87*
l'anima semplicetta che sa nulla,
 salvo che, mossa da lieto fattore,
 volontier torna a ciò che la trastulla. *90*
Di picciol bene in pria sente sapore;
 quivi s'inganna, e dietro ad esso corre,
 se guida o fren non torce suo amore. *93*
Onde convenne legge per fren porre;
 convenne rege aver, che discernesse
 de la vera cittade almen la torre. *96*
Le leggi son, ma chi pon mano ad esse?
 Nullo, però che 'l pastor che procede,
 rugumar può, ma non ha l'unghie fesse; *99*
per che la gente, che sua guida vede
 pur a quel ben fedire ond' ella è ghiotta,
 di quel si pasce, e più oltre non chiede. *102*
Ben puoi veder che la mala condotta
 è la cagion che 'l mondo ha fatto reo,
 e non natura che 'n voi sia corrotta. *105*
Soleva Roma, che 'l buon mondo feo,
 due soli aver, che l'una e l'altra strada
 facean vedere, e del mondo e di Deo. *108*

You lie subject, in your freedom, to a greater power and to a better nature, and that creates the mind in you which the heavens have not in their charge. Therefore if the present world goes astray, in you is the cause, in you let it be sought: and I will now be a true scout to you in this.

"From His hands, who fondly loves it before it exists, comes forth after the fashion of a child that sports, now weeping, now laughing, the simple little soul, which knows nothing, save that, proceeding from a glad Maker, it turns eagerly to what delights it. First it tastes the savor of a trifling good: there it is beguiled and runs after it, if guide or curb bend not its love. Wherefore it was needful to impose law as a bridle, it was needful to have a ruler who could discern at least the tower of the true city. Laws there are, but who puts his hand to them? None, because the shepherd that leads may chew the cud but has not the hoofs divided. Wherefore the people, who see their guide snatch only at that good whereof they are greedy, feed upon that, and seek no further. Well can you see that ill-guidance is what has made the world wicked, and not nature that is corrupt in you. Rome, which made the world good, was wont to have two Suns, which made visible both the one road and the other, that of the world and that of God.

L'un l'altro ha spento; ed è giunta la spada
col pasturale, e l'un con l'altro insieme
per viva forza mal convien che vada; *111*
però che, giunti, l'un l'altro non teme:
se non mi credi, pon mente a la spiga,
ch'ogn' erba si conosce per lo seme. *114*
In sul paese ch'Adice e Po riga,
solea valore e cortesia trovarsi,
prima che Federigo avesse briga; *117*
or può sicuramente indi passarsi
per qualunque lasciasse, per vergogna,
di ragionar coi buoni o d'appressarsi. *120*
Ben v'èn tre vecchi ancora in cui rampogna
l'antica età la nova, e par lor tardo
che Dio a miglior vita li ripogna: *123*
Currado da Palazzo e 'l buon Gherardo
e Guido da Castel, che mei si noma,
francescamente, il semplice Lombardo. *126*
Dì oggimai che la Chiesa di Roma,
per confondere in sé due reggimenti,
cade nel fango, e sé brutta e la soma." *129*
"O Marco mio," diss' io, "bene argomenti;
e or discerno perché dal retaggio
li figli di Levì furono essenti. *132*
Ma qual Gherardo è quel che tu per saggio
di' ch'è rimaso de la gente spenta,
in rimprovèro del secol selvaggio?" *135*
"O tuo parlar m'inganna, o el mi tenta,"
rispuose a me; "ché, parlandomi tosco,
par che del buon Gherardo nulla senta. *138*

The one has quenched the other, and the sword is joined to the crook: and the one together with the other must perforce go ill —since joined, the one does not fear the other. If you do not believe me, look well at the ear, for every plant is known by the seed.

"On the land that is watered by the Adige and the Po valor and courtesy were once to be found, before Frederick met with strife. Now anyone may safely pass there who out of shame would avoid speaking with the good or coming near them. There are yet indeed three old men in whom the ancient times rebuke the new, and it seems to them long till God remove them to a better life: Currado da Palazzo and the good Gherardo and Guido da Castel, who is better named, in the French fashion, the simple Lombard. Tell henceforth that the Church of Rome, by confounding in itself two governments, falls in the mire and befouls both itself and its burden."

"O Marco mine," I said, "you reason well; and now I perceive why the sons of Levi were excluded from inheritance. But what Gherardo is this who, you say, remains for sample of the extinct people, in reproach of the barbarous age?"

"Either your speech beguiles me, or it makes trial of me," he answered, "for you, speaking to me in Tuscan, seem to know nothing of the good Gherardo.

Per altro sopranome io nol conosco,
s'io nol togliessi da sua figlia Gaia.
Dio sia con voi, ché più non vegno vosco. *141*
Vedi l'albor che per lo fummo raia
già biancheggiare, e me convien partirmi
(l'angelo è ivi) prima ch'io li paia."
Così tornò, e più non volle udirmi. *145*

I know him by no other added name, unless I took it from his daughter Gaia. May God be with you, for I come with you no farther. Behold the brightness that rays through the smoke already whitening, and I must go—the angel is there—before I am seen by him."

So he turned back and would not hear me more.

RICORDITI, lettor, se mai ne l'alpe
  ti colse nebbia per la qual vedessi
  non altrimenti che per pelle talpe, *3*
come, quando i vapori umidi e spessi
  a diradar cominciansi, la spera
  del sol debilemente entra per essi; *6*
e fia la tua imagine leggera
  in giugnere a veder com' io rividi
  lo sole in pria, che già nel corcar era. *9*
Sì, pareggiando i miei co' passi fidi
  del mio maestro, usci' fuor di tal nube
  ai raggi morti già ne' bassi lidi. *12*
O imaginativa che ne rube
  talvolta sì di fuor, ch'om non s'accorge
  perché dintorno suonin mille tube, *15*
chi move te, se 'l senso non ti porge?
  Moveti lume che nel ciel s'informa,
  per sé o per voler che giù lo scorge. *18*
De l'empiezza di lei che mutò forma
  ne l'uccel ch'a cantar più si diletta,
  ne l'imagine mia apparve l'orma; *21*

# CANTO XVII

RECALL, reader, if ever in the mountains a mist has caught you, through which you could not see except as moles do through the skin, how, when the moist dense vapors begin to dissipate, the sphere of the sun enters feebly through them, and your fancy will quickly come to see how, at first, I saw the sun again, which was now at its setting. So, matching mine to the trusty steps of my master, I came forth from such a fog to the rays which were already dead on the low shores.

O imagination, that do sometimes so snatch us from outward things that we give no heed, though a thousand trumpets sound around us, who moves you if the sense affords you naught? A light moves you which takes form in heaven, of itself, or by a will that downward guides it.

Of her impious deed who changed her form into the bird that most delights to sing, the impress appeared in my imagination,

e qui fu la mia mente sì ristretta
dentro da sé, che di fuor non venìa
cosa che fosse allor da lei ricetta. 24
Poi piovve dentro a l'alta fantasia
un crucifisso, dispettoso e fero
ne la sua vista, e cotal si moria; 27
intorno ad esso era il grande Assüero,
Estèr sua sposa e 'l giusto Mardoceo,
che fu al dire e al far così intero. 30
E come questa imagine rompeo
sé per sé stessa, a guisa d'una bulla
cui manca l'acqua sotto qual si feo, 33
surse in mia visïone una fanciulla
piangendo forte, e dicea: "O regina,
perché per ira hai voluto esser nulla? 36
Ancisa t'hai per non perder Lavina;
or m'hai perduta! Io son essa che lutto,
madre, a la tua pria ch'a l'altrui ruina." 39
Come si frange il sonno ove di butto
nova luce percuote il viso chiuso,
che fratto guizza pria che muoia tutto; 42
così l'imaginar mio cadde giuso
tosto che lume il volto mi percosse,
maggior assai che quel ch'è in nostro uso. 45
I' mi volgea per veder ov' io fosse,
quando una voce disse "Qui si monta,"
che da ogne altro intento mi rimosse; 48
e fece la mia voglia tanto pronta
di riguardar chi era che parlava,
che mai non posa, se non si raffronta. 51

and at this my mind was so restrained within itself, that from outside came naught that was then received by it. Then rained down within the high fantasy one crucified, scornful and fierce in his mien, and so was he dying. Round about him were the great Ahasuerus, Esther his wife, and the just Mordecai who was in speech and deed so blameless. And when this imagination burst of itself, like a bubble for which the water fails beneath which it was made, there rose in my vision a maiden, weeping sorely, and she was saying, "O Queen, why through anger have you willed to be naught? You have killed yourself in order not to lose Lavinia: now you have lost me! I am she who mourns, mother, at yours, before another's ruin."

As sleep is broken, when on a sudden new light strikes on the closed eyes, and being broken, quivers before it wholly dies away, so my imagining fell down from me as soon as a light, brighter by far than that to which we are accustomed, smote on my face. I was turning to see where I was when a voice said, "Here is the ascent," which removed me from every other intent; and it gave to my desire to behold who it was that spoke such eagerness as never rests till it sees face to face.

Ma come al sol che nostra vista grava
  e per soverchio sua figura vela,
  così la mia virtù quivi mancava. 54
"Questo è divino spirito, che ne la
  via da ir sù ne drizza sanza prego,
  e col suo lume sé medesmo cela. 57
Sì fa con noi, come l'uom si fa sego;
  ché quale aspetta prego e l'uopo vede,
  malignamente già si mette al nego. 60
Or accordiamo a tanto invito il piede;
  procacciam di salir pria che s'abbui,
  ché poi non si poria, se 'l dì non riede." 63
Così disse il mio duca, e io con lui
  volgemmo i nostri passi ad una scala;
  e tosto ch'io al primo grado fui, 66
senti'mi presso quasi un muover d'ala
  e ventarmi nel viso e dir: "*Beati*
  *pacifici,* che son sanz' ira mala!" 69
Già eran sovra noi tanto levati
  li ultimi raggi che la notte segue,
  che le stelle apparivan da più lati. 72
"O virtù mia, perché sì ti dilegue?"
  fra me stesso dicea, ché mi sentiva
  la possa de le gambe posta in triegue. 75
Noi eravam dove più non saliva
  la scala sù, ed eravamo affissi,
  pur come nave ch'a la piaggia arriva. 78
E io attesi un poco, s'io udissi
  alcuna cosa nel novo girone;
  poi mi volsi al maestro mio, e dissi: 81

But, as at the sun which oppresses our sight, and veils its own form by excess, so was my power failing me.

"This is a divine spirit that directs us to the way of the ascent without our asking, and hides itself by its own light. It does with us as one man with another, for he that waits for the asking and sees the need already sets himself unkindly toward denial. Now let us accord our steps to such an invitation; let us strive to ascend before it grows dark, for then it would not be possible until the day returns." Thus spoke my leader, and together we turned our footsteps to a stairway; and as soon as I was on the first step, near me I felt as it were the motion of a wing fanning my face, and I heard the words, "*Beati pacifici*, who are without evil wrath."

Already the last rays before nightfall were lifted so high above us that the stars were appearing on many sides. "O my strength, why do you so melt away?" I said within myself, for I felt the power of my legs suspended. We stood where the stair went no higher and we were stopped there, even as a ship that arrives at the shore; and I listened a little if I might hear anything in the new circle. Then I turned to my master, and said,

"Dolce mio padre, dì, quale offensione
si purga qui nel giro dove semo?
Se i piè si stanno, non stea tuo sermone." 84
Ed elli a me: "L'amor del bene, scemo
del suo dover, quiritta si ristora;
qui si ribatte il mal tardato remo. 87
Ma perché più aperto intendi ancora,
volgi la mente a me, e prenderai
alcun buon frutto di nostra dimora." 90
"Né creator né creatura mai,"
cominciò el, "figliuol, fu sanza amore,
o naturale o d'animo; e tu 'l sai. 93
Lo naturale è sempre sanza errore,
ma l'altro puote errar per malo obietto
o per troppo o per poco di vigore. 96
Mentre ch'elli è nel primo ben diretto,
e ne' secondi sé stesso misura,
esser non può cagion di mal diletto; 99
ma quando al mal si torce, o con più cura
o con men che non dee corre nel bene,
contra 'l fattore adovra sua fattura. 102
Quinci comprender puoi ch'esser convene
amor sementa in voi d'ogne virtute
e d'ogne operazion che merta pene. 105
Or, perché mai non può da la salute
amor del suo subietto volger viso,
da l'odio proprio son le cose tute; 108
e perché intender non si può diviso,
e per sé stante, alcuno esser dal primo,
da quello odiare ogne effetto è deciso. 111

"My sweet father, say what offense is purged here in the circle where we are: if our feet are stayed, do not stay your speech."

And he to me, "The love of good which comes short of its duty is here restored: here the ill-slackened oar is plied anew. But that you may understand yet more clearly, turn your mind to me, and you shall gather some good fruit from our stay."

He began: "Neither Creator nor creature, my son, was ever without love, either natural or of the mind, and this you know. The natural is always without error; but the other may err either through an evil object, or through too much or too little vigor. While it is directed on the Primal Good, and on secondary goods observes right measure, it cannot be the cause of sinful pleasure. But when it is turned awry to evil, or speeds to good with more zeal, or with less, than it ought, against the Creator works His creature. Hence you can comprehend that love must needs be the seed in you of every virtue and of every action deserving punishment.

"Now, inasmuch as love can never turn its sight from the weal of its subject, all things are secure from self-hatred; and since no being can be conceived of as severed from the First, and as standing by itself, every creature is cut off from hatred of Him.

Resta, se dividendo bene stimo,
 che 'l mal che s'ama è del prossimo; ed esso
 amor nasce in tre modi in vostro limo. 114
È chi, per esser suo vicin soppresso,
 spera eccellenza, e sol per questo brama
 ch'el sia di sua grandezza in basso messo; 117
è chi podere, grazia, onore e fama
 teme di perder perch' altri sormonti,
 onde s'attrista sì che 'l contrario ama; 120
ed è chi per ingiuria par ch'aonti,
 sì che si fa de la vendetta ghiotto,
 e tal convien che 'l male altrui impronti. 123
Questo triforme amor qua giù di sotto
 si piange: or vo' che tu de l'altro intende,
 che corre al ben con ordine corrotto. 126
Ciascun confusamente un bene apprende
 nel qual si queti l'animo, e disira;
 per che di giugner lui ciascun contende. 129
Se lento amore a lui veder vi tira
 o a lui acquistar, questa cornice,
 dopo giusto penter, ve ne martira. 132
Altro ben è che non fa l'uom felice;
 non è felicità, non è la buona
 essenza, d'ogne ben frutto e radice. 135
L'amor ch'ad esso troppo s'abbandona,
 di sovr' a noi si piange per tre cerchi;
 ma come tripartito si ragiona,
tacciolo, acciò che tu per te ne cerchi." 139

It follows, if I distinguish rightly, that the evil we love is our neighbor's, and this love springs up in three ways in your clay. There is he that hopes to excel by the abasement of his neighbor, and solely for this desires that he be cast down from his greatness. There is he that fears to lose power, favor, honor, and fame, because another is exalted, by which he is so saddened that he loves the contrary. And there is he who seems so outraged by injury that he becomes greedy of vengeance, and such a one must needs contrive another's hurt. This threefold love is wept for down here below.

"Now I would have you hear of the other, which hastens toward the good in faulty measure. Each one apprehends vaguely a good wherein the mind may find rest, and this it desires; wherefore each one strives to attain thereto. If lukewarm love draws you to see it or to gain it, this terrace after due repentance torments you for it.

"Another good there is which does not make man happy, it is not happiness, it is not the good essence, the fruit and root of every good. The love which abandons itself to that is wept for above us in three circles, but how it is distinguished as threefold I do not say, that you may search it out for yourself."

# PURGATORIO

Posto avea fine al suo ragionamento
  l'alto dottore, e attento guardava
  ne la mia vista s'io parea contento; *3*
e io, cui nova sete ancor frugava,
  di fuor tacea, e dentro dicea: "Forse
  lo troppo dimandar ch'io fo li grava." *6*
Ma quel padre verace, che s'accorse
  del timido voler che non s'apriva,
  parlando, di parlare ardir mi porse. *9*
Ond' io: "Maestro, il mio veder s'avviva
  sì nel tuo lume, ch'io discerno chiaro
  quanto la tua ragion parta o descriva. *12*
Però ti prego, dolce padre caro,
  che mi dimostri amore, a cui reduci
  ogne buono operare e 'l suo contraro." *15*
"Drizza," disse, "ver' me l'agute luci
  de lo 'ntelletto, e fieti manifesto
  l'error de' ciechi che si fanno duci. *18*

# CANTO XVIII

THE LOFTY teacher had made an end of his discourse and was looking intently in my face to see if I was satisfied; and I, whom a fresh thirst was already goading, was silent outwardly, and within was saying, "Perhaps I irk him with too much questioning." But that true father, who was aware of the timid desire which did not declare itself, by speaking gave me courage to speak. Therefore I said, "Master, my sight is so quickened in your light that I discern clearly all that your discourse distinguishes or declares; wherefore, dear and gentle father, I pray that you expound love to me, to which you reduce every good action and its opposite."

"Direct on me the keen eyes of your understanding," he said, "and the error will be manifest to you of the blind who make themselves guides.

L'animo, ch'è creato ad amar presto,
ad ogne cosa è mobile che piace,
tosto che dal piacere in atto è desto. *21*
Vostra apprensiva da esser verace
tragge intenzione, e dentro a voi la spiega,
sì che l'animo ad essa volger face; *24*
e se, rivolto, inver' di lei si piega,
quel piegare è amor, quell' è natura
che per piacer di novo in voi si lega. *27*
Poi, come 'l foco movesi in altura
per la sua forma ch'è nata a salire
là dove più in sua matera dura, *30*
così l'animo preso entra in disire,
ch'è moto spiritale, e mai non posa
fin che la cosa amata il fa gioire. *33*
Or ti puote apparer quant' è nascosa
la veritate a la gente ch'avvera
ciascun amore in sé laudabil cosa; *36*
però che forse appar la sua matera
sempre esser buona, ma non ciascun segno
è buono, ancor che buona sia la cera." *39*
"Le tue parole e 'l mio seguace ingegno,"
rispuos' io lui, "m'hanno amor discoverto,
ma ciò m'ha fatto di dubbiar più pregno; *42*
ché, s'amore è di fuori a noi offerto
e l'anima non va con altro piede,
se dritta o torta va, non è suo merto." *45*
Ed elli a me: "Quanto ragion qui vede,
dir ti poss' io; da indi in là t'aspetta
pur a Beatrice, ch'è opra di fede. *48*

"The mind, which is created quick to love, is responsive to everything that pleases, as soon as by pleasure it is roused to action. Your faculty of apprehension draws an image from a real existence and displays it within you, so that it makes the mind turn to it; and if, thus turned, the mind inclines toward it, that inclination is love, that inclination is nature which is bound in you anew by pleasure. Then, even as fire moves upwards by reason of its form, being born to ascend thither where it lasts longest in its matter, so the captive mind enters into desire, which is a spiritual movement, and never rests until the thing loved makes it rejoice. Now it may be apparent to you how far the truth is hidden from the people who aver that every love is praiseworthy in itself, because perhaps its matter appears always to be good: but not every imprint is good, although the wax bc good."

"Your discourse and my understanding which has followed it," I replied, "have revealed love to me; but that has made me more full of doubt; for if love is offered to us from without, and if the soul walks with no other foot, it has no merit whether it go straight or crooked."

And he to me, "As far as reason sees here I can tell you; beyond that wait only for Beatrice, for it is a matter of faith.

Ogne forma sustanzïal, che setta
è da matera ed è con lei unita,
specifica vertute ha in sé colletta, 51
la qual sanza operar non è sentita,
né si dimostra mai che per effetto,
come per verdi fronde in pianta vita. 54
Però, là onde vegna lo 'ntelletto
de le prime notizie, omo non sape,
e de' primi appetibili l'affetto, 57
che sono in voi sì come studio in ape
di far lo mele; e questa prima voglia
merto di lode o di biasmo non cape. 60
Or perché a questa ogn' altra si raccoglia,
innata v'è la virtù che consiglia,
e de l'assenso de' tener la soglia. 63
Quest' è 'l principio là onde si piglia
ragion di meritare in voi, secondo
che buoni e rei amori accoglie e viglia. 66
Color che ragionando andaro al fondo,
s'accorser d'esta innata libertate;
però moralità lasciaro al mondo. 69
Onde, poniam che di necessitate
surga ogne amor che dentro a voi s'accende,
di ritenerlo è in voi la podestate. 72
La nobile virtù Beatrice intende
per lo libero arbitrio, e però guarda
che l'abbi a mente, s'a parlar ten prende." 75
La luna, quasi a mezza notte tarda,
facea le stelle a noi parer più rade,
fatta com' un secchion che tuttor arda; 78

"Every substantial form that is both distinct from matter and united with it, holds within itself a specific virtue, which is not perceived except through operation nor ever shows itself save by its effect, as life in a plant by the green leaves. Therefore, whence comes the intelligence of the first cognitions man does not know, nor whence the affection for the first objects of desire, which exist in you even as zeal in the bee for making honey; and this primal will admits no deserving of praise or blame. Now, in order that to this will every other will may be conformed, there is innate in you the faculty that counsels and that ought to hold the threshold of assent. This is the principle wherefrom is derived the reason of desert in you, according as it garners and winnows good and evil loves. They who in their reasoning went to the root of the matter took note of this innate liberty, and accordingly bequeathed ethics to the world. Wherefore, suppose that every love which is kindled in you arises of necessity, the power to arrest it is in you. This noble virtue Beatrice understands as the free will: and therefore look that you have it in mind if she should speak of it to you."

The moon, retarded almost to midnight, shaped like a bucket that continues to glow, made the stars appear scarcer to us,

e correa contra 'l ciel per quelle strade
che 'l sole infiamma allor che quel da Roma
tra ' Sardi e ' Corsi il vede quando cade. 81
E quell' ombra gentil per cui si noma
Pietola più che villa mantoana,
del mio carcar diposta avea la soma; 84
per ch'io, che la ragione aperta e piana
sovra le mie quistioni avea ricolta,
stava com' om che sonnolento vana. 87
Ma questa sonnolenza mi fu tolta
subitamente da gente che dopo
le nostre spalle a noi era già volta. 90
E quale Ismeno già vide e Asopo
lungo di sé di notte furia e calca,
pur che i Teban di Bacco avesser uopo, 93
cotal per quel giron suo passo falca,
per quel ch'io vidi di color, venendo,
cui buon volere e giusto amor cavalca. 96
Tosto fur sovr' a noi, perché correndo
si movea tutta quella turba magna;
e due dinanzi gridavan piangendo: 99
"Maria corse con fretta a la montagna;
e Cesare, per soggiogare Ilerda,
punse Marsilia e poi corse in Ispagna." 102
"Ratto, ratto, che 'l tempo non si perda
per poco amor," gridavan li altri appresso,
"che studio di ben far grazia rinverda." 105
"O gente in cui fervore aguto adesso
ricompie forse negligenza e indugio
da voi per tepidezza in ben far messo, 108

and her course against the heavens was on those paths which the sun inflames, when they in Rome see it between the Sardinians and the Corsicans at its setting. And that noble shade, through whom Pietola is more renowned than any Mantuan town, had put off the burden I had laid upon him; wherefore I, who had garnered clear and plain reasons to my questions, remained like one who rambles drowsily. But this drowsiness was taken suddenly from me by people who had now come round to us behind our backs. And even as Ismenus and Asopus saw of old a fury and a throng along their banks by night, if but the Thebans had need of Bacchus, suchwise, by what I saw of them, bending their way around that circle, were coming those whom right will and a just love bestride. Soon were they upon us, because all that great throng was moving at a run; and two in front were shouting in tears, "Mary ran with haste to the hill country," and "Caesar, to subdue Lerida, thrust at Marseilles and then ran on to Spain." "Swift, swift! let no time be lost through little love," cried the others following, "that zeal in doing well may renew grace."

"O people in whom keen fervor now perhaps makes good the negligence and delay used by you through lukewarmness in well-

questi che vive, e certo i' non vi bugio,
  vuole andar sù, pur che 'l sol ne riluca;
  però ne dite ond' è presso il pertugio." *111*
Parole furon queste del mio duca;
  e un di quelli spirti disse: "Vieni
  di retro a noi, e troverai la buca. *114*
Noi siam di voglia a muoverci sì pieni,
  che restar non potem; però perdona,
  se villania nostra giustizia tieni. *117*
Io fui abate in San Zeno a Verona
  sotto lo 'mperio del buon Barbarossa,
  di cui dolente ancor Milan ragiona. *120*
E tale ha già l'un piè dentro la fossa,
  che tosto piangerà quel monastero,
  e tristo fia d'avere avuta possa; *123*
perché suo figlio, mal del corpo intero,
  e de la mente peggio, e che mal nacque,
  ha posto in loco di suo pastor vero." *126*
Io non so se più disse o s'ei si tacque,
  tant' era già di là da noi trascorso;
  ma questo intesi, e ritener mi piacque. *129*
E quei che m'era ad ogne uopo soccorso
  disse: "Volgiti qua: vedine due
  venir dando a l'accidïa di morso." *132*
Di retro a tutti dicean: "Prima fue
  morta la gente a cui il mar s'aperse,
  che vedesse Iordan le rede sue. *135*
E quella che l'affanno non sofferse
  fino a la fine col figlio d'Anchise,
  sé stessa a vita sanza gloria offerse." *138*

doing, this one who lives—and indeed I do not lie to you—would go up as soon as the sun shines to us again; therefore tell us where the opening is at hand."

These were my leader's words; and one of the spirits said, "Come behind us, and you shall find the gap. We are so filled with desire to keep moving that we cannot stay; forgive, therefore, if you take our penance for rudeness. I was Abbot of San Zeno at Verona under the rule of the good Barbarossa, of whom Milan still talks with sorrow. And one there is that has already a foot in the grave who soon will lament on account of that monastery, and will be sad for having had power there, because his son, deformed in his whole body and worse in mind, and who was born in shame, he has put there in place of its lawful shepherd."

If he said more, or if he was silent, I do not know, so far already had he raced beyond us, but this much I heard and was pleased to retain. And he that was my succor in every need said, "Turn round here, see two of them who come giving a bite to sloth." Behind all the rest they were saying, "The people for whom the sea opened were dead before Jordan saw its heirs; and those who did not endure the toil to the end with Anchises' son gave themselves to a life without glory."

Poi quando fuor da noi tanto divise
  quell' ombre, che veder più non potiersi,
  novo pensiero dentro a me si mise, *141*
del qual più altri nacquero e diversi;
  e tanto d'uno in altro vaneggiai,
  che li occhi per vaghezza ricopersi,
e 'l pensamento in sogno trasmutai. *145*

Then when those shades were so far parted from us that they could no more be seen, a new thought arose within me, from which others many and diverse were born; and I so rambled from one to another that, wandering thus, I closed my eyes, and transmuted my musing into a dream.

# PURGATORIO

NE L'ORA che non può 'l calor dïurno
intepidar più 'l freddo de la luna,
vinto da terra, e talor da Saturno *3*
—quando i geomanti lor Maggior Fortuna
veggiono in orïente, innanzi a l'alba,
surger per via che poco le sta bruna— *6*
mi venne in sogno una femmina balba,
ne li occhi guercia, e sovra i piè distorta,
con le man monche, e di colore scialba. *9*
Io la mirava; e come 'l sol conforta
le fredde membra che la notte aggrava,
così lo sguardo mio le facea scorta *12*
la lingua, e poscia tutta la drizzava
in poco d'ora, e lo smarrito volto,
com' amor vuol, così le colorava. *15*
Poi ch'ell' avea 'l parlar così disciolto,
cominciava a cantar sì, che con pena
da lei avrei mio intento rivolto. *18*

# CANTO XIX

At the hour when the day's heat, overcome by Earth and at times by Saturn, can no more warm the cold of the moon—when the geomancers see their *Fortuna Major* rise in the East before dawn by a path which does not long stay dark for it—there came to me in a dream a woman, stammering, with eyes asquint and crooked on her feet, with maimed hands, and of sallow hue. I gazed upon her: and even as the sun revives cold limbs benumbed by night, so my look made ready her tongue, and then in but little time set her full straight, and colored her pallid face even as love requires. When she had her speech thus unloosed, she began to sing so that it would have been hard for me to turn my attention from her.

"Io son," cantava, "io son dolce serena,
che ' marinari in mezzo mar dismago;
tanto son di piacere a sentir piena! 21
Io volsi Ulisse del suo cammin vago
al canto mio; e qual meco s'ausa,
rado sen parte; sì tutto l'appago!" 24
Ancor non era sua bocca richiusa,
quand' una donna apparve santa e presta
lunghesso me per far colei confusa. 27
"O Virgilio, Virgilio, chi è questa?"
fieramente dicea; ed el venìa
con li occhi fitti pur in quella onesta. 30
L'altra prendea, e dinanzi l'apria
fendendo i drappi, e mostravami 'l ventre;
quel mi svegliò col puzzo che n'uscia. 33
Io mossi li occhi, e 'l buon maestro: "Almen tre
voci t'ho messe!" dicea, "Surgi e vieni;
troviam l'aperta per la qual tu entre." 36
Sù mi levai, e tutti eran già pieni
de l'alto dì i giron del sacro monte,
e andavam col sol novo a le reni. 39
Seguendo lui, portava la mia fronte
come colui che l'ha di pensier carca,
che fa di sé un mezzo arco di ponte; 42
quand' io udi' "Venite; qui si varca"
parlare in modo soave e benigno,
qual non si sente in questa mortal marca. 45
Con l'ali aperte, che parean di cigno,
volseci in sù colui che sì parlonne
tra due pareti del duro macigno. 48

"I am," she sang, "I am the sweet Siren who leads mariners astray in mid-sea, so full am I of pleasantness to hear. Ulysses, eager to journey on, I turned aside to my song; and whosoever abides with me rarely departs, so wholly do I satisfy him." Her mouth was not yet shut when a lady, holy and alert, appeared close beside me to put her to confusion. "O Virgil, Virgil, who is this?" she said sternly; and he came on with his eyes fixed only on that honest one. He seized the other and laid her bare in front, rending her garments and showing me her belly: this waked me with the stench that issued therefrom. I turned my eyes, and the good master said, "I have called you at least three times: arise and come, let us find the opening by which you may enter."

I rose up; and all the circles of the holy mountain were already filled with the high day, and we journeyed with the new sun at our back. Following him, I was bearing my brow like one that has it burdened with thought, who makes of himself a half-arch of a bridge, when I heard, "Come, here is the passage," spoken in a tone gentle and kind, such as is not heard in this mortal region. With open wings that seemed like a swan's he who thus had spoken to us turned us upward between the two walls of hard rock,

Mosse le penne poi e ventilonne,
"*Qui lugent*" affermando esser beati,
ch'avran di consolar l'anime donne. 51
"Che hai che pur inver' la terra guati?"
la guida mia incominciò a dirmi,
poco amendue da l'angel sormontati. 54
E io: "Con tanta sospeccion fa irmi
novella visïon ch'a sé mi piega,
sì ch'io non posso dal pensar partirmi." 57
"Vedesti," disse, "quell'antica strega
che sola sovr' a noi omai si piagne;
vedesti come l'uom da lei si slega. 60
Bastiti, e batti a terra le calcagne;
li occhi rivolgi al logoro che gira
lo rege etterno con le rote magne." 63
Quale 'l falcon, che prima a' piè si mira,
indi si volge al grido e si protende
per lo disio del pasto che là il tira, 66
tal mi fec' io; e tal, quanto si fende
la roccia per dar via a chi va suso,
n'andai infin dove 'l cerchiar si prende. 69
Com' io nel quinto giro fui dischiuso,
vidi gente per esso che piangea,
giacendo a terra tutta volta in giuso. 72
"*Adhaesit pavimento anima mea*"
sentia dir lor con sì alti sospiri,
che la parola a pena s'intendea. 75
"O eletti di Dio, li cui soffriri
e giustizia e speranza fa men duri,
drizzate noi verso li alti saliri." 78

then moved his feathers and fanned us, declaring "*Qui lugent*" to be blessed, for they shall have their souls possessed of consolation.

"What ails you that you keep gazing on the ground?" my guide began to say to me, when we had both climbed a little above the angel. And I, "In such apprehension I am made to go by a new vision, which bends me to itself so that I cannot leave off thinking on it."

"You have seen," he said, "that ancient witch who alone is now wept for above us: you have seen how man is freed from her. Let it suffice you, and strike your heels on the ground: turn your eyes to the lure which the eternal King spins with the mighty spheres." Like the falcon that first looks down, then turns at the cry and stretches forward, through desire of the food that draws him thither, such I became, and such, so far as the rock is cleft to afford a way to him who mounts, I went, up to where the circling is begun.

When I had come forth on the fifth round, I saw people upon it who were weeping, lying on the ground all turned downward. "*Adhaesit pavimento anima mea*," I heard them saying with sighs so deep that the words could hardly be distinguished.

"O elect of God, whose sufferings both justice and hope make less hard, direct us toward the high ascents."

"Se voi venite dal giacer sicuri,
e volete trovar la via più tosto,
le vostre destre sien sempre di fori." *81*
Così pregò 'l poeta, e sì risposto
poco dinanzi a noi ne fu; per ch'io
nel parlare avvisai l'altro nascosto, *84*
e volsi li occhi a li occhi al segnor mio:
ond' elli m'assentì con lieto cenno
ciò che chiedea la vista del disio. *87*
Poi ch'io potei di me fare a mio senno,
trassimi sovra quella creatura
le cui parole pria notar mi fenno, *90*
dicendo: "Spirto in cui pianger matura
quel sanza 'l quale a Dio tornar non pòssi,
sosta un poco per me tua maggior cura. *93*
Chi fosti e perché vòlti avete i dossi
al sù, mi dì, e se vuo' ch'io t'impetri
cosa di là ond' io vivendo mossi." *96*
Ed elli a me: "Perché i nostri diretri
rivolga il cielo a sé, saprai; ma prima
*scias quod ego fui successor Petri.* *99*
Intra Sïestri e Chiaveri s'adima
una fiumana bella, e del suo nome
lo titol del mio sangue fa sua cima. *102*
Un mese e poco più prova' io come
pesa il gran manto a chi dal fango il guarda,
che piuma sembran tutte l'altre some. *105*
La mia conversïone, omè!, fu tarda;
ma, come fatto fui roman pastore,
così scopersi la vita bugiarda. *108*

"If you come exempt from lying prostrate, and would most quickly find the way, let your right hand be ever to the outside." Thus the poet asked, and thus came the answer from a little way ahead; wherefore, by this speech, I marked what was concealed, then turned my eyes on the eyes of my lord: at which with a glad sign he gave assent to what the look of my desire was craving. And when I was free to do as I wished, I drew forward above that soul whose words before had made me take note of him, saying, "Spirit in whom weeping matures that without which there is no returning to God, suspend a little for me your greater care. Tell me who you were; and why you have your backs turned upwards, and whether you will have me obtain aught for you yonder whence I set out alive."

And he to me, "Why heaven turns our backs to itself you shall know; but first *scias quod ego fui successor Petri*. Between Sestri and Chiavari descends a fair river and of its name the title of my blood makes its top. One month, and little more, I learned how the great mantle weighs on him who keeps it from the mire, so that all other burdens seem a feather. My conversion, ah me! was tardy; but when I was made Roman Shepherd, then I found how false life is.

Vidi che lì non s'acquetava il core,
né più salir potiesi in quella vita;
per che di questa in me s'accese amore. *111*

Fino a quel punto misera e partita
da Dio anima fui, del tutto avara;
or, come vedi, qui ne son punita. *114*

Quel ch'avarizia fa, qui si dichiara
in purgazion de l'anime converse;
e nulla pena il monte ha più amara. *117*

Sì come l'occhio nostro non s'aderse
in alto, fisso a le cose terrene,
così giustizia qui a terra il merse. *120*

Come avarizia spense a ciascun bene
lo nostro amore, onde operar perdési,
così giustizia qui stretti ne tene, *123*

ne' piedi e ne le man legati e presi;
e quanto fia piacer del giusto Sire,
tanto staremo immobili e distesi." *126*

Io m'era inginocchiato e volea dire;
ma com' io cominciai ed el s'accorse,
solo ascoltando, del mio reverire, *129*

"Qual cagion," disse, "in giù così ti torse?"
E io a lui: "Per vostra dignitate
mia coscïenza dritto mi rimorse." *132*

"Drizza le gambe, lèvati sù, frate!"
rispuose; "non errar: conservo sono
teco e con li altri ad una podestate. *135*

Se mai quel santo evangelico suono
che dice '*Neque nubent*' intendesti,
ben puoi veder perch' io così ragiono. *138*

I saw that there the heart was not at rest; nor was it possible to mount higher in that life, wherefore the love of this was kindled in me. Up to that time I had been a wretched soul, parted from God and wholly avaricious. Now, as you see, I am here punished for it. What avarice does is displayed here in the purging of the down-turned souls, and the mountain has no more bitter penalty. Even as our eyes, fixed upon earthly things, were not lifted on high, so justice here has sunk them to the earth; even as avarice quenched all our love of good, so that our works were lost, so justice here holds us fast, bound and captive in feet and hands; and so long as it shall be the pleasure of the just Lord, so long shall we lie here outstretched and motionless."

I had kneeled, and wished to speak; but when I began, and he became aware, by the sound alone, of my reverence, "What cause," said he, "has thus bent you down?" And I to him, "Because of your dignity my conscience smote me for standing."

"Straighten your legs, rise up, brother," he replied, "do not err: I am fellow-servant with you and with the others unto one Power. If ever you have understood that holy gospel sound which says '*Neque nubent*,' you may well see why I speak thus.

Vattene omai: non vo' che più t'arresti;
  ché la tua stanza mio pianger disagia,
  col qual maturo ciò che tu dicesti. 141
Nepote ho io di là c'ha nome Alagia,
  buona da sé, pur che la nostra casa
  non faccia lei per essempro malvagia;
e questa sola di là m'è rimasa." 145

Go your way now: I would not have you stop longer, for your stay hinders my weeping, whereby I ripen that which you have spoken of. A niece I have yonder who is named Alagia, good in herself if only our house make her not wicked by example; and she alone remains to me yonder."

CONTRA miglior voler voler mal pugna;
onde contra 'l piacer mio, per piacerli,
trassi de l'acqua non sazia la spugna. *3*
Mossimi; e 'l duca mio si mosse per li
luoghi spediti pur lungo la roccia,
come si va per muro stretto a' merli; *6*
ché la gente che fonde a goccia a goccia
per li occhi il mal che tutto 'l mondo occupa,
da l'altra parte in fuor troppo s'approccia. *9*
Maladetta sie tu, antica lupa,
che più che tutte l'altre bestie hai preda
per la tua fame sanza fine cupa! *12*
O ciel, nel cui girar par che si creda
le condizion di qua giù trasmutarsi,
quando verrà per cui questa disceda? *15*
Noi andavam con passi lenti e scarsi,
e io attento a l'ombre, ch'i' sentia
pietosamente piangere e lagnarsi; *18*

# CANTO XX

AGAINST a better will the will fights ill: wherefore against my pleasure, to please him, I drew from the water the sponge unfilled. I moved on, and my leader moved on, keeping to the free spaces alongside the rock, as one goes on a wall close to the battlements; for the people who pour from their eyes drop by drop the evil that fills the whole world approach too near the edge on the other side.

Accursed be you, ancient wolf, who have more prey than all the other beasts, because of your hunger endlessly deep! O heaven, in whose revolution it seems conditions here below are thought to be changed, when will he come through whom she shall depart?

We were going on with slow and scant steps and I attentive to the shades whom I heard piteously weeping and complaining,

e per ventura udi' "Dolce Maria!"
  dinanzi a noi chiamar così nel pianto
  come fa donna che in parturir sia; 21
e seguitar: "Povera fosti tanto,
  quanto veder si può per quello ospizio
  dove sponesti il tuo portato santo." 24
Seguentemente intesi: "O buon Fabrizio,
  con povertà volesti anzi virtute
  che gran ricchezza posseder con vizio." 27
Queste parole m'eran sì piaciute,
  ch'io mi trassi oltre per aver contezza
  di quello spirto onde parean venute. 30
Esso parlava ancor de la larghezza
  che fece Niccolò a le pulcelle,
  per condurre ad onor lor giovinezza. 33
"O anima che tanto ben favelle,
  dimmi chi fosti," dissi, "e perché sola
  tu queste degne lode rinovelle. 36
Non fia sanza mercé la tua parola,
  s'io ritorno a compiér lo cammin corto
  di quella vita ch'al termine vola." 39
Ed elli: "Io ti dirò, non per conforto
  ch'io attenda di là, ma perché tanta
  grazia in te luce prima che sie morto. 42
Io fui radice de la mala pianta
  che la terra cristiana tutta aduggia,
  sì che buon frutto rado se ne schianta. 45
Ma se Doagio, Lilla, Guanto e Bruggia
  potesser, tosto ne saria vendetta;
  e io la cheggio a lui che tutto giuggia. 48

and by chance I heard one ahead of us crying out in his lament, "Sweet Mary," even as a woman does who is in travail; and continuing, "How poor you were may be seen from that hostelry where you laid down your holy burden." And following this I heard, "O good Fabricius, you chose to possess virtue with poverty rather than great riches with iniquity." These words so pleased me that I pressed forward to have acquaintance with that spirit from whom they seemed to come, and he went on to tell of the bounty which Nicholas gave to the maidens, to lead their youth to honor.

"O spirit that do discourse of so much good, tell me who you were," I said, "and why you alone renew these worthy praises. Your words shall not be without reward, if I return to complete the short way of that life which flies to its end."

And he, "I will tell you, not for any solace that I expect from yonder, but because such grace shines in you before you are dead. I was the root of the evil plant that overshadows all the Christian land so that good fruit is seldom plucked therefrom; but if Douai, Lille, Ghent, and Bruges had the strength, there would soon be vengeance on it: and this I implore of Him who judges all things.

Chiamato fui di là Ugo Ciappetta;
di me son nati i Filippi e i Luigi
per cui novellamente è Francia retta. 51
Figliuol fu' io d'un beccaio di Parigi:
quando li regi antichi venner meno
tutti, fuor ch'un renduto in panni bigi, 54
trova'mi stretto ne le mani il freno
del governo del regno, e tanta possa
di nuovo acquisto, e sì d'amici pieno, 57
ch'a la corona vedova promossa
la testa di mio figlio fu, dal quale
cominciar di costor le sacrate ossa. 60
Mentre che la gran dota provenzale
al sangue mio non tolse la vergogna,
poco valea, ma pur non facea male. 63
Lì cominciò con forza e con menzogna
la sua rapina; e poscia, per ammenda,
Pontì e Normandia prese e Guascogna. 66
Carlo venne in Italia e, per ammenda,
vittima fé di Curradino; e poi
ripinse al ciel Tommaso, per ammenda. 69
Tempo vegg' io, non molto dopo ancoi,
che tragge un altro Carlo fuor di Francia,
per far conoscer meglio e sé e ' suoi. 72
Sanz' arme n'esce e solo con la lancia
con la qual giostrò Giuda, e quella ponta
sì, ch'a Fiorenza fa scoppiar la pancia. 75
Quindi non terra, ma peccato e onta
guadagnerà, per sé tanto più grave,
quanto più lieve simil danno conta. 78

I was called Hugh Capet yonder; of me were born the Philips and the Louises, by whom of late France is ruled. I was the son of a butcher of Paris. When the ancient kings had all died out, save one, a gray-clad monk, I found tight in my hands the reins of the government of the realm, and with so much power from new possessions and with friends in such abundance that to the widowed crown my son's head was promoted, from whom began their consecrated bones.

"So long as the great dowry of Provence had not taken the sense of shame from my race, it was of little account, but still it did no evil. There by force and by fraud its rapine began; and then, for amends, it seized Ponthieu and Normandy and Gascony; Charles came into Italy and, for amends, made a victim of Conradin; and then, for amends, thrust Thomas back to Heaven. A time I see not long from this present day which brings another Charles out of France, to make both himself and his own the better known. Forth he comes unarmed save only with the lance with which Judas tilted, and he so couches it that he bursts the paunch of Florence; from this he shall gain, not land, but sin and shame, so much the heavier for him the lighter he reckons such wrong.

L'altro, che già uscì preso di nave,
veggio vender sua figlia e patteggiarne
come fanno i corsar de l'altre schiave. 81
O avarizia, che puoi tu più farne,
poscia c'ha' il mio sangue a te sì tratto,
che non si cura de la propria carne? 84
Perché men paia il mal futuro e 'l fatto,
veggio in Alagna intrar lo fiordaliso,
e nel vicario suo Cristo esser catto. 87
Veggiolo un'altra volta esser deriso;
veggio rinovellar l'aceto e 'l fiele,
e tra vivi ladroni esser anciso. 90
Veggio il novo Pilato sì crudele,
che ciò nol sazia, ma sanza decreto
portar nel Tempio le cupide vele. 93
O Segnor mio, quando sarò io lieto
a veder la vendetta che, nascosa,
fa dolce l'ira tua nel tuo secreto? 96
Ciò ch'io dicea di quell' unica sposa
de lo Spirito Santo e che ti fece
verso me volger per alcuna chiosa, 99
tanto è risposto a tutte nostre prece
quanto 'l dì dura; ma com' el s'annotta,
contrario suon prendemo in quella vece. 102
Noi repetiam Pigmalïon allotta,
cui traditore e ladro e paricida
fece la voglia sua de l'oro ghiotta; 105
e la miseria de l'avaro Mida,
che seguì a la sua dimanda gorda,
per la qual sempre convien che si rida. 108

The other, who once came forth a captive from a ship, I see selling his own daughter and haggling over her as do the corsairs with female slaves. O Avarice, what more can you do to us, since you have so drawn my race to yourself that it has no care for its own flesh? In order that the past and the future ill may seem less, I see the fleur-de-lis enter Alagna, and in His Vicar Christ made captive. I see Him mocked a second time; and I see renewed the vinegar and the gall, and Him slain between living thieves. I see the new Pilate so cruel that this does not sate him, but without decree he directs his greedy sails against the Temple. O my Lord, when shall I rejoice to see the vengeance which, concealed, makes sweet Thine anger in Thy secrecy?

"What I was saying of that only bride of the Holy Ghost, and which made you turn toward me for some gloss, so much is the answer to all our prayers, as long as the day lasts; but when the night comes, we take up a contrary sound instead: then we recall Pygmalion, whom insatiate lust of gold made traitor, thief, and parricide; and the misery of the avaricious Midas which followed on his greedy demand, whereat men must always laugh.

Del folle Acàn ciascun poi si ricorda,
 come furò le spoglie, sì che l'ira
 di Iosüè qui par ch'ancor lo morda. *111*
Indi accusiam col marito Saffira;
 lodiamo i calci ch'ebbe Elïodoro;
 e in infamia tutto 'l monte gira *114*
Polinestòr ch'ancise Polidoro;
 ultimamente ci si grida: 'Crasso,
 dilci, che 'l sai: di che sapore è l'oro?' *117*
Talor parla l'uno alto e l'altro basso,
 secondo l'affezion ch'ad ir ci sprona
 ora a maggiore e ora a minor passo: *120*
però al ben che 'l dì ci si ragiona,
 dianzi non era io sol; ma qui da presso
 non alzava la voce altra persona." *123*
Noi eravam partiti già da esso,
 e brigavam di soverchiar la strada
 tanto quanto al poder n'era permesso, *126*
quand' io senti', come cosa che cada,
 tremar lo monte; onde mi prese un gelo
 qual prender suol colui ch'a morte vada. *129*
Certo non si scoteo sì forte Delo,
 pria che Latona in lei facesse 'l nido
 a parturir li due occhi del cielo. *132*
Poi cominciò da tutte parti un grido
 tal, che 'l maestro inverso me si feo,
 dicendo: "Non dubbiar, mentr' io ti guido." *135*
"*Gloria in excelsis*" tutti "*Deo*"
 dicean, per quel ch'io da' vicin compresi,
 onde intender lo grido si poteo. *138*

Each then remembers the foolish Acan, how he stole the spoils, so that the wrath of Joshua seems to sting him here again. Then we accuse Sapphira with her husband; we celebrate the kicks which Heliodorus had; and in infamy the name of Polymestor who slew Polydorus circles all the mountain. Last, the cry here is, 'Tell us, Crassus, for you know, what is the savor of gold?' Sometimes we discourse, the one loud, the other low, according to the ardor that spurs us to speak, now with greater, now with lesser force; therefore, in the good we tell of here by day I was not alone before, but here nearby no other soul was raising his voice."

We were already parted from him and were striving to go forward as fast as we were able, when I felt the mountain shake like something that is falling; at which a chill seized me such as seizes one who goes to his death. Assuredly Delos was not shaken so violently before Latona made her nest therein to give birth to the two eyes of Heaven. Then began such a cry on all sides that my master drew toward me, saying, "Do not fear while I guide you." "*Gloria in excelsis, Deo*" all were saying, by what I understood from those nearby, where the cry could be heard.

No' istavamo immobili e sospesi
  come i pastor che prima udir quel canto,
  fin che 'l tremar cessò ed el compiési. *141*
Poi ripigliammo nostro cammin santo,
  guardando l'ombre che giacean per terra,
  tornate già in su l'usato pianto. *144*
Nulla ignoranza mai con tanta guerra
  mi fé desideroso di sapere,
  se la memoria mia in ciò non erra, *147*
quanta pareami allor, pensando, avere;
  né per la fretta dimandare er' oso,
  né per me lì potea cosa vedere:
così m'andava timido e pensoso. *151*

We stood motionless and in suspense, like the shepherds who first heard that song, until the quaking ceased and it was ended. Then we took up our holy way again, looking at the shades that lay on the ground, already returned to their wonted plaint. No ignorance—if my memory err not in this—did ever with so great assault make me desirous of knowing as it seemed I then experienced in thought. Nor, for our haste, did I dare ask, nor of myself could I see aught there. So I went on, timid and pensive.

# PURGATORIO

LA SETE natural che mai non sazia
se non con l'acqua onde la femminetta
samaritana domandò la grazia, *3*
mi travagliava, e pungeami la fretta
per la 'mpacciata via dietro al mio duca,
e condoleami a la giusta vendetta. *6*
Ed ecco, sì come ne scrive Luca
che Cristo apparve a' due ch'erano in via,
già surto fuor de la sepulcral buca, *9*
ci apparve un'ombra, e dietro a noi venìa,
dal piè guardando la turba che giace;
né ci addemmo di lei, sì parlò pria, *12*
dicendo: "O frati miei, Dio vi dea pace."
Noi ci volgemmo sùbiti, e Virgilio
rendéli 'l cenno ch'a ciò si conface. *15*
Poi cominciò: "Nel beato concilio
ti ponga in pace la verace corte
che me rilega ne l'etterno essilio." *18*
"Come!" diss' elli, e parte andavam forte:
"se voi siete ombre che Dio sù non degni,
chi v'ha per la sua scala tanto scorte?" *21*

# CANTO XXI

THE NATURAL thirst which is never quenched, save with the water whereof the poor Samaritan woman asked the grace, was tormenting me, and our haste was urging me along the encumbered way behind my leader, and I was grieving at the just vengeance; and lo, as Luke writes for us that Christ, new-risen from the sepulchral cave, appeared to the two who were on the way, a shade appeared to us, and he was coming on behind us while we were watching the crowd that lay at our feet, and we were not aware of him till he first spoke, saying "O my brothers, may God give you peace."

We turned quickly and Virgil answered him with the greeting that is fitting thereto; then he began, "May the true court which binds me in the eternal exile bring you in peace to the assembly of the blest."

"How," he said—and meanwhile we hastened on—"if you are shades whom God deigns not on high, who has brought you so far along His stairs?"

E 'l dottor mio: "Se tu riguardi a' segni
che questi porta e che l'angel profila,
ben vedrai che coi buon convien ch'e' regni. 24
Ma perché lei che dì e notte fila
non li avea tratta ancora la conocchia
che Cloto impone a ciascuno e compila, 27
l'anima sua, ch'è tua e mia serocchia,
venendo sù, non potea venir sola,
però ch'al nostro modo non adocchia. 30
Ond' io fui tratto fuor de l'ampia gola
d'inferno per mostrarli, e mosterrolli
oltre, quanto 'l potrà menar mia scola. 33
Ma dimmi, se tu sai, perché tai crolli
diè dianzi 'l monte, e perché tutto ad una
parve gridare infino a' suoi piè molli." 36
Sì mi diè, dimandando, per la cruna
del mio disio, che pur con la speranza
si fece la mia sete men digiuna. 39
Quei cominciò: "Cosa non è che sanza
ordine senta la religïone
de la montagna, o che sia fuor d'usanza. 42
Libero è qui da ogne alterazione:
di quel che 'l ciel da sé in sé riceve
esser ci puote, e non d'altro, cagione. 45
Per che non pioggia, non grando, non neve,
non rugiada, non brina più sù cade
che la scaletta di tre gradi breve; 48
nuvole spesse non paion né rade,
né coruscar, né figlia di Taumante,
che di là cangia sovente contrade; 51

And my teacher, "If you look at the marks which this man bears and which are traced by the angel, you will clearly see that he is to reign with the good. But since she who spins day and night had not yet drawn off for him the distaff which Clotho loads and compacts for everyone, his soul, which is your sister and mine, could not make the ascent alone, because it sees not after our fashion. Wherefore I was brought forth from Hell's wide jaws to guide him, and I will guide him onward as far as my school can lead him. But tell me, if you can, why the mountain quaked so just now, and why all seemed to shout at once, down to its moist base?"

Thus asking did he thread the needle's eye of my desire, and with hope alone my thirst was made less craving; and the other began, "The holy rule of the mountain suffers nothing that is without order or is outside its custom. This place is free from every change. That which heaven receives into itself from itself may here operate as cause, and naught else: wherefore neither rain, nor hail, nor snow, nor dew, nor hoarfrost falls any higher than the short little stairway of three steps. Clouds dense or thin do not appear, nor lightning-flash, nor Thaumas's daughter who often changes her region yonder;

secco vapor non surge più avante
ch'al sommo d'i tre gradi ch'io parlai,
dov' ha 'l vicario di Pietro le piante. 54
Trema forse più giù poco o assai;
ma per vento che 'n terra si nasconda,
non so come, qua sù non tremò mai. 57
Tremaci quando alcuna anima monda
sentesi, sì che surga o che si mova
per salir sù; e tal grido seconda. 60
De la mondizia sol voler fa prova,
che, tutto libero a mutar convento,
l'alma sorprende, e di voler le giova. 63
Prima vuol ben, ma non lascia il talento
che divina giustizia, contra voglia,
come fu al peccar, pone al tormento. 66
E io, che son giaciuto a questa doglia
cinquecent' anni e più, pur mo sentii
libera volontà di miglior soglia: 69
però sentisti il tremoto e li pii
spiriti per lo monte render lode
a quel Segnor, che tosto sù li 'nvii." 72
Così ne disse; e però ch'el si gode
tanto del ber quant' è grande la sete,
non saprei dir quant' el mi fece prode. 75
E 'l savio duca: "Omai veggio la rete
che qui vi 'mpiglia e come si scalappia,
perché ci trema e di che congaudete. 78
Ora chi fosti, piacciati ch'io sappia,
e perché tanti secoli giaciuto
qui se', ne le parole tue mi cappia." 81

nor does dry vapor rise beyond the highest of the three steps of which I spoke, where the vicar of Peter has his feet. It trembles perhaps lower down, little or much, but up here, from wind that is hidden in the earth, it never trembles, I know not how. It trembles here when some soul feels itself pure so that it may rise or set out for the ascent, and that shout follows. Of its purity the will alone gives proof, which takes by surprise the soul, wholly free now to change its convent, and avails it to will. It wills indeed before, but the desire consents not, which Divine Justice sets, counter to the will, toward the penalty, even as it was toward the sin. And I, who have lain in this pain five hundred years and more, only now felt free volition for a better threshold. Therefore you felt the earthquake and heard the pious spirits about the mountain give praises to that Lord—soon may He send them above!"

Thus he spoke to us; and since we enjoy more the draught in proportion as our thirst is great, I could not tell how much he profited me. And the wise leader, "Now I see the net that entangles you here, and how it is unmeshed, why it trembles here, and at what you rejoice together; and now be pleased to make me know who you are, and why you have lain here so many centuries let me gather from your words."

"Nel tempo che 'l buon Tito, con l'aiuto
del sommo rege, vendicò le fóra
ond' uscì 'l sangue per Giuda venduto, 84
col nome che più dura e più onora
era io di là," rispuose quello spirto,
"famoso assai, ma non con fede ancora. 87
Tanto fu dolce mio vocale spirto,
che, tolosano, a sé mi trasse Roma,
dove mertai le tempie ornar di mirto. 90
Stazio la gente ancor di là mi noma:
cantai di Tebe, e poi del grande Achille;
ma caddi in via con la seconda soma. 93
Al mio ardor fuor seme le faville,
che mi scaldar, de la divina fiamma
onde sono allumati più di mille; 96
de l'Eneïda dico, la qual mamma
fummi, e fummi nutrice, poetando:
sanz' essa non fermai peso di dramma. 99
E per esser vivuto di là quando
visse Virgilio, assentirei un sole
più che non deggio al mio uscir di bando." 102
Volser Virgilio a me queste parole
con viso che, tacendo, disse "Taci";
ma non può tutto la virtù che vuole; 105
ché riso e pianto son tanto seguaci
a la passion di che ciascun si spicca,
che men seguon voler ne' più veraci. 108
Io pur sorrisi come l'uom ch'ammicca;
per che l'ombra si tacque, e riguardommi
ne li occhi ove 'l sembiante più si ficca; 111

"In the time when the good Titus, with help of the Highest King, avenged the wounds whence issued the blood sold by Judas, I was famous enough yonder with the name which lasts longest and honors most," replied that spirit, "but not yet with faith. So sweet was my vocal spirit that me, a Toulousan, Rome drew to itself, where I was deemed worthy to have my brows adorned with myrtle. Men yonder still speak my name, which is Statius. I sang of Thebes, and then of the great Achilles, but I fell on the way with my second burden. The sparks which warmed me from the divine flame whereby more than a thousand have been kindled were the seeds of my poetic fire: I mean the *Aeneid*, which in poetry was both mother and nurse to me—without it I had achieved little of worth; and to have lived yonder when Virgil lived I would consent to one sun more than I owe to my coming forth from exile."

These words turned Virgil to me with a look that, silent, said, "Be silent." But the power that wills cannot do everything; for smiles and tears are such close followers on the emotion from which each springs, that in the most truthful they least follow the will. I only smiled, like one who makes a sign; at which the shade was silent, and looked into my eyes, where the expression is most fixed,

e "Se tanto labore in bene assommi,"
disse, "perché la tua faccia testeso
un lampeggiar di riso dimostrommi?" *114*
Or son io d'una parte e d'altra preso:
l'una mi fa tacer, l'altra scongiura
ch'io dica; ond' io sospiro, e sono inteso *117*
dal mio maestro, e "Non aver paura,"
mi dice, "di parlar; ma parla e digli
quel ch'e' dimanda con cotanta cura." *120*
Ond' io: "Forse che tu ti maravigli,
antico spirto, del rider ch'io fei;
ma più d'ammirazion vo' che ti pigli. *123*
Questi che guida in alto li occhi miei,
è quel Virgilio dal qual tu togliesti
forte a cantar de li uomini e d'i dèi. *126*
Se cagion altra al mio rider credesti,
lasciala per non vera, ed esser credi
quelle parole che di lui dicesti." *129*
Già s'inchinava ad abbracciar li piedi
al mio dottor, ma el li disse: "Frate,
non far, ché tu se' ombra e ombra vedi." *132*
Ed ei surgendo: "Or puoi la quantitate
comprender de l'amor ch'a te mi scalda,
quand' io dismento nostra vanitate,
trattando l'ombre come cosa salda." *136*

and, "So may your great labor end in good," he said, "why did your face just now show me the flash of a smile?"

Now am I caught on the one side and the other: the one makes me keep silence, the other conjures me to speak, so that I sigh and am understood by my master, and, "Do not fear to speak," he says to me, "but speak and tell him what he asks so earnestly." Wherefore I, "Perhaps you wonder, ancient spirit, at my smiling; but I would have yet more wonder seize you. This one who guides my eyes on high is that Virgil from whom you derived the strength to sing of men and of the gods; and if you did believe other cause for my smile, dismiss it as untrue, and believe it was those words which you spoke of him."

Already he was stooping to embrace my teacher's feet; but he said to him, "Brother, do not so, for you are a shade and a shade you see."

And he, rising, "Now you may comprehend the measure of the love that burns in me for you, when I forget our emptiness and treat shades as solid things."

PURGATORIO

GIÀ ERA l'angel dietro a noi rimaso,
l'angel che n'avea vòlti al sesto giro,
avendomi dal viso un colpo raso; 3
e quei c'hanno a giustizia lor disiro
detto n'avea beati, e le sue voci
con "*sitiunt*," sanz' altro, ciò forniro. 6
E io più lieve che per l'altre foci
m'andava, sì che sanz' alcun labore
seguiva in sù li spiriti veloci; 9
quando Virgilio incominciò: "Amore,
acceso di virtù, sempre altro accese,
pur che la fiamma sua paresse fore; 12
onde da l'ora che tra noi discese
nel limbo de lo 'nferno Giovenale,
che la tua affezion mi fé palese, 15
mia benvoglienza inverso te fu quale
più strinse mai di non vista persona,
sì ch'or mi parran corte queste scale. 18

# CANTO XXII

Now the angel who had directed us to the sixth circle was left behind us, having erased a stroke from my face, and he had declared to us that they whose desire is for righteousness are blessed, his words completing this with "*sitiunt*," without the rest. And I, lighter than at the other passages, went on so that without any toil I was following the fleet spirits upwards, when Virgil began, "Love, kindled by virtue, has ever kindled other love, if but its flame appear outwardly; wherefore, from the hour when Juvenal descended among us in the Limbo of Hell and made your affection known to me, my good will toward you has been such as never yet did bind to an unseen person, so that these stairs will now seem short to me.

Ma dimmi, e come amico mi perdona
se troppa sicurtà m'allarga il freno,
e come amico omai meco ragiona: 21
come poté trovar dentro al tuo seno
loco avarizia, tra cotanto senno
di quanto per tua cura fosti pieno?" 24
Queste parole Stazio mover fenno
un poco a riso pria; poscia rispuose:
"Ogne tuo dir d'amor m'è caro cenno. 27
Veramente più volte appaion cose
che danno a dubitar falsa matera
per le vere ragion che son nascose. 30
La tua dimanda tuo creder m'avvera
esser ch'i' fossi avaro in l'altra vita,
forse per quella cerchia dov' io era. 33
Or sappi ch'avarizia fu partita
troppo da me, e questa dismisura
migliaia di lunari hanno punita. 36
E se non fosse ch'io drizzai mia cura,
quand' io intesi là dove tu chiame,
crucciato quasi a l'umana natura: 39
'Per che non reggi tu, o sacra fame
de l'oro, l'appetito de' mortali?'
voltando sentirei le giostre grame. 42
Allor m'accorsi che troppo aprir l'ali
potean le mani a spendere, e pente'mi
così di quel come de li altri mali. 45
Quanti risurgeran coi crini scemi
per ignoranza, che di questa pecca
toglie 'l penter vivendo e ne li stremi! 48

But tell me—and as a friend pardon me if too great confidence slackens my rein, and talk with me now as with a friend—how could avarice find place in your breast, amid wisdom so great as that wherewith you were filled by your zeal?"

These words first made Statius begin to smile a little, then he replied, "Every word of yours is a dear token to me of love; but truly things oftentimes do so appear, their true reasons being hidden, that they give false matter for doubting. Your question makes plain to me your belief, perhaps because of that circle where I was, that I was avaricious in the other life. Now know that avarice was too far parted from me, and this want of measure thousands of courses of the moon have punished; and were it not that I set right my care, when I gave heed to the lines where you exclaim, angered as it were against human nature: 'To what do you not drive the appetite of mortals, O accursèd hunger of gold?' at the rolling I should feel the grievous jousts. It was then that I perceived that our hands could open their wings too wide in spending, and I repented of that as well as of other sins. How many will rise again with shorn locks, through ignorance, which takes away repentance of this sin, during life and at the last hour!

E sappie che la colpa che rimbecca
per dritta opposizione alcun peccato,
con esso insieme qui suo verde secca; *51*

però, s'io son tra quella gente stato
che piange l'avarizia, per purgarmi,
per lo contrario suo m'è incontrato." *54*

"Or quando tu cantasti le crude armi
de la doppia trestizia di Giocasta,"
disse 'l cantor de' buccolici carmi, *57*

"per quello che Clïò teco lì tasta,
non par che ti facesse ancor fedele
la fede, sanza qual ben far non basta. *60*

Se così è, qual sole o quai candele
ti stenebraron sì, che tu drizzasti
poscia di retro al pescator le vele?" *63*

Ed elli a lui: "Tu prima m'invïasti
verso Parnaso a ber ne le sue grotte,
e prima appresso Dio m'alluminasti. *66*

Facesti come quei che va di notte,
che porta il lume dietro e sé non giova,
ma dopo sé fa le persone dotte, *69*

quando dicesti: 'Secol si rinova;
torna giustizia e primo tempo umano,
e progenïe scende da ciel nova.' *72*

Per te poeta fui, per te cristiano:
ma perché veggi mei ciò ch'io disegno,
a colorare stenderò la mano. *75*

Già era 'l mondo tutto quanto pregno
de la vera credenza, seminata
per li messaggi de l'etterno regno; *78*

Know, too, that the fault which rebuts any sin with direct opposition dries up its verdure here along with it. Therefore, if I, to purge me, have been among that people who bewail their avarice, it is because of its contrary that this has befallen me."

"Now, when you sang of the cruel strife of Jocasta's twofold sorrow," said the singer of the Bucolic songs, "it does not appear, from that which Clio touches with you there, that the faith, without which good works suffice not, had yet made you faithful. If that is so, then what sun or what candles dispelled your darkness, so that thereafter you set your sails to follow the Fisherman?"

And he to him, "You it was who first sent me toward Parnassus to drink in its caves, and you who first did light me on to God. You were like one who goes by night and carries the light behind him and profits not himself, but makes those wise who follow him, when you said, 'The ages are renewed; Justice returns and the first age of man, and a new progeny descends from heaven.' Through you I was a poet, through you a Christian; but that you may see better what I outline, I will set my hand to color it. Already the whole world was big with the true faith, sown by the messengers of the eternal realm,

e la parola tua sopra toccata
  si consonava a' nuovi predicanti;
  ond' io a visitarli presi usata. *81*
Vennermi poi parendo tanto santi,
  che, quando Domizian li perseguette,
  sanza mio lagrimar non fur lor pianti; *84*
e mentre che di là per me si stette,
  io li sovvenni, e i lor dritti costumi
  fer dispregiare a me tutte altre sette. *87*
E pria ch'io conducessi i Greci a' fiumi
  di Tebe poetando, ebb' io battesmo;
  ma per paura chiuso cristian fu'mi, *90*
lungamente mostrando paganesmo;
  e questa tepidezza il quarto cerchio
  cerchiar mi fé più che 'l quarto centesmo. *93*
Tu dunque, che levato hai il coperchio
  che m'ascondeva quanto bene io dico,
  mentre che del salire avem soverchio, *96*
dimmi dov' è Terrenzio nostro antico,
  Cecilio e Plauto e Varro, se lo sai:
  dimmi se son dannati, e in qual vico." *99*
"Costoro e Persio e io e altri assai,"
  rispuose il duca mio, "siam con quel Greco
  che le Muse lattar più ch'altri mai, *102*
nel primo cinghio del carcere cieco;
  spesse fiate ragioniam del monte
  che sempre ha le nutrice nostre seco. *105*
Euripide v'è nosco e Antifonte,
  Simonide, Agatone e altri piùe
  Greci che già di lauro ornar la fronte. *108*

and those words of yours I have just spoken were so in accord with the new preachers that I began to frequent them. They came then to seem to me so holy that when Domitian persecuted them, their wailing was not without my tears, and while I remained yonder I succored them and their righteous lives made me scorn all other sects. And before I had led the Greeks to the rivers of Thebes in my verse, I received baptism; but, for fear, I was a secret Christian, long making show of paganism, and this lukewarmness made me circle round the fourth circle for more than four centuries. You, therefore, that did lift for me the covering that was hiding from me the great good I tell of, while we still have time to spare on the ascent, tell me, where is our ancient Terence, and Caecilius and Plautus and Varius, if you know; tell me if they are damned, and in which ward."

"These, and Persius and I and many others," replied my leader, "are with that Greek whom the Muses suckled more than any other, in the first circle of the dark prison; oftentimes we talk of that mountain which has our nurses ever with it. Euripides is with us there, and Antiphon, Simonides, Agathon, and many other Greeks who once decked their brows with laurel.

Quivi si veggion de le genti tue
Antigone, Deïfile e Argia,
e Ismene sì trista come fue. *111*
Védeisi quella che mostrò Langia;
èvvi la figlia di Tiresia, e Teti,
e con le suore sue Deïdamia." *114*
Tacevansi ambedue già li poeti,
di novo attenti a riguardar dintorno,
liberi da saliri e da pareti; *117*
e già le quattro ancelle eran del giorno
rimase a dietro, e la quinta era al temo,
drizzando pur in sù l'ardente corno, *120*
quando il mio duca: "Io credo ch'a lo stremo
le destre spalle volger ne convegna,
girando il monte come far solemo." *123*
Così l'usanza fu lì nostra insegna,
e prendemmo la via con men sospetto
per l'assentir di quell' anima degna. *126*
Elli givan dinanzi, e io soletto
di retro, e ascoltava i lor sermoni,
ch'a poetar mi davano intelletto. *129*
Ma tosto ruppe le dolci ragioni
un alber che trovammo in mezza strada,
con pomi a odorar soavi e buoni; *132*
e come abete in alto si digrada
di ramo in ramo, così quello in giuso,
cred' io, perché persona sù non vada. *135*
Dal lato onde 'l cammin nostro era chiuso,
cadea de l'alta roccia un liquor chiaro
e si spandeva per le foglie suso. *138*

There of your own people are seen Antigone, Deiphyle, Argia, and Ismene sad still as she was. There she is seen who showed Langia; there is the daughter of Tiresias and Thetis and Deidamia with her sisters."

Now were both poets silent, intent now on gazing round, freed from the ascent and the walls, and already four handmaids of the day were left behind and the fifth was at the chariot-pole, directing yet upward its flaming horn, when my leader said, "I think it behooves us to turn our right shoulders to the outer edge and to circle the mountain as we are wont." Thus usage was our guide there, and we went our way with less doubt because of the assent of that worthy soul.

They were going on in front, and I solitary behind, and I was listening to their speech which gave me understanding in poetry. But soon the pleasant converse was broken by a tree which we found in the midst of the way, with fruit sweet and good to smell. And as a fir-tree tapers upward from branch to branch, so downwards did that—I think so that none may climb it. On the side where our way was bounded there fell from the high rock a clear water which spread itself over the leaves above.

Li due poeti a l'alber s'appressaro;
e una voce per entro le fronde
gridò: "Di questo cibo avrete caro." 141

Poi disse: "Più pensava Maria onde
fosser le nozze orrevoli e intere,
ch'a la sua bocca, ch'or per voi risponde. 144

E le Romane antiche, per lor bere,
contente furon d'acqua; e Danïello
dispregiò cibo e acquistò savere. 147

Lo secol primo, quant' oro fu bello,
fé savorose con fame le ghiande,
e nettare con sete ogne ruscello. 150

Mele e locuste furon le vivande
che nodriro il Batista nel diserto;
per ch'elli è glorïoso e tanto grande
quanto per lo Vangelio v'è aperto." 154

The two poets approached the tree, and a voice from within the leaves cried, "Of this food you shall have want." Then it said, "Mary thought more how the wedding-feast might be honorable and complete, than of her own mouth, which now answers for you; and the Roman women of old were content with water for their drink; and Daniel despised food and gained wisdom. The first age was fair as gold: with hunger it made acorns savory, and with thirst made every streamlet nectar. Honey and locusts were the viands that nourished the Baptist in the desert; wherefore he is in glory and so great, as in the Gospel is revealed to you."

# PURGATORIO

MENTRE che li occhi per la fronda verde
ficcava ïo sì come far suole
chi dietro a li uccellin sua vita perde, *3*
lo più che padre mi dicea: "Figliuole,
vienne oramai, ché 'l tempo che n'è imposto
più utilmente compartir si vuole." *6*
Io volsi 'l viso, e 'l passo non men tosto,
appresso i savi, che parlavan sìe,
che l'andar mi facean di nullo costo. *9*
Ed ecco piangere e cantar s'udìe
"*Labïa mëa, Domine*" per modo
tal, che diletto e doglia parturìe. *12*
"O dolce padre, che è quel ch'i' odo?"
comincia' io; ed elli: "Ombre che vanno
forse di lor dover solvendo il nodo." *15*
Sì come i peregrin pensosi fanno,
giugnendo per cammin gente non nota,
che si volgono ad essa e non restanno, *18*

# CANTO XXIII

While I was peering thus intently through the green foliage, even as he is wont to do who wastes his life after the birds, my more than father said to me, "Son, come on now, for the time that is allotted us must be more usefully apportioned."

I turned my face, and my steps no less quickly, following after the sages whose talk was such that it made the going of no cost to me, when lo, in tears and song was heard: "*Labïa mëa Domine*," in such manner that it gave birth to joy and to grief. "O sweet father, what is this I hear?" I began; and he, "Shades who go perhaps loosening the knot of their debt."

Even as pilgrims who go absorbed in thought and, if they overtake strangers on the road, turn to them without stopping,

così di retro a noi, più tosto mota,
venendo e trapassando ci ammirava
d'anime turba tacita e devota. 21
Ne li occhi era ciascuna oscura e cava,
palida ne la faccia, e tanto scema
che da l'ossa la pelle s'informava. 24
Non credo che così a buccia strema
Erisittone fosse fatto secco,
per digiunar, quando più n'ebbe tema. 27
Io dicea fra me stesso pensando: "Ecco
la gente che perdé Ierusalemme,
quando Maria nel figlio diè di becco!" 30
Parean l'occhiaie anella sanza gemme:
chi nel viso de li uomini legge "omo"
ben avria quivi conosciuta l'emme. 33
Chi crederebbe che l'odor d'un pomo
sì governasse, generando brama,
e quel d'un'acqua, non sappiendo como? 36
Già era in ammirar che sì li affama,
per la cagione ancor non manifesta
di lor magrezza e di lor trista squama, 39
ed ecco del profondo de la testa
volse a me li occhi un'ombra e guardò fiso;
poi gridò forte: "Qual grazia m'è questa?" 42
Mai non l'avrei riconosciuto al viso;
ma ne la voce sua mi fu palese
ciò che l'aspetto in sé avea conquiso. 45
Questa favilla tutta mi raccese
mia conoscenza a la cangiata labbia,
e ravvisai la faccia di Forese. 48

so a crowd of souls, silent and devout, which came on behind us with greater speed and passed on, gazed at us in wonder. Each was dark and hollow in the eyes, pallid in the face and so wasted that the skin took its shape from the bones. I do not believe that Erysichthon became thus withered to the utter rind by hunger when he had most fear of it. I said to myself in thought, "Behold the people who lost Jerusalem, when Mary struck her beak into her son!" The sockets of their eyes seemed rings without gems: he who reads *OMO* in the face of man would there surely have recognized the *M*. Who, not knowing how, would believe that the scent of a fruit and that of a water, begetting desire, would have wrought thus?

I was now wondering what so famishes them, the cause of their leanness and their wretched scurf being unknown to me as yet, when lo, from the depths of his head a shade turned his eyes on me and looked at me fixedly, then cried loudly, "What a grace is this to me!" I should never have known him by his appearance, but in his voice was plain to me that which his countenance had suppressed in itself: this spark rekindled in me all my knowledge of the changed features, and I recognized the face of Forese.

"Deh, non contendere a l'asciutta scabbia
che mi scolora," pregava, "la pelle,
né a difetto di carne ch'io abbia; *51*
ma dimmi il ver di te, dì chi son quelle
due anime che là ti fanno scorta;
non rimaner che tu non mi favelle!" *54*
"La faccia tua, ch'io lagrimai già morta,
mi dà di pianger mo non minor doglia,"
rispuos' io lui, "veggendola sì torta. *57*
Però mi dì, per Dio, che sì vi sfoglia;
non mi far dir mentr' io mi maraviglio,
ché mal può dir chi è pien d'altra voglia." *60*
Ed elli a me: "De l'etterno consiglio
cade vertù ne l'acqua e ne la pianta
rimasa dietro, ond' io sì m'assottiglio. *63*
Tutta esta gente che piangendo canta
per seguitar la gola oltra misura,
in fame e 'n sete qui si rifà santa. *66*
Di bere e di mangiar n'accende cura
l'odor ch'esce del pomo e de lo sprazzo
che si distende su per sua verdura. *69*
E non pur una volta, questo spazzo
girando, si rinfresca nostra pena:
io dico pena, e dovria dir sollazzo, *72*
ché quella voglia a li alberi ci mena
che menò Cristo lieto a dire *'Elì,'*
quando ne liberò con la sua vena." *75*
E io a lui: "Forese, da quel dì
nel qual mutasti mondo a miglior vita,
cinqu' anni non son vòlti infino a qui. *78*

"Ah, strive not with the dry scab that discolors my skin," he begged, "nor with my lack of flesh, but tell me the truth about yourself, and tell me who are those two souls yonder that give you escort. Delay not to speak to me!"

"Your face, which once I wept for dead," I answered him, "now gives me no less cause for tears when I see it so disfigured. Therefore tell me, in God's name, what strips you so? Make me not talk while I am marveling, for ill can he speak who is full of other desire."

And he to me, "From the eternal counsel virtue descends into the water and into the tree left behind, whereby I waste away thus. All this people who weeping sing, sanctify themselves again in hunger and thirst, for having followed appetite to excess. The scent which comes from the fruit, and from the spray that is diffused over the green leaves, kindles within us a craving to eat and to drink; and not once only, as we circle this road, is our pain renewed—I say pain and ought to say solace: for that will leads us to the trees which led glad Christ to say '*Elì*,' when He delivered us with His blood."

And I to him, "Forese, from that day on which you changed the world for a better life, not five years have revolved till now.

Se prima fu la possa in te finita
di peccar più, che sovvenisse l'ora
del buon dolor ch'a Dio ne rimarita, 81
come se' tu qua sù venuto ancora?
Io ti credea trovar là giù di sotto,
dove tempo per tempo si ristora." 84
Ond' elli a me: "Sì tosto m'ha condotto
a ber lo dolce assenzo d'i martìri
la Nella mia con suo pianger dirotto. 87
Con suoi prieghi devoti e con sospiri
tratto m'ha de la costa ove s'aspetta,
e liberato m'ha de li altri giri. 90
Tanto è a Dio più cara e più diletta
la vedovella mia, che molto amai,
quanto in bene operare è più soletta; 93
ché la Barbagia di Sardigna assai
ne le femmine sue più è pudica
che la Barbagia dov' io la lasciai. 96
O dolce frate, che vuo' tu ch'io dica?
Tempo futuro m'è già nel cospetto,
cui non sarà quest' ora molto antica, 99
nel qual sarà in pergamo interdetto
a le sfacciate donne fiorentine
l'andar mostrando con le poppe il petto. 102
Quai barbare fuor mai, quai saracine,
cui bisognasse, par farle ir coperte,
o spiritali o altre discipline? 105
Ma se le svergognate fosser certe
di quel che 'l ciel veloce loro ammanna,
già per urlare avrian le bocche aperte; 108

If power to sin more came to an end in you before the hour supervened of the good sorrow that weds us anew to God, how is it you are come up here already? I had thought to find you down there below, where time is repaid for time."

And he to me, "Thus soon has led me to drink the sweet wormwood of the torments my Nella with her flood of tears; by her devout prayers and by her sighs she has brought me from the slope where they wait, and set me free from the other circles. So much more precious and beloved of God is my widow, whom I loved so well, as she is the more alone in good works: for the Barbagia of Sardinia is far more modest in its women than the Barbagia where I left her. O sweet brother, what would you have me say? Already in my vision is a future time, to which this hour shall not be very old, when the brazen-faced women of Florence shall be forbidden from the pulpit to go displaying their breasts with the paps. What Barbarian, what Saracen women were there ever, who required either spiritual or other discipline to make them go covered? But if the shameless creatures were assured of what swift heaven is preparing for them, already would they have their mouths open to howl;

ché, se l'antiveder qui non m'inganna,
 prima fien triste che le guance impeli
 colui che mo si consola con nanna. *111*
Deh, frate, or fa che più non mi ti celi!
 vedi che non pur io, ma questa gente
 tutta rimira là dove 'l sol veli." *114*
Per ch'io a lui: "Se tu riduci a mente
 qual fosti meco, e qual io teco fui,
 ancor fia grave il memorar presente. *117*
Di quella vita mi volse costui
 che mi va innanzi, l'altr' ier, quando tonda
 vi si mostrò la suora di colui," *120*
e 'l sol mostrai; "costui per la profonda
 notte menato m'ha d'i veri morti
 con questa vera carne che 'l seconda. *123*
Indi m'han tratto sù li suoi conforti,
 salendo e rigirando la montagna
 che drizza voi che 'l mondo fece torti. *126*
Tanto dice di farmi sua compagna
 che io sarò là dove fia Beatrice;
 quivi convien che sanza lui rimagna. *129*
Virgilio è questi che così mi dice,"
 e addita'lo; "e quest' altro è quell' ombra
 per cuï scosse dianzi ogne pendice
lo vostro regno, che da sé lo sgombra." *133*

for if our foresight here beguiles me not, they shall be sorrowing before he shall cover his cheeks with hair who is now consoled with lullabies. Ah, brother, now no longer conceal yourself from me! You see how not only I, but all these people are gazing there where you veil the sun."

Wherefore I to him, "If you bring back to mind what you have been with me and what I have been with you, the present memory will still be grievous. From that life he who goes before me turned me the other day, when the sister of him," and I pointed to the sun, "showed full to you. He it is that has led me through the profound night of the truly dead, in this true flesh which follows him. From there his counsels have drawn me up, ascending and circling this mountain, which makes you straight whom the world made crooked. So long he says that he will bear me company until I shall be there where Beatrice will be: there must I remain bereft of him. Virgil is he who tells me this," and I pointed to him, "and this other is that shade for whom just now your realm shook all its slopes, releasing him from itself."

NÉ 'L DIR l'andar, né l'andar lui più lento
facea, ma ragionando andavam forte,
sì come nave pinta da buon vento; *3*
e l'ombre, che parean cose rimorte,
per le fosse de li occhi ammirazione
traean di me, di mio vivere accorte. *6*
E io, continüando al mio sermone,
dissi: "Ella sen va sù forse più tarda
che non farebbe, per altrui cagione. *9*
Ma dimmi, se tu sai, dov' è Piccarda;
dimmi s'io veggio da notar persona
tra questa gente che sì mi riguarda." *12*
"La mia sorella, che tra bella e buona
non so qual fosse più, trïunfa lieta
ne l'alto Olimpo già di sua corona." *15*
Sì disse prima; e poi: "Qui non si vieta
di nominar ciascun, da ch'è sì munta
nostra sembianza via per la dïeta. *18*

# CANTO XXIV

SPEECH made not the going, nor did the going make that more slow; but, talking, we went on apace even as a ship driven by a fair wind. And the shades, that seemed things twice dead, darted wonder at me from the depths of their eyes, perceiving that I was alive. And I, continuing my discourse, said, "He goes up perchance for another's sake more slowly than he would do. But, tell me, if you know, where is Piccarda; and tell me if I see any person of note among this folk that so gazes at me."

"My sister, who whether she was more fair or good I do not know, triumphs already on high Olympus, rejoicing in her crown." So he said first, and then, "Here it is not forbidden to name each other, since our features are so wrung by the fast.

"Questi," e mostrò col dito, "è Bonagiunta,
  Bonagiunta da Lucca; e quella faccia
  di là da lui più che l'altre trapunta *21*
ebbe la Santa Chiesa in le sue braccia:
  dal Torso fu, e purga per digiuno
  l'anguille di Bolsena e la vernaccia." *24*
Molti altri mi nomò ad uno ad uno;
  e del nomar parean tutti contenti,
  sì ch'io però non vidi un atto bruno. *27*
Vidi per fame a vòto usar li denti
  Ubaldin da la Pila e Bonifazio
  che pasturò col rocco molte genti. *30*
Vidi messer Marchese, ch'ebbe spazio
  già di bere a Forlì con men secchezza,
  e si fu tal, che non si sentì sazio. *33*
Ma come fa chi guarda e poi s'apprezza
  più d'un che d'altro, fei a quel da Lucca,
  che più parea di me aver contezza. *36*
El mormorava; e non so che "Gentucca"
  sentiv' io là, ov' el sentia la piaga
  de la giustizia che sì li pilucca. *39*
"O anima," diss' io, "che par sì vaga
  di parlar meco, fa sì ch'io t'intenda,
  e te e me col tuo parlare appaga." *42*
"Femmina è nata, e non porta ancor benda,"
  cominciò el, "che ti farà piacere
  la mia città, come ch'om la riprenda. *45*
Tu te n'andrai con questo antivedere:
  se nel mio mormorar prendesti errore,
  dichiareranti ancor le cose vere. *48*

This," and he pointed with his finger, "is Bonagiunta, Bonagiunta of Lucca; and that face beyond him, more drawn than the others, had Holy Church in his arms: he was from Tours; and by fasting he purges the eels of Bolsena and the Vernaccia wine." Many others he named to me, one by one, and at their naming all appeared content, so that for this I saw not one dark look. I saw, plying their teeth on the void for very hunger, Ubaldin da la Pila and Bonifazio who shepherded many people with his staff. I saw Messer Marchese, who once had leisure for drinking at Forlì with less thirst, and yet was such that he felt not sated. But as he does who looks, and then esteems one more than another, so did I to him of Lucca, who seemed to have most knowledge of me. He was murmuring, and I know not what, save that I heard "Gentucca" there where he felt the pang of the justice which so strips them.

"O soul," said I, "that seem so eager to talk with me, speak so that I may hear you, and satisfy both yourself and me by your speech."

"A woman is born and wears not yet the veil," he began, "who shall make my city pleasing to you, however men may blame it. You shall go hence with this prophecy; if you have taken my murmuring in error, the real events will yet make it clear to you.

Ma dì s'i' veggio qui colui che fore
  trasse le nove rime, cominciando
  '*Donne ch'avete intelletto d'amore.*'" 51
E io a lui: "I' mi son un che, quando
  Amor mi spira, noto, e a quel modo
  ch'e' ditta dentro vo significando." 54
"O frate, issa vegg' io," diss' elli, "il nodo
  che 'l Notaro e Guittone e me ritenne
  di qua dal dolce stil novo ch'i' odo! 57
Io veggio ben come le vostre penne
  di retro al dittator sen vanno strette,
  che de le nostre certo non avvenne; 60
e qual più a gradire oltre si mette,
  non vede più da l'uno a l'altro stilo";
  e, quasi contentato, si tacette. 63
Come li augei che vernan lungo 'l Nilo,
  alcuna volta in aere fanno schiera,
  poi volan più a fretta e vanno in filo, 66
così tutta la gente che lì era,
  volgendo 'l viso, raffrettò suo passo,
  e per magrezza e per voler leggera. 69
E come l'uom che di trottare è lasso,
  lascia andar li compagni, e si passeggia
  fin che si sfoghi l'affollar del casso, 72
sì lasciò trapassar la santa greggia
  Forese, e dietro meco sen veniva,
  dicendo: "Quando fia ch'io ti riveggia?" 75
"Non so," rispuos' io lui, "quant' io mi viva;
  ma già non fia il tornar mio tantosto,
  ch'io non sia col voler prima a la riva; 78

But tell me if I see here him who brought forth the new rhymes, beginning: 'Ladies that have understanding of love'?"

And I to him, "I am one who, when Love inspires me, takes note, and goes setting it forth after the fashion which he dictates within me."

"O brother," he said, "now I see the knot which kept the Notary, and Guittone, and me, short of the sweet new style that I hear. Clearly I see how your pens follow close after him who dictates, which certainly befell not with ours—and he who sets himself to seek farther can see no other difference between the one style and the other." And, as if satisfied, he was silent.

As the birds that winter along the Nile sometimes make a flock in the air, then fly in greater haste and go in file, so all that people there, light both through leanness and through desire, turning away their faces, quickened again their pace. And as one who is weary of running lets his companions go on, and walks until the panting of his chest be eased, so Forese let that holy flock pass by, and came on behind with me, saying, "When shall it be that I see you again?"

"I do not know how long I may live," I answered him, "but truly my return here will not be so speedy that in desire I shall not be sooner at the shore,

però che 'l loco u' fui a viver posto,
di giorno in giorno più di ben si spolpa,
e a trista ruina par disposto." 81
"Or va," diss' el; "che quei che più n'ha colpa,
vegg' ïo a coda d'una bestia tratto
inver' la valle ove mai non si scolpa. 84
La bestia ad ogne passo va più ratto,
crescendo sempre, fin ch'ella il percuote,
e lascia il corpo vilmente disfatto. 87
Non hanno molto a volger quelle ruote,"
e drizzò li occhi al ciel, "che ti fia chiaro
ciò che 'l mio dir più dichiarar non puote. 90
Tu ti rimani omai; ché 'l tempo è caro
in questo regno, sì ch'io perdo troppo
venendo teco sì a paro a paro." 93
Qual esce alcuna volta di gualoppo
lo cavalier di schiera che cavalchi,
e va per farsi onor del primo intoppo, 96
tal si partì da noi con maggior valchi;
e io rimasi in via con esso i due
che fuor del mondo sì gran marescalchi. 99
E quando innanzi a noi intrato fue,
che li occhi miei si fero a lui seguaci,
come la mente a le parole sue, 102
parvermi i rami gravidi e vivaci
d'un altro pomo, e non molto lontani
per esser pur allora vòlto in laci. 105
Vidi gente sott' esso alzar le mani
e gridar non so che verso le fronde,
quasi bramosi fantolini e vani 108

because the place where I was put to live is, day by day, more stripped of good and seems doomed to wretched ruin."

"Now go," said he, "for him who is most in fault I see dragged at the tail of a beast, toward the valley where there is no absolving. The beast at every step goes faster, increasing ever till it dashes him and leaves his body hideously disfigured. Those wheels have not long to revolve"—and he lifted his eyes up to the heavens—"before that will be clear to you which my speech cannot further declare. Now do you remain behind, for time is precious in this realm, so that I lose too much by coming with you thus at equal pace."

As a horseman sometimes issues forth from a troop that is riding and goes to win the honor of the first encounter, so he parted from us with greater strides, and I remained on the way with those two who were such great marshals of the world. And when he had gone on so far ahead of us that my eyes became such followers of him, as my mind was of his words, the laden and verdant branches of another tree appeared to me, and not far distant, because only then had I come round there. Beneath it I saw people lifting up their hands and crying I know not what toward the leaves, like eager and fond little children,

che pregano, e 'l pregato non risponde,
  ma, per fare esser ben la voglia acuta,
  tien alto lor disio e nol nasconde. *111*
Poi si partì sì come ricreduta;
  e noi venimmo al grande arbore adesso,
  che tanti prieghi e lagrime rifiuta. *114*
"Trapassate oltre sanza farvi presso:
  legno è più sù che fu morso da Eva,
  e questa pianta si levò da esso." *117*
Sì tra le frasche non so chi diceva;
  per che Virgilio e Stazio e io, ristretti,
  oltre andavam dal lato che si leva. *120*
"Ricordivi," dicea, "d'i maladetti
  nei nuvoli formati, che, satolli,
  Tesëo combatter co' doppi petti; *123*
e de li Ebrei ch'al ber si mostrar molli,
  per che no i volle Gedeon compagni,
  quando inver' Madïan discese i colli." *126*
Sì accostati a l'un d'i due vivagni
  passammo, udendo colpe de la gola
  seguite già da miseri guadagni. *129*
Poi, rallargati per la strada sola,
  ben mille passi e più ci portar oltre,
  contemplando ciascun sanza parola. *132*
"Che andate pensando sì voi sol tre?"
  sùbita voce disse; ond' io mi scossi
  come fan bestie spaventate e poltre. *135*
Drizzai la testa per veder chi fossi;
  e già mai non si videro in fornace
  vetri o metalli sì lucenti e rossi, *138*

who beg, and he of whom they beg answers not, but to make their longing full keen, holds aloft what they desire and hides it not. Then they departed, as if undeceived. And now we came to the great tree which rejects so many prayers and tears.

"Pass farther onward, without drawing near. A tree is higher up that was eaten of by Eve, and this plant was raised from it." Thus among the branches I know not who spoke; wherefore Virgil and Statius and I, drawing close together, went onward along the side that rises.

"Remember," the voice was saying, "the accursèd ones that were formed in the clouds who, when gorged, fought Theseus with their double breasts; and the Hebrews who at the drinking showed themselves soft, wherefore Gideon would not have them for comrades when he came down the hills to Midian."

Thus, keeping close to one side of the way, we passed by, hearing sins of gluttony, once followed by woeful gains. Then, spread out along the solitary way, full a thousand paces and more bore us onward, each of us in meditation without a word.

"Why go you thus in thought, you three alone?" said a sudden voice; whereat I started as do frightened and skittish beasts. I raised my head to see who it was, and never in a furnace was glass or metal seen so glowing and red

com' io vidi un che dicea: "S'a voi piace
montare in sù, qui si convien dar volta;
quinci si va chi vuole andar per pace." *141*

L'aspetto suo m'avea la vista tolta;
per ch'io mi volsi dietro a' miei dottori,
com' om che va secondo ch'elli ascolta. *144*

E quale, annunziatrice de li albori,
l'aura di maggio movesi e olezza,
tutta impregnata da l'erba e da' fiori; *147*

tal mi senti' un vento dar per mezza
la fronte, e ben senti' mover la piuma,
che fé sentir d'ambrosïa l'orezza. *159*

E senti' dir: "Beati cui alluma
tanto di grazia, che l'amor del gusto
nel petto lor troppo disir non fuma,
esurïendo sempre quanto è giusto!" *154*

as one I saw who said, "If it please you to mount up, here must you make the turn: this way he goes who desires to go for peace." His countenance had bereft me of sight, wherefore I turned and followed my teachers like one who goes according as he hears.

And as, heralding the dawn, the breeze of May stirs and smells sweet, all impregnate with grass and with flowers, such a wind I felt strike full on my brow, and right well I felt the pinions move, which wafted ambrosial fragrance to my senses; and I heard say, "Blessed are they who are so illumined by grace that the love of taste kindles not too great desire in their breasts, and who hunger always so far as is just."

ORA ERA onde 'l salir non volea storpio;
chè 'l sole avëa il cerchio di merigge
lasciato al Tauro e la notte a lo Scorpio: 3
per che, come fa l'uom che non s'affigge
ma vassi a la via sua, che che li appaia,
se di bisogno stimolo il trafigge, 6
così intrammo noi per la callaia,
uno innanzi altro prendendo la scala
che per artezza i salitor dispaia. 9
E quale il cicognin che leva l'ala
per voglia di volare, e non s'attenta
d'abbandonar lo nido, e giù la cala; 12
tal era io con voglia accesa e spenta
di dimandar, venendo infino a l'atto
che fa colui ch'a dicer s'argomenta. 15
Non lasciò, per l'andar che fosse ratto,
lo dolce padre mio, ma disse: "Scocca
l'arco del dir, che 'nfino al ferro hai tratto." 18
Allor sicuramente apri' la bocca
e cominciai: "Come si può far magro
là dove l'uopo di nodrir non tocca?" 21

# CANTO XXV

It was now an hour when the ascent brooked no impediment, for the meridian circle had been left by the sun to the Bull, and by the night to the Scorpion. Therefore, like one that does not stop but, whatever may appear to him, goes on his way, if the goad of necessity prick him, so did we enter through the gap, one before the other, taking the stairway which by its straitness unpairs the climbers. And as the little stork that lifts its wing through desire to fly and, not venturing to abandon the nest, drops it again, even so was I, with desire to ask, kindled and quenched, going as far as the movement he makes who is preparing to speak. Nor, though our gait was swift, did my sweet father forbear, but said, "Discharge the bow of your speech which you have drawn to the iron."

Then I opened my mouth confidently and began, "How can one grow lean there where the need of nourishment is not felt?"

"Se t'ammentassi come Meleagro
si consumò al consumar d'un stizzo,
non fora," disse, "a te questo sì agro; 24
e se pensassi come, al vostro guizzo,
guizza dentro a lo specchio vostra image,
ciò che par duro ti parrebbe vizzo. 27
Ma perché dentro a tuo voler t'adage,
ecco qui Stazio; e io lui chiamo e prego
che sia or sanator de le tue piage." 30
"Se la veduta etterna li dislego,"
rispuose Stazio, "là dove tu sie,
discolpi me non potert' io far nego." 33
Poi cominciò: "Se le parole mie,
figlio, la mente tua guarda e riceve,
lume ti fiero al come che tu die. 36
Sangue perfetto, che poi non si beve
da l'assetate vene, e si rimane
quasi alimento che di mensa leve, 39
prende nel core a tutte membra umane
virtute informativa, come quello
ch'a farsi quelle per le vene vane. 42
Ancor digesto, scende ov' è più bello
tacer che dire; e quindi poscia geme
sovr' altrui sangue in natural vasello. 45
Ivi s'accoglie l'uno e l'altro insieme,
l'un disposto a patire, e l'altro a fare
per lo perfetto loco onde si preme; 48
e, giunto lui, comincia ad operare
coagulando prima, e poi avviva
ciò che per sua matera fé constare. 51

"If you would call to mind how Meleager was consumed at the consuming of a firebrand," he said, "this would not be so difficult to you; and if you would think how, at your every movement, your image moves within the mirror, that which seems hard would seem easy to you. But, in order that you may find rest in your desire, here is Statius, and I call on him and pray that he be now the healer of your wounds."

"If I explain to him the eternal view," replied Statius, "where you are present, let my excuse be that I cannot deny you."

Then he began, "If, son, your mind regards and receives my words, they will enlighten you on the 'how' of what you ask. The perfect blood, which never is drunk by the thirsty veins and is left behind as it were food which one removes from the table, acquires in the heart an informing power for all the bodily members, like that blood which flows through the veins to become those members. Digested yet again, it descends there whereof to be silent is more seemly than to speak; and thence afterwards drops upon other's blood, in natural vessel. There the one is mingled with the other, one designed to be passive, the other to be active, by reason of the perfect place whence it springs; and, conjoined with the former, the latter begins to operate, first by coagulating, then by quickening that to which it has given consistency to serve as its material.

Anima fatta la virtute attiva
qual d'una pianta, in tanto differente,
che questa è in via e quella è già a riva, *54*
tanto ovra poi, che già si move e sente,
come spungo marino; e indi imprende
ad organar le posse ond' è semente. *57*
Or si spiega, figliuolo, or si distende
la virtù ch'è dal cor del generante,
dove natura a tutte membra intende. *60*
Ma come d'animal divegna fante,
non vedi tu ancor: quest' è tal punto,
che più savio di te fé già errante, *63*
sì che per sua dottrina fé disgiunto
da l'anima il possibile intelletto,
perché da lui non vide organo assunto. *66*
Apri a la verità che viene il petto;
e sappi che, sì tosto come al feto
l'articular del cerebro è perfetto, *69*
lo motor primo a lui si volge lieto
sovra tant' arte di natura, e spira
spirito novo, di vertù repleto, *72*
che ciò che trova attivo quivi, tira
in sua sustanzia, e fassi un'alma sola,
che vive e sente e sé in sé rigira. *75*
E perché meno ammiri la parola,
guarda il calor del sol che si fa vino,
giunto a l'omor che de la vite cola. *78*
Quando Làchesis non ha più del lino,
solvesi da la carne, e in virtute
ne porta seco e l'umano e 'l divino: *81*

The active virtue having become a soul, like that of a plant (but in so far different that this is on the way, and that has already arrived) so works then that now it moves and feels, like a sea-fungus; then it proceeds to develop organs for the powers of which it is the germ. Now, son, expands, now distends, the virtue which proceeds from the heart of the begetter, where nature makes provision for all the members. But how from animal it becomes a human being you do not see yet: this is such a point that once it made one wiser than you to err, so that in his teaching he separated the possible intellect from the soul because he saw no organ assumed by it.

"Open your breast to the truth which is coming, and know that, so soon as in the foetus the articulation of the brain is perfect, the First Mover turns to it with joy over such art of nature, and breathes into it a new spirit replete with virtue, which absorbs that which is active there into its own substance, and makes one single soul which lives and feels and circles on itself. And that you may marvel less at my words, look at the sun's heat, which is made wine when combined with the juice that flows from the vine.

"And when Lachesis has no more thread, the soul is loosed from the flesh and carries with it, in potency, both the human and the divine;

l'altre potenze tutte quante mute;
memoria, intelligenza e volontade
in atto molto più che prima agute. 84
Sanza restarsi, per sé stessa cade
mirabilmente a l'una de le rive;
quivi conosce prima le sue strade. 87
Tosto che loco lì la circunscrive,
la virtù formativa raggia intorno
così e quanto ne le membra vive. 90
E come l'aere, quand' è ben pïorno,
per l'altrui raggio che 'n sé si reflette,
di diversi color diventa addorno; 93
così l'aere vicin quivi si mette
e in quella forma ch'è in lui suggella
virtüalmente l'alma che ristette; 96
e simigliante poi a la fiammella
che segue il foco là 'vunque si muta,
segue lo spirto sua forma novella. 99
Però che quindi ha poscia sua paruta,
è chiamata ombra; e quindi organa poi
ciascun sentire infino a la veduta. 102
Quindi parliamo e quindi ridiam noi;
quindi facciam le lagrime e ' sospiri
che per lo monte aver sentiti puoi. 105
Secondo che ci affliggono i disiri
e li altri affetti, l'ombra si figura;
e quest' è la cagion di che tu miri." 108
E già venuto a l'ultima tortura
s'era per noi, e vòlto a la man destra,
ed eravamo attenti ad altra cura. 111

the other faculties all of them mute, but memory, intellect, and will far more acute in action than before. Without staying, it falls of itself marvelously to one of the banks. Here it first knows its own roads. As soon as space encompasses it there, the formative virtue radiates around, in form and quantity as in the living members. And as the air, when it is full of moisture, becomes adorned with various colors by another's rays which are reflected in it, so here the neighboring air shapes itself in that form which is virtually imprinted on it by the soul that stopped there; and then, like the flame which follows the fire wheresoever it moves, the spirit is followed by its new form. Inasmuch as therefrom it has its semblance, it is called a shade, and therefrom it forms the organs of every sense, even to the sight. By this we speak and by this we laugh, by this we make the tears and sighs which you may have heard about the mountain. According as the desires and the other affections prick us, the shade takes its form; and this is the cause of that at which you marvel."

And now we had come to the last circuit and had turned to the right and were intent on other care.

Quivi la ripa fiamma in fuor balestra,
e la cornice spira fiato in suso
che la reflette e via da lei sequestra; *114*
ond' ir ne convenia dal lato schiuso
ad uno ad uno; e io temëa 'l foco
quinci, e quindi temeva cader giuso. *117*
Lo duca mio dicea: "Per questo loco
si vuol tenere a li occhi stretto il freno,
però ch'errar potrebbesi per poco." *120*
"*Summae Deus clementïae*" nel seno
al grande ardore allora udi' cantando,
che di volger mi fé caler non meno; *123*
e vidi spirti per la fiamma andando;
per ch'io guardava a loro e a' miei passi,
compartendo la vista a quando a quando. *126*
Appresso il fine ch'a quell' inno fassi,
gridavano alto: "*Virum non cognosco*";
indi ricominciavan l'inno bassi. *129*
Finitolo, anco gridavano: "Al bosco
si tenne Diana, ed Elice caccionne
che di Venere avea sentito il tòsco." *132*
Indi al cantar tornavano; indi donne
gridavano e mariti che fuor casti
come virtute e matrimonio imponne. *135*
E questo modo credo che lor basti
per tutto il tempo che 'l foco li abbruscia:
con tal cura conviene e con tai pasti
che la piaga da sezzo si ricuscia. *139*

Here the bank flashes forth flames, and the edge of the terrace sends a blast upwards which bends them back and sequesters a path from them; wherefore it behooved us to go on the side that was free, one by one, and on the one side I feared the fire, and on the other I feared I might fall off. My leader said, "Along this place the rein must be kept tight on the eyes, for one might easily take a false step."

"*Summae Deus clementiae*" I then heard sung in the heart of the great burning, which made me no less eager to turn; and I saw spirits going through the fire, wherefore I looked at them and at my steps, with divided gaze from time to time. After the end which is made to that hymn, they cried aloud, "*Virum non cognosco*," then softly began the hymn again. When it was finished, they further cried, "Diana kept to the woods and chased Helice forth, who had felt the poison of Venus." Then they returned to their singing; then they cried wives and husbands who were chaste, even as virtue and marriage enjoin upon us. And this fashion, I believe, suffices them for all the time the fire burns them: with such treatment and with such diet must the last wound of all be healed.

MENTRE che sì per l'orlo, uno innanzi altro,
ce n'andavamo, e spesso il buon maestro
diceami: "Guarda: giovi ch'io ti scaltro"; 3
feriami il sole in su l'omero destro,
che già, raggiando, tutto l'occidente
mutava in bianco aspetto di cilestro; 6
e io facea con l'ombra più rovente
parer la fiamma; e pur a tanto indizio
vidi molt' ombre, andando, poner mente. 9
Questa fu la cagion che diede inizio
loro a parlar di me; e cominciarsi
a dir: "Colui non par corpo fittizio"; 12
poi verso me, quanto potëan farsi,
certi si fero, sempre con riguardo
di non uscir dove non fosser arsi. 15
"O tu che vai, non per esser più tardo,
ma forse reverente, a li altri dopo,
rispondi a me che 'n sete e 'n foco ardo. 18

# CANTO XXVI

WHILE we were advancing thus along the brink, one before the other, the good master often saying to me, "Take heed: let my warning avail you," the sun was striking me on my right shoulder, for now its beams were changing the whole face of the West from azure to white. And with my shadow I made the flame appear more glowing, and merely at this slight sign I saw many shades, as they went on, give heed. This it was that first brought them to speak of me, and they began to say to each other, "That one does not seem a shadowy body"; then certain of them came as far as they could toward me, ever careful not to come out where they would not be burned.

"O you who go behind the others, not from tardiness but perhaps from reverence, answer me who burn in thirst and in fire;

Né solo a me la tua risposta è uopo;
  ché tutti questi n'hanno maggior sete
  che d'acqua fredda Indo o Etïopo. 21
Dinne com' è che fai di te parete
  al sol, pur come tu non fossi ancora
  di morte intrato dentro da la rete." 24
Sì mi parlava un d'essi; e io mi fora
  già manifesto, s'io non fossi atteso
  ad altra novità ch'apparve allora; 27
ché per lo mezzo del cammino acceso
  venne gente col viso incontro a questa,
  la qual mi fece a rimirar sospeso. 30
Lì veggio d'ogne parte farsi presta
  ciascun' ombra e basciarsi una con una
  sanza restar, contente a brieve festa; 33
così per entro loro schiera bruna
  s'ammusa l'una con l'altra formica,
  forse a spïar lor via e lor fortuna. 36
Tosto che parton l'accoglienza amica,
  prima che 'l primo passo lì trascorra,
  sopragridar ciascuna s'affatica: 39
la nova gente: "Soddoma e Gomorra";
  e l'altra: "Ne la vacca entra Pasife,
  perché 'l torello a sua lussuria corra." 42
Poi, come grue ch'a le montagne Rife
  volasser parte, e parte inver' l'arene,
  queste del gel, quelle del sole schife, 45
l'una gente sen va, l'altra sen vene;
  e tornan, lagrimando, a' primi canti
  e al gridar che più lor si convene; 48

nor to me alone is your answer needful, for all these others have greater thirst thereof than Indian or Ethiopian for cold water. Tell us how it is that you make a wall of yourself to the sun, quite as if you had not yet entered into death's net." Thus one of them spoke to me, and now I should have made myself known, had I not been intent on another strange thing which then appeared: for through the middle of the burning road people were coming with their faces opposite to these, and made me gaze in suspense. There on every side I see all the shades making haste and kissing one another, without stopping, content with brief greeting: thus within their dark band one ant touches muzzle with another, perhaps to spy out their way and their fortune.

As soon as they end the friendly greeting and before the first step there speeds onward, each one tries to shout the loudest: the new-come people "Sodom and Gomorrah," and the other, "Pasiphaë enters into the cow, that the bull may hasten to her lust." Then, like cranes that should fly, some to the Riphaean mountains and others toward the sands, these shy of the frost, those of the sun, the one people passes on, the other comes away, and they return weeping to their former chants and to the cry that most befits them.

e raccostansi a me, come davanti,
essi medesmi che m'avean pregato,
attenti ad ascoltar ne' lor sembianti. 51
Io, che due volte avea visto lor grato,
incominciai: "O anime sicure
d'aver, quando che sia, di pace stato, 54
non son rimase acerbe né mature
le membra mie di là, ma son qui meco
col sangue suo e con le sue giunture. 57
Quinci sù vo per non esser più cieco;
donna è di sopra che m'acquista grazia,
per che 'l mortal per vostro mondo reco. 60
Ma se la vostra maggior voglia sazia
tosto divegna, sì che 'l ciel v'alberghi
ch'è pien d'amore e più ampio si spazia, 63
ditemi, acciò ch'ancor carte ne verghi,
chi siete voi, e chi è quella turba
che se ne va di retro a' vostri terghi." 66
Non altrimenti stupido si turba
lo montanaro, e rimirando ammuta,
quando rozzo e salvatico s'inurba, 69
che ciascun' ombra fece in sua paruta;
ma poi che furon di stupore scarche,
lo qual ne li alti cuor tosto s'attuta, 72
"Beato te, che de le nostre marche,"
ricominciò colei che pria m'inchiese,
"per morir meglio, esperïenza imbarche! 75
La gente che non vien con noi, offese
di ciò per che già Cesar, trïunfando,
'Regina' contra sé chiamar s'intese: 78

And those same who had entreated me drew near to me as before, by their looks eager to listen.

Having twice seen their desire, I began, "O souls, certain of gaining, whensoever it may be, a state of peace, my limbs have not remained yonder green or ripe, but are here with me, with their blood and their joints. I go up hence in order to be blind no longer. A lady is above who wins grace for me, whereby I bring my mortal part through your world. But—so may your greatest longing soon be satisfied, so that the heaven harbor you which is full of love and widest spreads—tell me, so that I may yet trace it on paper, who you are, and what is that throng that is going away behind your backs."

Not otherwise is the astonished mountaineer overawed, and gazing round is dumb, when rude and rustic he enters the city, than was each shade in his looks; but when they were unburdened of amazement, which in lofty hearts is quickly stilled, "Blessed are you," he began again who had questioned me before, "who in order to die better do ship experience of our regions! The people who do not come with us offended in that for which Caesar in his triumph once heard 'Queen' cried out against him;

però si parton 'Soddoma' gridando,
rimproverando a sé com' hai udito,
e aiutan l'arsura vergognando. *81*
Nostro peccato fu ermafrodito;
ma perché non servammo umana legge,
seguendo come bestie l'appetito, *84*
in obbrobrio di noi, per noi si legge,
quando partinci, il nome di colei
che s'imbestiò ne le 'mbestiate schegge. *87*
Or sai nostri atti e di che fummo rei:
se forse a nome vuo' saper chi semo,
tempo non è di dire, e non saprei. *90*
Farotti ben di me volere scemo:
son Guido Guinizzelli, e già mi purgo
per ben dolermi prima ch'a lo stremo." *93*
Quali ne la tristizia di Ligurgo
si fer due figli a riveder la madre,
tal mi fec' io, ma non a tanto insurgo, *96*
quand' io odo nomar sé stesso il padre
mio e de li altri miei miglior che mai
rime d'amor usar dolci e leggiadre; *99*
e sanza udire e dir pensoso andai
lunga fiata rimirando lui,
né, per lo foco, in là più m'appressai. *102*
Poi che di riguardar pasciuto fui,
tutto m'offersi pronto al suo servigio
con l'affermar che fa credere altrui. *105*
Ed elli a me: "Tu lasci tal vestigio,
per quel ch'i' odo, in me, e tanto chiaro,
che Letè nol può tòrre né far bigio. *108*

therefore they go off crying 'Sodom,' reproving themselves as you have heard, and they help the burning with their shame. Our sin was hermaphrodite: but because we observed not human law, following appetite like beasts, when we part from them, the name of her who bestialized herself in the beast-shaped planks is uttered by us, in opprobrium of ourselves. Now you know our deeds, and of what we were guilty; if perchance you wish to know by name who we are, there is no time to tell, nor could I. Concerning me I will indeed satisfy your wish: I am Guido Guinizzelli, and already I make my purgation because of good repentance before the end."

As in the sorrow of Lycurgus two sons became on beholding their mother again, so I became, but I do not rise to such heights, when I hear name himself the father of me and of others my betters who ever used sweet and gracious rhymes of love; and without hearing or speaking, I went pondering, gazing a long time at him; nor did I draw nearer to him, because of the fire. When I had fed my sight on him, I offered myself wholly ready for his service, with the oath that compels another's belief.

And he to me, "You leave, by that which I hear, traces so deep and clear in me that Lethe cannot take them away or make them dim;

Ma se le tue parole or ver giuraro,
  dimmi che è cagion per che dimostri
  nel dire e nel guardar d'avermi caro." *111*
E io a lui: "Li dolci detti vostri,
  che, quanto durerà l'uso moderno,
  faranno cari ancora i loro incostri." *114*
"O frate," disse, "questi ch'io ti cerno
  col dito," e additò un spirto innanzi,
  "fu miglior fabbro del parlar materno. *117*
Versi d'amore e prose di romanzi
  soverchiò tutti; e lascia dir li stolti
  che quel di Lemosì credon ch'avanzi. *120*
A voce più ch'al ver drizzan li volti,
  e così ferman sua oppinïone
  prima ch'arte o ragion per lor s'ascolti. *123*
Così fer molti antichi di Guittone,
  di grido in grido pur lui dando pregio,
  fin che l'ha vinto il ver con più persone. *126*
Or se tu hai sì ampio privilegio,
  che licito ti sia l'andare al chiostro
  nel quale è Cristo abate del collegio, *129*
falli per me un dir d'un paternostro,
  quanto bisogna a noi di questo mondo,
  dove poter peccar non è più nostro." *132*
Poi, forse per dar luogo altrui secondo
  che presso avea, disparve per lo foco,
  come per l'acqua il pesce andando al fondo. *135*
Io mi fei al mostrato innanzi un poco,
  e dissi ch'al suo nome il mio disire
  apparecchiava grazïoso loco. *138*

but if your words just now swore truth, tell me for what reason you show yourself, by speech and look, to hold me dear."

And I to him, "Your sweet verses, which so long as modern use shall last, will make dear their very ink."

"O brother," he said, "he there whom I point out to you"—and he pointed to a spirit ahead—"was a better craftsman of the mother tongue: verses of love and tales of romance he surpassed them all—and let the fools talk who think that he of Limoges excels. They give heed to rumor rather than to truth, and thus settle their opinion before listening to art or reason. Thus did many of our fathers with Guittone, from cry to cry giving the prize to him alone, until with most the truth prevailed. Now, if you have such ample privilege that you are permitted to go to the cloister wherein Christ is abbot of the college, say there a paternoster for me, so far as is needful to us of this world where power to sin is no more ours." Then, perhaps to give place to another following close behind, he vanished through the flames like a fish that goes through the water to the bottom.

I moved forward a little towards him that had been pointed out to me, and said that for his name my desire was making ready a grateful place.

El cominciò liberamente a dire:
"*Tan m'abellis vostre cortes deman,*
*qu'ieu no me puesc ni voill a vos cobrire.* 141
*Ieu sui Arnaut, que plor e vau cantan;*
*consiros vei la passada folor,*
*e vei jausen lo joi qu'esper, denan.* 144
*Ara vos prec, per aquella valor*
*que vos guida al som de l'escalina,*
*sovenha vos a temps de ma dolor!*"
Poi s'ascose nel foco che li affina. 148

He began graciously to say, "So does your courteous request please me that I neither can nor would conceal myself from you. I am Arnaut, who weep and sing as I go; contritely I see my past folly, and joyously I see before me the joy that I await. Now I pray you, by that power which guides you to the summit of the stair, in due time be heedful of my pain." Then he hid himself in the fire that purifies them.

Sì come quando i primi raggi vibra
  là dove il suo fattor lo sangue sparse,
  cadendo Ibero sotto l'alta Libra, 3
e l'onde in Gange da nona rïarse,
  sì stava il sole; onde 'l giorno sen giva,
  come l'angel di Dio lieto ci apparse. 6
Fuor de la fiamma stava in su la riva,
  e cantava "*Beati mundo corde!*"
  in voce assai più che la nostra viva. 9
Poscia "Più non si va, se pria non morde,
  anime sante, il foco: intrate in esso,
  e al cantar di là non siate sorde," 12
ci disse come noi li fummo presso;
  per ch'io divenni tal, quando lo 'ntesi,
  qual è colui che ne la fossa è messo. 15
In su le man commesse mi protesi,
  guardando il foco e imaginando forte
  umani corpi già veduti accesi. 18

# CANTO XXVII

As WHEN it darts forth its first beams there where its Maker shed His blood, while Ebro falls beneath the lofty Scales and the waves in the Ganges are scorched by noon, so stood the sun, so that the day was departing when the glad angel of God appeared to us. He stood outside the flames on the bank and sang "*Beati mundo corde*" in a voice far more living than ours. Then, "No farther may you go, holy souls, if first the fire sting not; enter into it, and to the singing beyond be not deaf," he said to us, when we were near him; whereat I became such, on hearing him, as is he who is put into the pit. I bent forward over my clasped hands, gazing at the fire and vividly imagining human bodies once seen burned.

Volsersi verso me le buone scorte;
e Virgilio mi disse: "Figliuol mio,
qui può esser tormento, ma non morte. 21
Ricorditi, ricorditi! E se io
sovresso Gerïon ti guidai salvo,
che farò ora presso più a Dio? 24
Credi per certo che se dentro a l'alvo
di questa fiamma stessi ben mille anni,
non ti potrebbe far d'un capel calvo. 27
E se tu forse credi ch'io t'inganni,
fatti ver' lei, e fatti far credenza
con le tue mani al lembo d'i tuoi panni. 30
Pon giù omai, pon giù ogne temenza;
volgiti in qua e vieni: entra sicuro!"
E io pur fermo e contra coscïenza. 33
Quando mi vide star pur fermo e duro,
turbato un poco disse: "Or vedi, figlio:
tra Bëatrice e te è questo muro." 36
Come al nome di Tisbe aperse il ciglio
Piramo in su la morte, e riguardolla,
allor che 'l gelso diventò vermiglio; 39
così, la mia durezza fatta solla,
mi volsi al savio duca, udendo il nome
che ne la mente sempre mi rampolla. 42
Ond' ei crollò la fronte e disse: "Come!
volenci star di qua?"; indi sorrise
come al fanciul si fa ch'è vinto al pome. 45
Poi dentro al foco innanzi mi si mise,
pregando Stazio che venisse retro,
che pria per lunga strada ci divise. 48

The good escorts turned to me, and Virgil said to me, "My son, here may be torment, but not death. Remember, remember . . . and if on Geryon I guided you safely, what shall I do now nearer to God? Be well assured that if within the belly of this flame you should stay full a thousand years, it could not make you bald of one hair. And if perchance you think that I deceive you, go close to it and try it with your own hands on the edge of your garment. Put away now, put away all fear, turn hitherward, come, enter with confidence." And I still adamant and against my conscience.

When he saw me stand there unmoved and stubborn, he said, a little vexed, "Now see, son, between Beatrice and you is this wall."

As at the name of Thisbe, Pyramus, at the point of death, opened his eyelids and looked at her, when the mulberry turned red, so, my stubbornness being softened, I turned to the wise leader when I heard the name which ever springs up in my mind; at which he shook his head and said, "What? Do we desire to stay on this side?" then smiled as one does to a child that is won with an apple.

Then he entered into the fire in front of me, asking Statius, who for a long way had been between us, to come behind.

Sì com' fui dentro, in un bogliente vetro
gittato mi sarei per rinfrescarmi,
tant' era ivi lo 'ncendio sanza metro. 51
Lo dolce padre mio, per confortarmi,
pur di Beatrice ragionando andava,
dicendo: "Li occhi suoi già veder parmi." 54
Guidavaci una voce che cantava
di là; e noi, attenti pur a lei,
venimmo fuor là ove si montava. 57
"*Venite, benedicti Patris mei*,"
sonò dentro a un lume che lì era,
tal che mi vinse e guardar nol potei. 60
"Lo sol sen va," soggiunse, "e vien la sera;
non v'arrestate, ma studiate il passo,
mentre che l'occidente non si annera." 63
Dritta salia la via per entro 'l sasso
verso tal parte ch'io toglieva i raggi
dinanzi a me del sol ch'era già basso. 66
E di pochi scaglion levammo i saggi,
che 'l sol corcar, per l'ombra che si spense,
sentimmo dietro e io e li miei saggi. 69
E pria che 'n tutte le sue parti immense
fosse orizzonte fatto d'uno aspetto,
e notte avesse tutte sue dispense, 72
ciascun di noi d'un grado fece letto;
ché la natura del monte ci affranse
la possa del salir più e 'l diletto. 75
Quali si stanno ruminando manse
le capre, state rapide e proterve
sovra le cime avante che sien pranse, 78

As soon as I was in it I would have flung myself into molten glass to cool me, so without measure was the burning there. My sweet father, to encourage me, went on discoursing of Beatrice, saying, "Already I seem to behold her eyes." A voice was guiding us, which was singing on the other side; and we, ever attentive to it, came forth where the ascent began. "*Venite, benedicti Patris mei,*" sounded from within a light that was there, such that it overcame me and I could not look on it. "The sun is sinking," it added, "and the evening comes; do not stop, but hasten your steps before the west grows dark."

The way went straight up through the rock in such a direction that I was intercepting before me the rays of the sun, which was now low. And of few steps had we made assay when I and my sages perceived, by the shadow which had vanished, that the sun had set behind us. And before the horizon in all its vast range had become of one hue, and night held all her dominions, each of us made his bed of a step, for the law of the mountain took from us the strength as well as the desire to climb farther.

As goats, which have been swift and wayward on the peaks before they are fed, become tranquil as they ruminate,

tacite a l'ombra, mentre che 'l sol ferve,
  guardate dal pastor, che 'n su la verga
  poggiato s'è e lor di posa serve; *81*
e quale il mandrïan che fori alberga,
  lungo il pecuglio suo queto pernotta,
  guardando perché fiera non lo sperga; *84*
tali eravamo tutti e tre allotta,
  io come capra, ed ei come pastori,
  fasciati quinci e quindi d'alta grotta. *87*
Poco parer potea lì del di fori;
  ma, per quel poco, vedea io le stelle
  di lor solere e più chiare e maggiori. *90*
Sì ruminando e sì mirando in quelle,
  mi prese il sonno; il sonno che sovente,
  anzi che 'l fatto sia, sa le novelle. *93*
Ne l'ora, credo, che de l'orïente
  prima raggiò nel monte Citerea,
  che di foco d'amor par sempre ardente, *96*
giovane e bella in sogno mi parea
  donna vedere andar per una landa
  cogliendo fiori; e cantando dicea: *99*
"Sappia qualunque il mio nome dimanda
  ch'i' mi son Lia, e vo movendo intorno
  le belle mani a farmi una ghirlanda. *102*
Per piacermi a lo specchio, qui m'addorno;
  ma mia suora Rachel mai non si smaga
  dal suo miraglio, e siede tutto giorno. *105*
Ell' è d'i suoi belli occhi veder vaga
  com' io de l'addornarmi con le mani;
  lei lo vedere, e me l'ovrare appaga." *108*

silent in the shade while the sun is hot, guarded by the shepherd who leans upon his staff and tends their repose; and as the herdsman, who lodges out of doors, passes the night beside his quiet flock, watching lest a wild beast scatter it, such were we then all three, I as a goat and they as shepherds, bounded by the high rock on this side and on that. Little of the outside could be seen there, but through that little I saw the stars brighter and larger than their wont. As I was thus ruminating, and thus gazing at them, sleep fell on me, sleep which often knows the news before the event.

In the hour, I think, when Cytherea, who seems always burning with the fire of love, first shone on the mountain from the east, I seemed to see in a dream a lady young and beautiful going through a meadow gathering flowers and, singing, she was saying, "Whoso asks my name, let him know that I am Leah, and I go moving my fair hands around to make myself a garland. To please me at the glass I adorn me here, but my sister Rachel never leaves her mirror and sits all day. She is fain to behold her fair eyes, as I am to deck me with my hands: she with seeing, I with doing am satisfied."

E già per li splendori antelucani,
  che tanto a' pellegrin surgon più grati,
  quanto, tornando, albergan men lontani, *111*
le tenebre fuggian da tutti lati,
  e 'l sonno mio con esse; ond' io leva'mi,
  veggendo i gran maestri già levati. *114*
"Quel dolce pome che per tanti rami
  cercando va la cura de' mortali,
  oggi porrà in pace le tue fami." *117*
Virgilio inverso me queste cotali
  parole usò; e mai non furo strenne
  che fosser di piacere a queste iguali. *120*
Tanto voler sopra voler mi venne
  de l'esser sù, ch'ad ogne passo poi
  al volo mi sentia crescer le penne. *123*
Come la scala tutta sotto noi
  fu corsa e fummo in su 'l grado superno,
  in me ficcò Virgilio li occhi suoi, *126*
e disse: "Il temporal foco e l'etterno
  veduto hai, figlio; e se' venuto in parte
  dov' io per me più oltre non discerno. *129*
Tratto t'ho qui con ingegno e con arte;
  lo tuo piacere omai prendi per duce;
  fuor se' de l'erte vie, fuor se' de l'arte. *132*
Vedi lo sol che 'n fronte ti riluce;
  vedi l'erbette, i fiori e li arbuscelli
  che qui la terra sol da sé produce. *135*
Mentre che vegnan lieti li occhi belli
  che, lagrimando, a te venir mi fenno,
  seder ti puoi e puoi andar tra elli. *138*

And now before the splendors which precede the dawn, and rise the more welcome to pilgrims as, returning, they lodge less far from home, the shades of night fled away on every side, and my sleep with them; whereupon I rose, seeing the great masters already risen.

"That sweet fruit which the care of mortals goes seeking on so many branches, this day shall give your hungerings peace." Such were Virgil's words to me, and never were there gifts that could be equal in pleasure to these. Such wish upon wish came to me to be above, that at every step thereafter I felt my feathers growing for the flight.

When all the stair was sped beneath us and we were on the topmost step, Virgil fixed his eyes on me and said, "The temporal fire and the eternal you have seen, my son, and are come to a part where I of myself discern no farther onward. I have brought you here with understanding and with art. Take henceforth your own pleasure for your guide. Forth you are from the steep ways, forth from the narrow. See the sun that shines on your brow, see the tender grass, the flowers, the shrubs, which here the earth of itself alone produces: till the beautiful eyes come rejoicing which weeping made me come to you, you may sit or go among them.

Non aspettar mio dir più né mio cenno;
libero, dritto e sano è tuo arbitrio,
e fallo fora non fare a suo senno:
per ch'io te sovra te corono e mitrio." *142*

No longer expect word or sign from me. Free, upright, and whole is your will, and it would be wrong not to act according to its pleasure; wherefore I crown and miter you over yourself."

Vago già di cercar dentro e dintorno
   la divina foresta spessa e viva,
   ch'a li occhi temperava il novo giorno, *3*
sanza più aspettar, lasciai la riva,
   prendendo la campagna lento lento
   su per lo suol che d'ogne parte auliva. *6*
Un'aura dolce, sanza mutamento
   avere in sé, mi feria per la fronte
   non di più colpo che soave vento; *9*
per cui le fronde, tremolando, pronte
   tutte quante piegavano a la parte
   u' la prim' ombra gitta il santo monte; *12*
non però dal loro esser dritto sparte
   tanto, che li augelletti per le cime
   lasciasser d'operare ogne lor arte; *15*
ma con piena letizia l'ore prime,
   cantando, ricevieno intra le foglie,
   che tenevan bordone a le sue rime, *18*

# CANTO XXVIII

Eager now to search within and round about the divine forest green and dense, which tempered the new day to my eyes, without waiting longer I left the bank, taking the level ground very slowly over the soil that everywhere gives forth fragrance. A sweet breeze that had no variation in itself was striking on my brow with the force only of a gentle wind, by which the fluttering boughs all bent freely toward the quarter where the holy mountain casts its first shadow; yet were they not so deflected from their upright state that the little birds among the tops ceased practicing all their arts, but singing they greeted the morning hours with full joy among the leaves, which kept such burden to their rhymes

tal qual di ramo in ramo si raccoglie
per la pineta in su 'l lito di Chiassi,
quand' Ëolo scilocco fuor discioglie. 21
Già m'avean trasportato i lenti passi
dentro a la selva antica tanto, ch'io
non potea rivedere ond' io mi 'ntrassi; 24
ed ecco più andar mi tolse un rio,
che 'nver' sinistra con sue picciole onde
piegava l'erba che 'n sua ripa uscìo. 27
Tutte l'acque che son di qua più monde,
parrieno avere in sé mistura alcuna
verso di quella, che nulla nasconde, 30
avvegna che si mova bruna bruna
sotto l'ombra perpetüa, che mai
raggiar non lascia sole ivi né luna. 33
Coi piè ristetti e con li occhi passai
di là dal fiumicello, per mirare
la gran varïazion d'i freschi mai; 36
e là m'apparve, sì com' elli appare
subitamente cosa che disvia
per maraviglia tutto altro pensare, 39
una donna soletta che si gia
e cantando e scegliendo fior da fiore
ond' era pinta tutta la sua via. 42
"Deh, bella donna, che a' raggi d'amore
ti scaldi, s'i' vo' credere a' sembianti
che soglion esser testimon del core, 45
vegnati in voglia di trarreti avanti,"
diss' io a lei, "verso questa rivera,
tanto ch'io possa intender che tu canti. 48

as gathers from branch to branch through the pine forest on Chiassi's shore when Aeolus lets forth Sirocco.

Now my slow steps had carried me on into the ancient wood so far that I could not see back to where I had entered it, when lo, a stream took from me further progress, which with its little waves was bending leftwards the grass that grew on its bank. All the waters which here are purest would seem to have some defilement in them, compared with that, which conceals nothing, although it flows quite dark under the perpetual shade, which never lets sun or moon beam enter there.

With feet I stayed and with my eyes I passed to the other side of the rivulet to look at the great variety of the fresh-flowering boughs; and there appeared to me there, as appears of a sudden a thing that for wonder drives away every other thought, a lady all alone, who went singing and culling flower from flower, with which all her path was painted.

"Pray, fair lady, who do warm yourself at love's beams, if I may believe outward looks which are wont to be testimony of the heart," I said to her, "may it please you to draw forward to this stream so near that I may understand what you sing.

Tu mi fai rimembrar dove e qual era
Proserpina nel tempo che perdette
la madre lei, ed ella primavera." 51
Come si volge, con le piante strette
a terra e intra sé, donna che balli,
e piede innanzi piede a pena mette, 54
volsesi in su i vermigli e in su i gialli
fioretti verso me, non altrimenti
che vergine chè li occhi onesti avvalli; 57
e fece i prieghi miei esser contenti,
sì appressando sé, che 'l dolce suono
veniva a me co' suoi intendimenti. 60
Tosto che fu là dove l'erbe sono
bagnate già da l'onde del bel fiume,
di levar li occhi suoi mi fece dono. 63
Non credo che splendesse tanto lume
sotto le ciglia a Venere, trafitta
dal figlio fuor di tutto suo costume. 66
Ella ridea da l'altra riva dritta,
trattando più color con le sue mani,
che l'alta terra sanza seme gitta. 69
Tre passi ci facea il fiume lontani;
ma Elesponto, là 've passò Serse,
ancora freno a tutti orgogli umani, 72
più odio da Leandro non sofferse
per mareggiare intra Sesto e Abido,
che quel da me perch' allor non s'aperse. 75
"Voi siete nuovi, e forse perch' io rido,"
cominciò ella, "in questo luogo eletto
a l'umana natura per suo nido, 78

You make me recall where and what Proserpine was at the time her mother lost her, and she the spring."

As in a dance a lady turns with feet close to the ground and to each other, and hardly sets foot before foot, she turned upon the red and yellow flowerlets toward me, like a virgin that lowers her modest eyes, and gave satisfaction to my prayer, drawing so near that the sweet sound reached me with its meaning. As soon as she was there where the grass was just bathed by the waves of the fair stream, she bestowed on me the gift of lifting her eyes. I do not believe that so great a light shone forth under the eyelids of Venus, transfixed by her son against all his custom. She was smiling as she stood there on the opposite bank, arranging in her hands the many colors which that high land brings forth without seed. The river kept us three paces apart, but Hellespont where Xerxes passed it—ever a curb on all human pride—did not suffer more hatred from Leander for its swelling waters between Sestos and Abydos than that from me because it did not open then.

"You are newcomers," she began, "and, perhaps, why I am smiling in this place chosen for nest of the human race

maravigliando tienvi alcun sospetto;
ma luce rende il salmo *Delectasti*,
che puote disnebbiar vostro intelletto. *81*
E tu che se' dinanzi e mi pregasti,
dì s'altro vuoli udir; ch'i' venni presta
ad ogne tua question tanto che basti." *84*
"L'acqua," diss' io, "e 'l suon de la foresta
impugnan dentro a me novella fede
di cosa ch'io udi' contraria a questa." *87*
Ond' ella: "Io dicerò come procede
per sua cagion ciò ch'ammirar ti face,
e purgherò la nebbia che ti fiede. *90*
Lo sommo Ben, che solo esso a sé piace,
fé l'uom buono e a bene, e questo loco
diede per arr' a lui d'etterna pace. *93*
Per sua difalta qui dimorò poco;
per sua difalta in pianto e in affanno
cambiò onesto riso e dolce gioco. *96*
Perché 'l turbar che sotto da sé fanno
l'essalazion de l'acqua e de la terra,
che quanto posson dietro al calor vanno, *99*
a l'uomo non facesse alcuna guerra,
questo monte salìo verso 'l ciel tanto,
e libero n'è d'indi ove si serra. *102*
Or perché in circuito tutto quanto
l'aere si volge con la prima volta,
se non li è rotto il cerchio d'alcun canto, *105*
in questa altezza ch'è tutta disciolta
ne l'aere vivo, tal moto percuote,
e fa sonar la selva perch' è folta; *108*

some doubt holds you wondering; but the psalm *Delectasti* gives light that may dispel the cloud from your minds. And you that are in front, and did entreat me, say if you would hear more, for I have come ready to all your questions till you are satisfied."

"The water," I said, "and the sound of the forest contend in me with a recent belief in a thing I have heard contrary to this." Whereon she, "I will tell you how that which makes you wonder proceeds from its cause, and I will clear away the mist that offends you.

"The highest Good, who Himself alone does please Himself, made man good, and for good, and gave him this place as an earnest of eternal peace. Through his fault he had short stay here; through his fault he exchanged honest joy and sweet sport for tears and toil. In order that the disturbance which the exhalations of the water and of the earth (which follow so far as they can the heat) produce below might do no hurt to man, this mountain rose thus high toward heaven, and stands clear of them from where it is locked. Now, because all the air revolves in a circuit with the first circling, if its revolution is not interrupted at any point, such movement strikes upon this height, which is wholly free in the pure air, and this motion causes the forest, because it is dense, to resound;

e la percossa pianta tanto puote,
  che de la sua virtute l'aura impregna
  e quella poi, girando, intorno scuote; *111*
e l'altra terra, secondo ch'è degna
  per sé e per suo ciel, concepe e figlia
  di diverse virtù diverse legna. *114*
Non parrebbe di là poi maraviglia,
  udito questo, quando alcuna pianta
  sanza seme palese vi s'appiglia. *117*
E saper dei che la campagna santa
  dove tu se', d'ogne semenza è piena,
  e frutto ha in sé che di là non si schianta. *120*
L'acqua che vedi non surge di vena
  che ristori vapor che gel converta,
  come fiume ch'acquista e perde lena; *123*
ma esce di fontana salda e certa,
  che tanto dal voler di Dio riprende,
  quant' ella versa da due parti aperta. *126*
Da questa parte con virtù discende
  che toglie altrui memoria del peccato;
  da l'altra d'ogne ben fatto la rende. *129*
Quinci Letè; così da l'altro lato
  Eünoè si chiama, e non adopra
  se quinci e quindi pria non è gustato: *132*
a tutti altri sapori esto è di sopra.
  E avvegna ch'assai possa esser sazia
  la sete tua perch' io più non ti scuopra, *135*
darotti un corollario ancor per grazia;
  né credo che 'l mio dir ti sia men caro,
  se oltre promession teco si spazia. *138*

and the plant, being struck thus, has such potency that with its virtue it impregnates the breeze, and this then in its whirling scatters it abroad; and the rest of the earth, according to its fitness in itself and in its sky, conceives and brings forth from diverse virtues diverse growths. It should, then, not seem a marvel on earth, this being heard, when some plant takes root there without visible seed. And you should know that the holy plain, where you are, is full of every seed, and has in it fruit that yonder is not plucked.

"The water you see springs not from a vein that is restored by vapor which cold condenses, like a stream that gains and loses force, but issues from a fountain constant and sure which by the will of God regains as much as it pours forth freely on two sides. On this side it descends with virtue that takes from one the memory of sin; on the other side it restores the memory of every good deed. Here Lethe, so on the other side Eunoe it is called; and it works not if first it be not tasted on this side and on that. Its savor surpasses every other sweetness. And notwithstanding that your thirst might be fully satisfied even if I disclosed no more to you, I will yet give you a corollary for grace, nor do I think my speech will be less welcome to you if it reaches beyond my promise.

Quelli ch'anticamente poetaro
  l'età de l'oro e suo stato felice,
  forse in Parnaso esto loco sognaro. *141*
Qui fu innocente l'umana radice;
  qui primavera sempre e ogne frutto;
  nettare è questo di che ciascun dice." *144*
Io mi rivolsi 'n dietro allora tutto
  a' miei poeti, e vidi che con riso
  udito avëan l'ultimo costrutto;
poi a la bella donna torna' il viso. *148*

"They who in olden times sang of the Age of Gold and its happy state perhaps in Parnassus dreamed of this place. Here the root of mankind was innocent; here is always spring, and every fruit; this is the nectar of which each tells."

I turned then right round to my poets, and saw that with a smile they had heard these last words; then to the fair lady I turned my face.

# PURGATORIO

CANTANDO come donna innamorata,
continüò col fin di sue parole:
"*Beati quorum tecta sunt peccata!*" *3*
E come ninfe che si givan sole
per le salvatiche ombre, disïando
qual di veder, qual di fuggir lo sole, *6*
allor si mosse contra 'l fiume, andando
su per la riva; e io pari di lei,
picciol passo con picciol seguitando. *9*
Non eran cento tra ' suoi passi e ' miei,
quando le ripe igualmente dier volta,
per modo ch'a levante mi rendei. *12*
Né ancor fu così nostra via molta,
quando la donna tutta a me si torse,
dicendo: "Frate mio, guarda e ascolta." *15*
Ed ecco un lustro sùbito trascorse
da tutte parti per la gran foresta,
tal che di balenar mi mise in forse. *18*

# CANTO XXIX

SINGING like a lady enamored, she continued, at the end of her words, "*Beati quorum tecta sunt peccata!*" and, like nymphs who used to wend alone through the woodland shades, this one desiring to see and that to avoid the sun, she moved on, then, counter to the stream, going along the bank, and I abreast of her, matching her little steps with mine. We had not taken a hundred between us when the banks made an equal bend in such a way that I faced the East again; nor yet was our way thus very far when the lady turned full round to me, saying, "My brother, look and listen!" And lo! a sudden brightness flooded the great forest on all sides, such that it put me in doubt if it were lightning;

Ma perché 'l balenar, come vien, resta,
e quel, durando, più e più splendeva,
nel mio pensier dicea: "Che cosa è questa?" *21*

E una melodia dolce correva
per l'aere luminoso; onde buon zelo
mi fé riprender l'ardimento d'Eva, *24*

che là dove ubidia la terra e 'l cielo,
femmina, sola e pur testé formata,
non sofferse di star sotto alcun velo; *27*

sotto 'l qual se divota fosse stata,
avrei quelle ineffabili delizie
sentite prima e più lunga fïata. *30*

Mentr' io m'andava tra tante primizie
de l'etterno piacer tutto sospeso,
e disïoso ancora a più letizie, *33*

dinanzi a noi, tal quale un foco acceso,
ci si fé l'aere sotto i verdi rami;
e 'l dolce suon per canti era già inteso. *36*

O sacrosante Vergini, se fami,
freddi o vigilie mai per voi soffersi,
cagion mi sprona ch'io mercé vi chiami. *39*

Or convien che Elicona per me versi,
e Uranìe m'aiuti col suo coro
forti cose a pensar mettere in versi. *42*

Poco più oltre, sette alberi d'oro
falsava nel parere il lungo tratto
del mezzo ch'era ancor tra noi e loro; *45*

ma quand' i' fui sì presso di lor fatto,
che l'obietto comun, che 'l senso inganna,
non perdea per distanza alcun suo atto, *48*

but since lightning ceases even as it comes, and this, lasting, became more and more resplendent, in my thought I said, "What thing is this!" And a sweet melody ran through the luminous air; wherefore good zeal made me reprove Eve's daring, that, there where earth and heaven were obedient, a woman, alone and but then formed, did not bear to remain under any veil, under which, if she had been devout, I should have tasted those ineffable delights before, and for a longer time. While I went on among so many first-fruits of the eternal pleasure, all enrapt, and still desirous of more joys, in front of us the air under the green boughs became like a flaming fire to us, and the sweet sound was now heard as a song.

O most holy Virgins, if hunger, cold, or vigils I have ever endured for you, the occasion spurs me to claim my reward. Now it is meet that Helicon stream forth for me, and Urania aid me with her choir to put in verse things difficult to think.

A little farther on, a delusive semblance of seven trees of gold was caused by the long space still intervening between us and them; but when I had come so near that the common object, which deceives the sense, lost not by distance any of its features,

la virtù ch'a ragion discorso ammanna,
  sì com' elli eran candelabri apprese,
  e ne le voci del cantare "*Osanna.*" 51
Di sopra fiammeggiava il bello arnese
  più chiaro assai che luna per sereno
  di mezza notte nel suo mezzo mese. 54
Io mi rivolsi d'ammirazion pieno
  al buon Virgilio, ed esso mi rispuose
  con vista carca di stupor non meno. 57
Indi rendei l'aspetto a l'alte cose
  che si movieno incontr' a noi sì tardi,
  che foran vinte da novelle spose. 60
La donna mi sgridò: "Perché pur ardi
  sì ne l'affetto de le vive luci,
  e ciò che vien di retro a lor non guardi?" 63
Genti vid' io allor, come a lor duci,
  venire appresso, vestite di bianco;
  e tal candor di qua già mai non fuci. 66
L'acqua imprendëa dal sinistro fianco,
  e rendea me la mia sinistra costa,
  s'io riguardava in lei, come specchio anco. 69
Quand' io da la mia riva ebbi tal posta,
  che solo il fiume mi facea distante,
  per veder meglio ai passi diedi sosta, 72
e vidi le fiammelle andar davante,
  lasciando dietro a sé l'aere dipinto,
  e di tratti pennelli avean sembiante; 75
sì che lì sopra rimanea distinto
  di sette liste, tutte in quei colori
  onde fa l'arco il Sole e Delia il cinto. 78

the faculty that prepares matter for reason made them out to be candlesticks, even as they were, and in the words of the chant "Hosanna." Above flamed the splendid array, brighter by far than the moon in a clear midnight sky in her mid-month. I turned round full of wonder to the good Virgil, and he answered me with a look no less charged with amazement; then I turned my face again to the high things, which moved towards us so slowly that they would have been outstripped by new-made brides. The lady chid me, "Why are you so eager only for the sight of the living lights, and do not heed that which comes after them?" Then I saw people, following as after their leaders, clad in white, and a whiteness so pure never was here. The water was taking in my image on the left, and like a mirror reflected to me my left side if I looked in it. When I was at a point on my bank where only the stream separated me, I held my steps in order to see better, and I saw the flames advance, leaving the air behind them painted, and they looked like moving paint brushes, so that overhead it remained streaked with seven bands in all those colors whereof the sun makes his bow, and Delia her girdle.

Questi ostendali in dietro eran maggiori
che la mia vista; e, quanto a mio avviso,
diece passi distavan quei di fori. 81

Sotto così bel ciel com' io diviso
ventiquattro seniori, a due a due,
coronati venien di fiordaliso. 84

Tutti cantavan: "*Benedicta* tue
ne le figlie d'Adamo, e benedette
sieno in etterno le bellezze tue!" 87

Poscia che i fiori e l'altre fresche erbette
a rimpetto di me da l'altra sponda
libere fuor da quelle genti elette, 90

sì come luce luce in ciel seconda,
vennero appresso lor quattro animali,
coronati ciascun di verde fronda. 93

Ognuno era pennuto di sei ali;
le penne piene d'occhi; e li occhi d'Argo,
se fosser vivi, sarebber cotali. 96

A descriver lor forme più non spargo
rime, lettor; ch'altra spesa mi strigne,
tanto ch'a questa non posso esser largo; 99

ma leggi Ezechïel, che li dipigne
come li vide da la fredda parte
venir con vento e con nube e con igne; 102

e quali i troverai ne le sue carte,
tali eran quivi, salvo ch'a le penne
Giovanni è meco e da lui si diparte. 105

Lo spazio dentro a lor quattro contenne
un carro, in su due rote, trïunfale,
ch'al collo d'un grifon tirato venne. 108

These banners went back farther than my sight and, as well as I could judge, the outermost were ten paces apart. Beneath so fair a sky as I describe came four and twenty elders, two by two, crowned with lilies; all were singing, "Blessed art thou among the daughters of Adam, and blessed forever be thy beauties."

When the flowers and the other fresh herbage opposite me on the other bank were left clear of those chosen people, even as star follows star in the heavens, four living creatures came after them, each crowned with green leaves; and each of them was plumed with six wings, the plumes full of eyes, and the eyes of Argus, were they alive, would be such. To describe their forms, reader, I do not lay out more rhymes, for other spending constrains me so that I cannot be lavish in this; but read Ezekiel who depicts them as he saw them come from the cold parts, with wind and cloud and fire; and such as you shall find them on his pages, such were they here, except that, as to the wings, John is with me, and differs from him.

The space within the four of them contained a triumphal chariot on two wheels, which came drawn at the neck of a griffin;

Esso tendeva in sù l'una e l'altra ale
tra la mezzana e le tre e tre liste,
sì ch'a nulla, fendendo, facea male. *111*
Tanto salivan che non eran viste;
le membra d'oro avea quant' era uccello,
e bianche l'altre, di vermiglio miste. *114*
Non che Roma di carro così bello
rallegrasse Affricano, o vero Augusto,
ma quel del Sol saria pover con ello; *117*
quel del Sol che, svïando, fu combusto
per l'orazion de la Terra devota,
quando fu Giove arcanamente giusto. *120*
Tre donne in giro da la destra rota
venian danzando; l'una tanto rossa
ch'a pena fora dentro al foco nota; *123*
l'altr' era come se le carni e l'ossa
fossero state di smeraldo fatte;
la terza parea neve testé mossa; *126*
e or parëan da la bianca tratte,
or da la rossa; e dal canto di questa
l'altre toglien l'andare e tarde e ratte. *129*
Da la sinistra quattro facean festa,
in porpore vestite, dietro al modo
d'una di lor ch'avea tre occhi in testa. *132*
Appresso tutto il pertrattato nodo
vidi due vecchi in abito dispari,
ma pari in atto e onesto e sodo. *135*
L'un si mostrava alcun de' famigliari
di quel sommo Ipocràte che natura
a li animali fé ch'ell' ha più cari; *138*

and he stretched upwards one wing and the other between the middle and the three and three bands so that he did harm to none by cleaving. So high they rose that they were lost to sight; he had his members of gold so far as he was bird, and the rest was white mixed with red. Not only did Rome never gladden an Africanus or an Augustus with a chariot so splendid, but even that of the Sun would be poor to it—that of the Sun which, going astray, was consumed at devout Earth's prayer, when Jove in his secrecy was just.

Three ladies came dancing in a round at the right wheel, one of them so ruddy that she would hardly have been noted in the fire; another was as if her flesh and bones had been of emerald; the third seemed new-fallen snow; and they seemed to be led, now by the white, now by the red, and from this one's song the others took their movement fast and slow. By the left wheel four other ladies made festival, clothed in purple, following the measure of one of them that had three eyes in her head.

Behind the whole group I have described I saw two old men, unlike in dress but alike in bearing, venerable and grave: the one showed himself of the household of that great Hippocrates whom nature made for the creatures she holds dearest;

mostrava l'altro la contraria cura
  con una spada lucida e aguta,
  tal che di qua dal rio mi fé paura. *141*

Poi vidi quattro in umile paruta;
  e di retro da tutti un vecchio solo
  venir, dormendo, con la faccia arguta. *144*

E questi sette col primaio stuolo
  erano abitüati, ma di gigli
  dintorno al capo non facëan brolo, *147*

anzi di rose e d'altri fior vermigli;
  giurato avria poco lontano aspetto
  che tutti ardesser di sopra da' cigli. *150*

E quando il carro a me fu a rimpetto,
  un tuon s'udì, e quelle genti degne
  parvero aver l'andar più interdetto,

fermandosi ivi con le prime insegne. *154*

the other showed the contrary care, with a sharp and shining sword, such that on this side of the stream it made me afraid. Then I saw four of lowly aspect; and behind them all an old man coming alone, asleep, with keen visage. And these seven were clad like the first band, but they had no garland of lilies around their heads, rather of roses and of other red flowers: one who viewed them from short distance would have sworn that all were aflame above their eyebrows. And when the chariot was opposite to me, a thunderclap was heard: and those worthy folk seemed to have their further march forbidden, stopping there along with the banners in front.

QUANDO il settentrïon del primo cielo,
che né occaso mai seppe né orto
né d'altra nebbia che di colpa velo, 3
e che faceva lì ciascuno accorto
di suo dover, come 'l più basso face
qual temon gira per venire a porto, 6
fermo s'affisse: la gente verace,
venuta prima tra 'l grifone ed esso,
al carro volse sé come a sua pace; 9
e un di loro, quasi da ciel messo,
"*Veni, sponsa, de Libano*" cantando
gridò tre volte, e tutti li altri appresso. 12
Quali i beati al novissimo bando
surgeran presti ognun di sua caverna,
la revestita voce alleluiando, 15
cotali in su la divina basterna
si levar cento, *ad vocem tanti senis*,
ministri e messaggier di vita etterna. 18

# CANTO XXX

When the Wain of the first heaven, which never knew setting or rising, or veil of other cloud than of sin, and which there made each one aware of his duty, even as the lower wain guides him who turns the helm to come into port, had stopped still, the truthful people, who had come first between the griffin and it, turned to the chariot as to their peace, and one of them, as if sent from Heaven, singing cried thrice, "*Veni, sponsa de Libano*," and all the others after.

As the blessed at the last Trump will rise ready each from his tomb, singing Hallelujah with reclad voice, so upon the divine chariot, *ad vocem tanti senis*, rose up a hundred ministers and messengers of life eternal,

Tutti dicean: "*Benedictus qui venis!*"
e fior gittando e di sopra e dintorno,
"*Manibus*, oh, *date lilïa plenis!*" 21

Io vidi già nel cominciar del giorno
la parte orïental tutta rosata,
e l'altro ciel di bel sereno addorno; 24

e la faccia del sol nascere ombrata,
sì che per temperanza di vapori
l'occhio la sostenea lunga fïata: 27

così dentro una nuvola di fiori
che da le mani angeliche saliva
e ricadeva in giù dentro e di fori, 30

sovra candido vel cinta d'uliva
donna m'apparve, sotto verde manto
vestita di color di fiamma viva. 33

E lo spirito mio, che già cotanto
tempo era stato ch'a la sua presenza
non era di stupor, tremando, affranto, 36

sanza de li occhi aver più conoscenza,
per occulta virtù che da lei mosse,
d'antico amor sentì la gran potenza. 39

Tosto che ne la vista mi percosse
l'alta virtù che già m'avea trafitto
prima ch'io fuor di püerizia fosse, 42

volsimi a la sinistra col respitto
col quale il fantolin corre a la mamma
quando ha paura o quando elli è afflitto, 45

per dicere a Virgilio: "Men che dramma
di sangue m'è rimaso che non tremi:
conosco i segni de l'antica fiamma." 48

who all cried, "*Benedictus qui venis*" and, scattering flowers up and around, "*Manibus*, oh, *date lilia plenis*."

Sometimes I have seen at the beginning of the day the eastern region all rosy, while the rest of the heaven was adorned with fair clear sky, and the face of the sun rise shaded, so that through the tempering of vapors the eye sustained it a long while: so within a cloud of flowers, which rose from the angelic hands and fell down again within and without, olive-crowned over a white veil a lady appeared to me, clad, under a green mantle, with hue of living flame; and my spirit, which now for so long a time trembling with awe in her presence had not been overcome, without having more knowledge by the eyes, through occult virtue that proceeded from her, felt old love's great power. As soon as on my sight the lofty virtue smote that had already pierced me before I was out of my boyhood, I turned to the left with the confidence of a little child that runs to his mother when he is frightened or in distress, to say to Virgil, "Not a drop of blood is left in me that does not tremble: I know the tokens of the ancient flame."

Ma Virgilio n'avea lasciati scemi
di sé, Virgilio dolcissimo patre,
Virgilio a cui per mia salute die'mi; 51
né quantunque perdeo l'antica matre,
valse a le guance nette di rugiada
che, lagrimando, non tornasser atre. 54
"Dante, perché Virgilio se ne vada,
non pianger anco, non piangere ancora;
ché pianger ti conven per altra spada." 57
Quasi ammiraglio che in poppa e in prora
viene a veder la gente che ministra
per li altri legni, e a ben far l'incora; 60
in su la sponda del carro sinistra,
quando mi volsi al suon del nome mio,
che di necessità qui si registra, 63
vidi la donna che pria m'appario
velata sotto l'angelica festa,
drizzar li occhi ver' me di qua dal rio. 66
Tutto che 'l vel che le scendea di testa,
cerchiato de le fronde di Minerva,
non la lasciasse parer manifesta, 69
regalmente ne l'atto ancor proterva
continüò come colui che dice
e 'l più caldo parlar dietro reserva: 72
"Guardaci ben! Ben son, ben son Beatrice.
Come degnasti d'accedere al monte?
non sapei tu che qui è l'uom felice?" 75
Li occhi mi cadder giù nel chiaro fonte;
ma veggendomi in esso, i trassi a l'erba,
tanta vergogna mi gravò la fronte. 78

But Virgil had left us bereft of himself, Virgil sweetest father, Virgil to whom I gave myself for my salvation; nor did all that our ancient mother lost keep my dew-washed cheeks from turning dark again with tears.

"Dante, because Virgil leaves you, do not weep yet, do not weep yet, for you must weep for another sword!"

Like an admiral who goes to stern and bow to see the men that are serving on the other ships, and encourages them to do well, so on the left side of the chariot—when I turned at the sound of my name, which of necessity is registered here—I saw the lady, who first appeared to me veiled under the angelic festival, direct her eyes to me beyond the stream. Although the veil that fell from her head, encircled with Minerva's leaves, did not let her be seen distinctly, royally and ever stern in her mien, she continued, like one who speaks and keeps back the hottest words till the last, "Look at me well: indeed I am, indeed I am Beatrice! How did you deign to climb the mountain? Did you not know that here man is happy?" My eyes fell down to the clear fount, but, seeing myself in it, I drew them back to the grass, so great shame weighed on my brow;

Così la madre al figlio par superba,
com' ella parve a me; perché d'amaro
sente il sapor de la pietade acerba. *81*

Ella si tacque; e li angeli cantaro
di sùbito "*In te, Domine, speravi*";
ma oltre "*pedes meos*" non passaro. *84*

Sì come neve tra le vive travi
per lo dosso d'Italia si congela,
soffiata e stretta da li venti schiavi, *87*

poi, liquefatta, in sé stessa trapela,
pur che la terra che perde ombra spiri,
sì che par foco fonder la candela; *90*

così fui sanza lagrime e sospiri
anzi 'l cantar di quei che notan sempre
dietro a le note de li etterni giri; *93*

ma poi che 'ntesi ne le dolci tempre
lor compartire a me, par che se detto
avesser: "Donna, perché sì lo stempre?" *96*

lo gel che m'era intorno al cor ristretto,
spirito e acqua fessi, e con angoscia
de la bocca e de li occhi uscì del petto. *99*

Ella, pur ferma in su la detta coscia
del carro stando, a le sustanze pie
volse le sue parole così poscia: *102*

"Voi vigilate ne l'etterno die,
sì che notte né sonno a voi non fura
passo che faccia il secol per sue vie; *105*

onde la mia risposta è con più cura
che m'intenda colui che di là piagne,
perché sia colpa e duol d'una misura. *108*

so does the mother seem harsh to her child as she seemed to me, for bitter tastes the savor of stern pity.

She was silent; and the angels of a sudden sang, "*In te, Domine, speravi,*" but beyond "*pedes meos*" they did not pass. Even as the snow, among the living rafters upon the back of Italy, is congealed, blown and packed by Slavonian winds, then melting, trickles through itself, if only the land that loses shadow breathes, so that it seems a fire that melts the candle; so was I without tears or sighs before the song of those who ever sing in harmony with the eternal spheres. But when I heard how in their sweet notes they took my part, quite as if they had said, "Lady, why do you so confound him?" the ice that was bound tight around my heart became breath and water, and with anguish poured from my breast through my mouth and eyes.

She, still standing motionless on the aforesaid side of the chariot, then turned her words to the pitying angels thus: "You watch in the everlasting day, so that nor night nor slumber steals from you one step which the world makes along its ways; wherefore my answer is more concerned that he who weeps yonder should understand me, so that fault and grief may be of one measure.

Non pur per ovra de le rote magne,
  che drizzan ciascun seme ad alcun fine
  secondo che le stelle son compagne, *111*
ma per larghezza di grazie divine,
  che sì alti vapori hanno a lor piova,
  che nostre viste là non van vicine, *114*
questi fu tal ne la sua vita nova
  virtüalmente, ch'ogne abito destro
  fatto averebbe in lui mirabil prova. *117*
Ma tanto più maligno e più silvestro
  si fa 'l terren col mal seme e non cólto,
  quant' elli ha più di buon vigor terrestro. *120*
Alcun tempo il sostenni col mio volto:
  mostrando li occhi giovanetti a lui,
  meco il menava in dritta parte vòlto. *123*
Sì tosto come in su la soglia fui
  di mia seconda etade e mutai vita,
  questi si tolse a me, e diessi altrui. *126*
Quando di carne a spirto era salita,
  e bellezza e virtù cresciuta m'era,
  fu' io a lui men cara e men gradita; *129*
e volse i passi suoi per via non vera,
  imagini di ben seguendo false,
  che nulla promession rendono intera. *132*
Né l'impetrare ispirazion mi valse,
  con le quali e in sogno e altrimenti
  lo rivocai: sì poco a lui ne calse! *135*
Tanto giù cadde, che tutti argomenti
  a la salute sua eran già corti,
  fuor che mostrarli le perdute genti. *138*

Not only through the working of the great wheels, which direct every seed to some end according as the stars are its companions, but through largess of divine graces, which have for their rain vapors so lofty that our sight goes not near thereto, this man was such in his new life, virtually, that every right disposition would have made marvelous proof in him. But so much the more rank and wild becomes the land, ill-sown and untilled, as it has more of good strength of soil. For a time I sustained him with my countenance: showing him my youthful eyes I led him with me turned toward the right goal. So soon as I was on the threshold of my second age and had changed life, this one took himself from me and gave himself to others. When from flesh to spirit I had ascended, and beauty and virtue were increased in me, I was less dear and less pleasing to him and he turned his steps along a way not true, following false images of good, which pay no promise in full. Nor did it avail me to obtain inspirations with which, both in dream and otherwise, I called him back, so little did he heed them. He fell so low that all means for his salvation were now short, save to show him the lost people.

Per questo visitai l'uscio d'i morti,
  e a colui che l'ha qua sù condotto,
  li preghi miei, piangendo, furon porti. *141*
Alto fato di Dio sarebbe rotto,
  se Letè si passasse e tal vivanda
  fosse gustata sanza alcuno scotto
di pentimento che lagrime spanda." *145*

For this I visited the gate of the dead, and to him who has conducted him up hither my prayers were offered with tears. The high decree of God would be broken if Lethe were passed and such viands were tasted without some scot of penitence that may pour forth tears."

# PURGATORIO

"O TU CHE se' di là dal fiume sacro,"
volgendo suo parlare a me per punta,
che pur per taglio m'era paruto acro, *3*
ricominciò, seguendo sanza cunta,
"dì, dì se questo è vero; a tanta accusa
tua confession conviene esser congiunta." *6*
Era la mia virtù tanto confusa,
che la voce si mosse, e pria si spense
che da li organi suoi fosse dischiusa. *9*
Poco sofferse; poi disse: "Che pense?
Rispondi a me; ché le memorie triste
in te non sono ancor da l'acqua offense." *12*
Confusione e paura insieme miste
mi pinsero un tal "sì" fuor de la bocca,
al quale intender fuor mestier le viste. *15*
Come balestro frange, quando scocca
da troppa tesa, la sua corda e l'arco,
e con men foga l'asta il segno tocca, *18*

# CANTO XXXI

"O YOU who are on that side of the sacred river," she began again, turning against me the point of her speech, which even with the edge had seemed sharp to me; and continuing without pause, "Say, say, if this is true: to such an accusation your confession must be joined."

My power was so confounded that my voice moved and became extinct before it was set free from its organs. She forebore but little, then said, "What are you thinking? Answer me, for the sad memories in you are not yet destroyed by the water." Confusion and fear, together mingled, drove forth from my mouth a *Yes* such that the eyes were needed to hear it.

As a crossbow breaks its cord and the bow when it shoots with too great tension, and the shaft hits the mark with less force,

sì scoppia' io sottesso grave carco,
fuori sgorgando lagrime e sospiri,
e la voce allentò per lo suo varco. *21*

Ond' ella a me: "Per entro i mie' disiri,
che ti menavano ad amar lo bene
di là dal qual non è a che s'aspiri, *24*

quai fossi attraversati o quai catene
trovasti, per che del passare innanzi
dovessiti così spogliar la spene? *27*

E quali agevolezze o quali avanzi
ne la fronte de li altri si mostraro,
per che dovessi lor passeggiare anzi?" *30*

Dopo la tratta d'un sospiro amaro,
a pena ebbi la voce che rispuose,
e le labbra a fatica la formaro. *33*

Piangendo dissi: "Le presenti cose
col falso lor piacer volser miei passi,
tosto che 'l vostro viso si nascose." *36*

Ed ella: "Se tacessi o se negassi
ciò che confessi, non fora men nota
la colpa tua: da tal giudice sassi! *39*

Ma quando scoppia de la propria gota
l'accusa del peccato, in nostra corte
rivolge sé contra 'l taglio la rota. *42*

Tuttavia, perché mo vergogna porte
del tuo errore, e perché altra volta,
udendo le serene, sie più forte, *45*

pon giù il seme del piangere e ascolta:
sì udirai come in contraria parte
mover dovieti mia carne sepolta. *48*

so did I burst under that heavy load, pouring forth tears and sighs, and my voice failed along its passage. Wherefore she to me, "Within your desires of me that were leading you to love that Good beyond which there is nothing to which man may aspire, what pits did you find athwart your path, or what chains, that you had thus to strip you of the hope of passing onward? And what attractions or what advantages were displayed on the brow of others, that you were obliged to dally before them?"

After drawing a bitter sigh, I barely had the voice to make answer, and my lips shaped it with difficulty. Weeping I said, "The present things, with their false pleasure, turned my steps aside, as soon as your countenance was hidden."

And she, "Had you been silent, or had you denied that which you confess, your fault would not be less noted, by such a Judge is it known. But when accusation of the sin bursts from one's own cheek, in our court the grindstone turns itself back against the edge. Still, that you may now bear shame for your error, and another time, hearing the Sirens, may be stronger, lay aside the seed of tears and listen: so shall you hear how in opposite direction my buried flesh ought to have moved you.

Mai non t'appresentò natura o arte
piacer, quanto le belle membra in ch'io
rinchiusa fui, e che so' 'n terra sparte; 51
e se 'l sommo piacer sì ti fallio
per la mia morte, qual cosa mortale
dovea poi trarre te nel suo disio? 54
Ben ti dovevi, per lo primo strale
de le cose fallaci, levar suso
di retro a me che non era più tale. 57
Non ti dovea gravar le penne in giuso,
ad aspettar più colpo, o pargoletta
o altra novità con sì breve uso. 60
Novo augelletto due o tre aspetta;
ma dinanzi da li occhi d'i pennuti
rete si spiega indarno o si saetta." 63
Quali fanciulli, vergognando, muti
con li occhi a terra stannosi, ascoltando
e sé riconoscendo e ripentuti, 66
tal mi stav' io; ed ella disse: "Quando
per udir se' dolente, alza la barba,
e prenderai più doglia riguardando." 69
Con men di resistenza si dibarba
robusto cerro, o vero al nostral vento
o vero a quel de la terra di Iarba, 72
ch'io non levai al suo comando il mento;
e quando per la barba il viso chiese,
ben conobbi il velen de l'argomento. 75
E come la mia faccia si distese,
posarsi quelle prime creature
da loro aspersïon l'occhio comprese; 78

"Never did nature or art present to you beauty so great as the fair members in which I was enclosed and now are scattered to dust. And if the highest beauty thus failed you by my death, what mortal thing should then have drawn you into desire for it? Truly, at the first arrow of deceitful things you ought to have risen up, following me who was no longer such. Young damsel or other novelty of such brief enjoyment should not have weighed down your wings to await more shots. The young bird waits two or three, but before the eyes of the full-fledged in vain is net spread or arrow shot."

As children stand ashamed and dumb, with eyes on the ground, listening conscience-stricken and repentant, so stood I. And she said, "Since you are grieved through hearing, lift up your beard and you will receive more grief through seeing."

With less resistance is the sturdy oak uprooted, whether by wind of ours or by that which blows from Iarbas' land, than at her command I raised my chin; and when by the beard she asked for my face, well I knew the venom of the argument. When my face was lifted up, my sight perceived those primal creatures resting from their strewing;

e le mie luci, ancor poco sicure,
vider Beatrice volta in su la fiera
ch'è sola una persona in due nature. *81*

Sotto 'l suo velo e oltre la rivera
vincer pariemi più sé stessa antica,
vincer che l'altre qui, quand' ella c'era. *84*

Di penter sì mi punse ivi l'ortica,
che di tutte altre cose qual mi torse
più nel suo amor, più mi si fé nemica. *87*

Tanta riconoscenza il cor mi morse,
ch'io caddi vinto; e quale allora femmi,
salsi colei che la cagion mi porse. *90*

Poi, quando il cor virtù di fuor rendemmi,
la donna ch'io avea trovata sola
sopra me vidi, e dicea: "Tiemmi, tiemmi!" *93*

Tratto m'avea nel fiume infin la gola,
e tirandosi me dietro sen giva
sovresso l'acqua lieve come scola. *96*

Quando fui presso a la beata riva,
"*Asperges me*" sì dolcemente udissi,
che nol so rimembrar, non ch'io lo scriva. *99*

La bella donna ne le braccia aprissi;
abbracciommi la testa e mi sommerse
ove convenne ch'io l'acqua inghiottissi. *102*

Indi mi tolse, e bagnato m'offerse
dentro a la danza de le quattro belle;
e ciascuna del braccio mi coperse. *105*

"Noi siam qui ninfe e nel ciel siamo stelle;
pria che Beatrice discendesse al mondo,
fummo ordinate a lei per sue ancelle. *108*

and my eyes, still little assured, saw Beatrice turned toward the animal that is one person in two natures. Beneath her veil and beyond the stream she seemed to me to surpass more her former self than she surpassed the others here when she was with us; and the nettle of remorse so stung me there that of all other things, that which had most turned me to love of it became most hateful to me. Such contrition stung my heart that I fell overcome; and what I then became she knows who was the cause of it.

Then when my heart had restored my outward sense I saw above me the lady I had found alone and she was saying, "Cling, cling to me!" She had brought me into the river up to the throat and, drawing me behind her, was moving over the water as light as a shuttle. When I was close to the blessed shore, I heard "*Asperges me*" sung so sweetly that I cannot remember it, far less write it. The fair lady opened her arms, clasped my head and dipped me under, where it behooved me to swallow of the water. Then she drew me forth and led me bathed into the dance of the four fair ones, and each of them covered me with her arm. "Here we are nymphs and in heaven we are stars: before Beatrice descended to the world we were ordained to her for her handmaids.

Merrenti a li occhi suoi; ma nel giocondo
lume ch'è dentro aguzzeranno i tuoi
le tre di là, che miran più profondo." 111
Così cantando cominciaro; e poi
al petto del grifon seco menarmi,
ove Beatrice stava volta a noi. 114
Disser: "Fa che le viste non risparmi;
posto t'avem dinanzi a li smeraldi
ond' Amor già ti trasse le sue armi." 117
Mille disiri più che fiamma caldi
strinsermi li occhi a li occhi rilucenti,
che pur sopra 'l grifone stavan saldi. 120
Come in lo specchio il sol, non altrimenti
la doppia fiera dentro vi raggiava,
or con altri, or con altri reggimenti. 123
Pensa, lettor, s'io mi maravigliava,
quando vedea la cosa in sé star queta,
e ne l'idolo suo si trasmutava. 126
Mentre che piena di stupore e lieta
l'anima mia gustava di quel cibo
che, saziando di sé, di sé asseta, 129
sé dimostrando di più alto tribo
ne li atti, l'altre tre si fero avanti,
danzando al loro angelico caribo. 132
"Volgi, Beatrice, volgi li occhi santi,"
era la sua canzone, "al tuo fedele
che, per vederti, ha mossi passi tanti! 135
Per grazia fa noi grazia che disvele
a lui la bocca tua, sì che discerna
la seconda bellezza che tu cele." 138

We will bring you to her eyes; but in the joyous light which is within them the three on the other side, who look deeper, shall quicken yours." Thus they began to sing, then brought me with them to the breast of the griffin, where Beatrice stood turned towards us. "See that you spare not your gaze," they said, "we have placed you before the emeralds from which Love once shot his darts at you."

A thousand desires hotter than flame held my eyes on the shining eyes that remained ever fixed on the griffin. As the sun in a mirror, so was the twofold animal gleaming therewithin, now with the one, now with the other bearing. Think, reader, if I marveled when I saw the thing stand still in itself, and in its image changing.

While my soul, full of amazement and gladness, was tasting of that food which, sating of itself, causes hunger for itself, the other three, showing themselves by their bearing to be of a higher order, came forward, dancing to their angelic roundelay. "Turn, Beatrice, turn your holy eyes upon your faithful one," was their song, "who has moved so many steps to see you. For grace do us the grace to unveil to him your mouth, that he may discern the second beauty which you conceal."

O isplendor di viva luce etterna,
  chi palido si fece sotto l'ombra
  sì di Parnaso, o bevve in sua cisterna, *141*
che non paresse aver la mente ingombra,
  tentando a render te qual tu paresti
  là dove armonizzando il ciel t'adombra,
quando ne l'aere aperto ti solvesti? *145*

O splendor of living light eternal! Who has ever grown so pale under the shade of Parnassus or drunk so deep at its well, that he would not seem to have his mind encumbered, on trying to render you as you appeared, when in the free air you did disclose yourself, there where in its harmony that heaven overshadows you!

# PURGATORIO

TANT' eran li occhi miei fissi e attenti
a disbramarsi la decenne sete,
che li altri sensi m'eran tutti spenti. *3*
Ed essi quinci e quindi avien parete
di non caler—così lo santo riso
a sé traéli con l'antica rete!— *6*
quando per forza mi fu vòlto il viso
ver' la sinistra mia da quelle dee,
perch' io udi' da loro un "Troppo fiso!" *9*
e la disposizion ch'a veder èe
ne li occhi pur testé dal sol percossi,
sanza la vista alquanto esser mi fée. *12*
Ma poi ch'al poco il viso riformossi
(e dico "al poco" per rispetto al molto
sensibile onde a forza mi rimossi), *15*
vidi 'n sul braccio destro esser rivolto
lo glorïoso essercito, e tornarsi
col sole e con le sette fiamme al volto. *18*

# CANTO XXXII

So FIXED and intent were my eyes in satisfying their ten-year thirst, that every other sense was quenched in me; and they themselves had a wall of indifference, on one side and on the other, so did the holy smile draw them to itself with the old net, when my face was turned perforce to my left by those goddesses, for I heard from them a "Too fixedly!" And the condition of the sight that is in eyes just smitten by the sun left me for a time without vision. But after my sight had adjusted itself to the lesser object—lesser, I mean, with regard to the greater from which I was forced to withdraw—I saw that the glorious army had wheeled on its right and was returning with the sun and the seven flames in its face.

Come sotto li scudi per salvarsi
volgesi schiera, e sé gira col segno,
prima che possa tutta in sé mutarsi; 21
quella milizia del celeste regno
che procedeva, tutta trapassonne
pria che piegasse il carro il primo legno. 24
Indi a le rote si tornar le donne,
e 'l grifon mosse il benedetto carco
sì, che però nulla penna crollonne. 27
La bella donna che mi trasse al varco
e Stazio e io seguitavam la rota
che fé l'orbita sua con minore arco. 30
Sì passeggiando l'alta selva vòta,
colpa di quella ch'al serpente crese,
temprava i passi un'angelica nota. 33
Forse in tre voli tanto spazio prese
disfrenata saetta, quanto eramo
rimossi, quando Bëatrice scese. 36
Io senti' mormorare a tutti "Adamo";
poi cerchiaro una pianta dispogliata
di foglie e d'altra fronda in ciascun ramo. 39
La coma sua, che tanto si dilata
più quanto più è sù, fora da l'Indi
ne' boschi lor per altezza ammirata. 42
"Beato se', grifon, che non discindi
col becco d'esto legno dolce al gusto,
poscia che mal si torce il ventre quindi." 45
Così dintorno a l'albero robusto
gridaron li altri; e l'animal binato:
"Sì si conserva il seme d'ogne giusto." 48

As under their shields a troop wheels about to save itself and turns with its standard before it can completely face round, that soldiery of the celestial realm which was in advance had wholly gone past us before the chariot bent round its pole. Then the ladies returned to the wheels and the griffin moved his blessed burden, on such wise however that no feather of him was ruffled. The fair lady who had drawn me at the ford, and Statius and I, were following the wheel that made its turn with the smaller arc, and as we passed through the lofty wood, empty through fault of her who believed the serpent, an angelic song set the time to our steps. Perhaps three flights of an arrow loosed from the string would cover such distance as we had advanced, when Beatrice descended. I heard "Adam" murmured by all, then they encircled a tree stripped of its flowers and of its foliage in every bough. Its branches, which so much the wider spread the higher up they are, would be marveled at for height by the Indians in their woods.

"Blessed art thou, Griffin, that dost not pluck with thy beak from this tree, sweet to the taste, for the belly is ill racked thereby." Thus around the sturdy tree cried the others; and the animal of two natures, "So is preserved the seed of all righteousness";

E vòlto al temo ch'elli avea tirato,
trasselo al piè de la vedova frasca,
e quel di lei a lei lasciò legato. 51
Come le nostre piante, quando casca
giù la gran luce mischiata con quella
che raggia dietro a la celeste lasca, 54
turgide fansi, e poi si rinovella
di suo color ciascuna, pria che 'l sole
giunga li suoi corsier sotto altra stella; 57
men che di rose e più che di vïole
colore aprendo, s'innovò la pianta,
che prima avea le ramora sì sole. 60
Io non lo 'ntesi, né qui non si canta
l'inno che quella gente allor cantaro,
né la nota soffersi tutta quanta. 63
S'io potessi ritrar come assonnaro
li occhi spietati udendo di Siringa,
li occhi a cui pur vegghiar costò sì caro; 66
come pintor che con essempro pinga,
disegnerei com' io m'addormentai;
ma qual vuol sia che l'assonnar ben finga. 69
Però trascorro a quando mi svegliai,
e dico ch'un splendor mi squarciò 'l velo
del sonno, e un chiamar: "Surgi: che fai?" 72
Quali a veder de' fioretti del melo
che del suo pome li angeli fa ghiotti
e perpetüe nozze fa nel cielo, 75
Pietro e Giovanni e Iacopo condotti
e vinti, ritornaro a la parola
da la qual furon maggior sonni rotti, 78

and turning to the pole which he had pulled, he drew it to the foot of the widowed trunk and that which was of it he left bound to it.

As our plants, when the great light falls downward mingled with that which shines behind the celestial Carp, begin to swell, and then renew themselves, each in its own color, before the sun yokes his coursers under other stars; so, disclosing a hue less than of roses and more than of violets, the tree was renewed that first had its branches so bare. I did not understand the hymn, and it is not sung here, which that company then sang, nor did I bear to hear the music to the end.

If I could portray how the pitiless eyes sank to slumber, hearing of Syrinx, the eyes whose long vigil cost so dear, like a painter who paints from a model I would picture how I fell asleep: but whoso would, let him be one that can depict slumber well. I pass on, therefore, to when I awoke, and tell that a splendor rent the veil of my sleep, and a call, "Arise, what are you doing?"

As when brought to see some of the blossoms of the apple tree that makes the angels greedy of its fruit and holds perpetual wedding feasts in Heaven, Peter and John and James were overpowered, and came to themselves again at the word by which deeper slumbers were broken,

e videro scemata loro scuola
così di Moïsè come d'Elia,
e al maestro suo cangiata stola; 81
tal torna' io, e vidi quella pia
sovra me starsi che conducitrice
fu de' miei passi lungo 'l fiume pria. 84
E tutto in dubbio dissi: "Ov' è Beatrice?"
Ond' ella: "Vedi lei sotto la fronda
nova sedere in su la sua radice. 87
Vedi la compagnia che la circonda:
li altri dopo 'l grifon sen vanno suso
con più dolce canzone e più profonda." 90
E se più fu lo suo parlar diffuso,
non so, però che già ne li occhi m'era
quella ch'ad altro intender m'avea chiuso. 93
Sola sedeasi in su la terra vera,
come guardia lasciata lì del plaustro
che legar vidi a la biforme fera. 96
In cerchio le facevan di sé claustro
le sette ninfe, con quei lumi in mano
che son sicuri d'Aquilone e d'Austro. 99
"Qui sarai tu poco tempo silvano;
e sarai meco sanza fine cive
di quella Roma onde Cristo è romano. 102
Però, in pro del mondo che mal vive,
al carro tieni or li occhi, e quel che vedi,
ritornato di là, fa che tu scrive." 105
Così Beatrice; e io, che tutto ai piedi
d'i suoi comandamenti era divoto,
la mente e li occhi ov' ella volle diedi. 108

and saw their company diminished alike by Moses and Elias, and their Master's raiment changed, so I came to myself, and saw standing over me that compassionate lady who first had been my guide along the stream; and all in doubt I said, "Where is Beatrice?" And she, "See her beneath the new foliage, seated upon its root; see the company that encircles her: the rest are rising on high behind the griffin, with sweeter song and more profound." And if her speech continued longer I do not know, for already in my eyes was she who had shut me off from every other care. She was sitting there alone on the bare ground, like a guard left there of the chariot which I had seen bound by the biformed animal. In a circle the seven nymphs were making of themselves an enclosure for her, with those lights in their hands that are safe from Aquilo and from Auster.

"Here shall you be short time a forester, and you shall be with me forever a citizen of that Rome whereof Christ is Roman. Therefore, for profit of the world that lives ill, hold your eyes now on the chariot, and what you see, mind that you write it when you have returned yonder." Thus Beatrice; and I, who at the feet of her commands was all devout, gave my mind and my eyes whither she willed.

Non scese mai con sì veloce moto
foco di spessa nube, quando piove
da quel confine che più va remoto, 111
com' io vidi calar l'uccel di Giove
per l'alber giù, rompendo de la scorza,
non che d'i fiori e de le foglie nove; 114
e ferì 'l carro di tutta sua forza;
ond' el piegò come nave in fortuna,
vinta da l'onda, or da poggia, or da orza. 117
Poscia vidi avventarsi ne la cuna
del trïunfal veiculo una volpe
che d'ogne pasto buon parea digiuna; 120
ma, riprendendo lei di laide colpe,
la donna mia la volse in tanta futa
quanto sofferser l'ossa sanza polpe. 123
Poscia per indi ond' era pria venuta,
l'aguglia vidi scender giù ne l'arca
del carro e lasciar lei di sé pennuta; 126
e qual esce di cuor che si rammarca,
tal voce uscì del cielo e cotal disse:
"O navicella mia, com' mal se' carca!" 129
Poi parve a me che la terra s'aprisse
tr'ambo le ruote, e vidi uscirne un drago
che per lo carro sù la coda fisse; 132
e come vespa che ritragge l'ago,
a sé traendo la coda maligna,
trasse del fondo, e gissen vago vago. 135
Quel che rimase, come da gramigna
vivace terra, da la piuma, offerta
forse con intenzion sana e benigna, 138

Never with so swift a motion did fire descend from dense cloud, when it falls from the confine that stretches most remote, as I saw the bird of Jove swoop downward through the tree, rending the bark as well as the flowers and the new leaves, and it struck the chariot with all its force, so that it reeled like a ship in a tempest, driven by the waves, now to starboard, now to larboard. Then I saw leap into the body of the triumphal vehicle a fox that seemed starved of all good nourishment; but my lady, rebuking it for its foul offenses, turned it to such flight as its fleshless bones allowed. Then, from there whence it had come before, I saw the eagle descend into the body of the chariot and leave it feathered with its plumage. And a voice such as issues from a heart that is afflicted came from Heaven, and it said, "O little bark of mine, how ill are you laden!" Then it seemed to me that the earth opened between the two wheels, and I saw a dragon issue therefrom, which drove its tail upward through the chariot, and, like a wasp that retracts its sting, drawing to itself its malignant tail, tore out part of the bottom and made off, all content. What was left was covered again, as live soil with grass, with the plumage, offered perhaps with sincere and kind intent,

si ricoperse, e funne ricoperta
e l'una e l'altra rota e 'l temo, in tanto
che più tiene un sospir la bocca aperta. *141*

Trasformato così 'l dificio santo
mise fuor teste per le parti sue,
tre sovra 'l temo e una in ciascun canto. *144*

Le prime eran cornute come bue,
ma le quattro un sol corno avean per fronte:
simile mostro visto ancor non fue. *147*

Sicura, quasi rocca in alto monte,
seder sovresso una puttana sciolta
m'apparve con le ciglia intorno pronte; *150*

e come perché non li fosse tolta,
vidi di costa a lei dritto un gigante;
e basciavansi insieme alcuna volta. *153*

Ma perché l'occhio cupido e vagante
a me rivolse, quel feroce drudo
la flagellò dal capo infin le piante; *156*

poi, di sospetto pieno e d'ira crudo,
disciolse il mostro, e trassel per la selva,
tanto che sol di lei mi fece scudo
a la puttana e a la nova belva. *160*

and both one and the other wheel were covered with it in less time than a sigh keeps open the mouth. Thus transformed, the holy structure put forth heads upon its parts, three on the pole and one on each corner: the three were horned like oxen, but the four had a single horn on the forehead. Such a monster was never seen before. Secure, like a fortress on a high mountain, there appeared to me an ungirt harlot sitting upon it, with eyes quick to rove around; and, as if in order that she should not be taken from him, I saw standing at her side a giant, and they kissed each other again and again. But because she turned her lustful and wandering eye on me, that fierce paramour beat her from head to foot. Then, full of jealousy and fierce with rage, he loosed the monster and drew it through the wood so far that only of that he made a shield from me for the harlot and for the strange beast.

"*Deus, venerunt gentes,*" alternando
or tre or quattro dolce salmodia,
le donne incominciaro, e lagrimando; *3*
e Bëatrice, sospirosa e pia,
quelle ascoltava sì fatta, che poco
più a la croce si cambiò Maria. *6*
Ma poi che l'altre vergini dier loco
a lei di dir, levata dritta in pè,
rispuose, colorata come foco: *9*
"*Modicum, et non videbitis me*;
*et iterum,* sorelle mie dilette,
*modicum, et vos videbitis me.*" *12*
Poi le si mise innanzi tutte e sette,
e dopo sé, solo accennando, mosse
me e la donna e 'l savio che ristette. *15*
Così sen giva; e non credo che fosse
lo decimo suo passo in terra posto,
quando con li occhi li occhi mi percosse; *18*

## CANTO XXXIII

"D*eus, venerunt gentes,*" the ladies began, alternating, now three now four, a sweet psalmody, and weeping. And Beatrice, sighing and compassionate, was listening to them, so moved that little more did Mary change at the Cross. But when the other virgins gave place to her to speak, uprisen erect on her feet, she answered, colored like fire, "*Modicum et non videbitis me, et iterum,* my beloved sisters, *modicum et vos videbitis me.*" Then she set all the seven in front of her; and behind her, merely beckoning, she placed me and the lady and the sage who remained. Thus she went on, and I do not think she had taken the tenth step on the ground when with her eyes she smote on mine,

e con tranquillo aspetto "Vien più tosto,"
mi disse, "tanto che, s'io parlo teco,
ad ascoltarmi tu sie ben disposto." 21
Sì com' io fui, com' io dovëa, seco,
dissemi: "Frate, perché non t'attenti
a domandarmi omai venendo meco?" 24
Come a color che troppo reverenti
dinanzi a suo maggior parlando sono,
che non traggon la voce viva ai denti, 27
avvenne a me, che sanza intero suono
incominciai: "Madonna, mia bisogna
voi conoscete, e ciò ch'ad essa è buono." 30
Ed ella a me: "Da tema e da vergogna
voglio che tu omai ti disviluppe,
sì che non parli più com' om che sogna. 33
Sappi che 'l vaso che 'l serpente ruppe,
fu e non è; ma chi n'ha colpa, creda
che vendetta di Dio non teme suppe. 36
Non sarà tutto tempo sanza reda
l'aguglia che lasciò le penne al carro,
per che divenne mostro e poscia preda; 39
ch'io veggio certamente, e però il narro,
a darne tempo già stelle propinque,
secure d'ogn' intoppo e d'ogne sbarro, 42
nel quale un cinquecento diece e cinque,
messo di Dio, anciderà la fuia
con quel gigante che con lei delinque. 45
E forse che la mia narrazion buia,
qual Temi e Sfinge, men ti persuade,
perch' a lor modo lo 'ntelletto attuia; 48

and with tranquil look said to me, "Come more quickly, so that if I speak with you, you be well placed to listen to me." As soon as I was with her, as it was my duty to be, she said to me, "Brother, why, coming now with me, do you not venture to ask of me?"

As with those who with excessive reverence are speaking in the presence of their superiors so that they do not bring the voice whole to their lips, so it was with me, and without full utterance I began, "My lady, my need you know and that which is good for it." And she to me, "From fear and from shame I wish that you henceforth divest yourself, so that you may no more speak like one who is dreaming. Know that the vessel which the serpent broke was, and is not: but let him whose fault it is believe that God's vengeance fears no hindrance. Not for all time shall be without an heir the eagle that left its feathers on the chariot, whereby it became a monster and then a prey: for I see surely, and therefore I tell of it, stars already close at hand, secure from all check and hindrance, that shall bring us a time wherein a Five Hundred, Ten, and Five, sent by God, shall slay the thievish woman, with that giant who sins with her. And perhaps my prophecy, obscure as Themis and Sphinx, persuades you less because, after their fashion, it darkens your mind;

ma tosto fier li fatti le Naiade,
  che solveranno questo enigma forte
  sanza danno di pecore o di biade. *51*
Tu nota; e sì come da me son porte,
  così queste parole segna a' vivi
  del viver ch'è un correre a la morte. *54*
E aggi a mente, quando tu le scrivi,
  di non celar qual hai vista la pianta
  ch'è or due volte dirubata quivi. *57*
Qualunque ruba quella o quella schianta,
  con bestemmia di fatto offende a Dio,
  che solo a l'uso suo la creò santa. *60*
Per morder quella, in pena e in disio
  cinquemilia anni e più l'anima prima
  bramò colui che 'l morso in sé punio. *63*
Dorme lo 'ngegno tuo, se non estima
  per singular cagione essere eccelsa
  lei tanto e sì travolta ne la cima. *66*
E se stati non fossero acqua d'Elsa
  li pensier vani intorno a la tua mente,
  e 'l piacer loro un Piramo a la gelsa, *69*
per tante circostanze solamente
  la giustizia di Dio, ne l'interdetto,
  conosceresti a l'arbor moralmente. *72*
Ma perch' io veggio te ne lo 'ntelletto
  fatto di pietra e, impetrato, tinto,
  sì che t'abbaglia il lume del mio detto, *75*
voglio anco, e se non scritto, almen dipinto,
  che 'l te ne porti dentro a te per quello
  che si reca il bordon di palma cinto." *78*

but soon the facts shall be the Naiads that will solve this hard enigma, without loss of flocks or of harvest. Do you note, and even as these words are uttered by me, so teach them to those who live the life that is a race to death; and have in mind, when you write them, not to hide what you have seen of the tree which has now twice over been despoiled here. Whosoever robs that tree, or rends it, offends with blasphemy of act against God, who for His own sole use created it holy. For tasting of that tree the first soul longed in pain and in desire five thousand years and more for Him who punished on Himself that taste. Your wit sleeps if it deem not that for a special reason it is of such loftiness and thus inverted at its top; and if your vain thoughts had not been as water of Elsa round about your mind, and their pleasantness as Pyramus to the mulberry, by so many circumstances only you would recognize, in the moral sense, the justice of God in the interdict on the tree. But since I see you turned to stone in your mind, and stonelike, such in hue that the light of my word dazes you, I would also have you bear it away within you—and if not written, at least depicted—for the reason that the pilgrim's staff is brought back wreathed with palm."

E io: "Sì come cera da suggello,
che la figura impressa non trasmuta,
segnato è or da voi lo mio cervello. 81
Ma perchè tanto sovra mia veduta
vostra parola disïata vola,
che più la perde quanto più s'aiuta?" 84
"Perché conoschi," disse, "quella scuola
c'hai seguitata, e veggi sua dottrina
come può seguitar la mia parola; 87
e veggi vostra via da la divina
distar cotanto, quanto si discorda
da terra il ciel che più alto festina." 90
Ond' io rispuosi lei: "Non mi ricorda
ch'i' stranïasse me già mai da voi,
né honne coscïenza che rimorda." 93
"E se tu ricordar non te ne puoi,"
sorridendo rispuose, "or ti rammenta
come bevesti di Letè ancoi; 96
e se dal fummo foco s'argomenta,
cotesta oblivïon chiaro conchiude
colpa ne la tua voglia altrove attenta. 99
Veramente oramai saranno nude
le mie parole, quanto converrassi
quelle scovrire a la tua vista rude." 102
E più corusco e con più lenti passi
teneva il sole il cerchio di merigge,
che qua e là, come li aspetti, fassi, 105
quando s'affisser, sì come s'affigge
chi va dinanzi a gente per iscorta
se trova novitate o sue vestigge, 108

And I, "Even as wax under the seal, that does not change the imprinted figure, my brain is now stamped by you; but why do your longed-for words soar so far beyond my sight, that the more it strains the more it loses them?"

"In order that you may know," she said, "that school which you have followed, and may see if its teaching can follow my word, and see your way so far distant from the divine way, as the heaven that highest spins is remote from earth."

Whereon I answered her, "I do not remember that I ever estranged me from you, nor have I conscience thereof that gnaws me."

"And if you cannot remember it," smiling she replied, "bethink you now how you have drunk of Lethe this very day; and if from smoke fire is argued, this forgetfulness clearly proves fault in your will elsewhere intent. But henceforth my words shall be as simple as may be needful to make them plain to your rude sight."

Now more refulgent and with slower steps the sun held the meridian circle, which shifts here and there with the point of view, when, just as one going before a company for escort, stops if he comes on some strange thing or traces thereof,

le sette donne al fin d'un'ombra smorta,
qual sotto foglie verdi e rami nigri
sovra suoi freddi rivi l'alpe porta. 111
Dinanzi ad esse Ëufratès e Tigri
veder mi parve uscir d'una fontana,
e, quasi amici, dipartirsi pigri. 114
"O luce, o gloria de la gente umana,
che acqua è questa che qui si dispiega
da un principio e sé da sé lontana?" 117
Per cotal priego detto mi fu: "Priega
Matelda che 'l ti dica." E qui rispuose,
come fa chi da colpa si dislega, 120
la bella donna: "Questo e altre cose
dette li son per me; e son sicura
che l'acqua di Letè non gliel nascose." 123
E Bëatrice: "Forse maggior cura,
che spesse volte la memoria priva,
fatt' ha la mente sua ne li occhi oscura. 126
Ma vedi Eünoè che là diriva:
menalo ad esso, e come tu se' usa,
la tramortita sua virtù ravviva." 129
Come anima gentil, che non fa scusa,
ma fa sua voglia de la voglia altrui
tosto che è per segno fuor dischiusa; 132
così, poi che da essa preso fui,
la bella donna mossesi, e a Stazio
donnescamente disse: "Vien con lui." 135
S'io avessi, lettor, più lungo spazio
da scrivere, i' pur cantere' in parte
lo dolce ber che mai non m'avria sazio; 138

the seven ladies stopped at the edge of a pale shade, such as beneath green leaves and dark boughs the mountains cast over their cold streams. In front of them it seemed to me I saw Euphrates and Tigris issue from one fountain, and, like friends, slowly part from one another.

"O light, O glory of the human race, what water is this that pours here from one source and from itself withdraws itself?" To my question she replied, "Ask Matelda to tell you." And here the beautiful lady answered, as one freeing herself from blame, "This and other things I have told him, and I am certain that Lethe's water did not hide it from him."

And Beatrice, "Perhaps some greater care, which often robs the memory, has darkened the eyes of his mind. But see Eunoe that flows forth there: bring him thereto, and, as you are wont, revive his weakened faculties."

As a gentle spirit that makes no excuse, but makes its will of another's will, as soon as that is disclosed by outward sign, so the fair lady, after I was taken by her, moved on, and with womanly grace said to Statius, "Come with him."

If, reader, I had greater space for writing, I would yet partly sing the sweet draught which never would have sated me;

ma perché piene son tutte le carte
  ordite a questa cantica seconda,
  non mi lascia più ir lo fren de l'arte. *141*
Io ritornai da la santissima onda
  rifatto sì come piante novelle
  rinovellate di novella fronda,
puro e disposto a salire a le stelle. *145*

but since all the pages ordained for this second canticle are filled, the curb of art lets me go no further. I came forth from the most holy waves, renovated even as new trees renewed with new foliage, pure and ready to rise to the stars.

# INDEX

This list includes the names of persons and places mentioned in the *Purgatorio*. All names are given in their conventional English form where possible, according to the translation in this volume. Even though a name may occur more than once in a single passage or Canto, only its first occurrence there is listed. Italicized numbers of Cantos and verses indicate indirect reference to a person or place in the verse cited.

INDEX

# INDEX